One Call

Wendy Williams

Troubador Publishing Ltd
Unit E2 Airfield Business Park,
Harrison Road, Market Harborough,
Leicestershire. LE16 7UL
Tel: 0116 2792299
Email: books@troubador.co.uk
Web: www.troubador.co.uk/matador

ISBN 978 1805140 900

British Library Cataloguing in Publication Data.
A catalogue record for this book is available from the British Library.

Printed and bound in Great Britain by CMP UK
Typeset in 10.5pt Adobe Garamond Pro by Troubador Publishing Ltd, Leicester, UK

Matador is an imprint of Troubador Publishing Ltd

For Eleanor and Amelia
Always

1

'**P**olice emergency.'

Silence. That happens. For all sorts of reasons. The call flashed up as a triple nine, so Hannah tries again.

'You're through to the police. Do you need police assistance?'

Still nothing. This is odd. Hannah is trained to listen and there's always something; background noise, muffled voices, sounds of distress, music, car engines, something, anything. Not right now. The first trickles of a shiver creep down her spine. Hannah is alert, still. She senses the colleagues who are not on calls responding to her tension. Their heads turn, their eyes on Hannah.

'Caller, can you hear me?'

Hannah could end the call, but something stops her. Something about the silence. It feels physical, frightening.

A shocked silence.

She shuffles to the edge of her seat as if bringing her body closer to the computer screens will help. Hunched forward, eyes closed, her chin dropped towards her chest. They all do it. It does nothing to improve hearing but somehow hunkering down and blocking out the surrounding bustle from a dozen other call handlers, despatchers, supervisors, and police officers brings the caller closer. Hannah is practised at shutting everyone else out. Her call, this call, is the only one that matters.

It's two forty-five in the morning. Late bars are closing, but night clubs still buzz with hyped-up individuals who don't know if it's day or night. They're too drunk to know the difference between a life-and-death emergency call and a giggle with friends. And much, much too stupid to care.

But after a year or two on the job instincts deep within the gut work overtime. Hannah can't say why she thinks this is a genuine call rather than a prank, why her senses are on high alert. It's a visceral reaction. There's a tone to the silence.

A sound.

A single breath. And another. Frantic, irregular breathing. Someone is afraid, or in shock, or hurt. Or all three.

What an ordinary night this had been. Routine. A quiet shift.

Colleagues chatting and sharing sweeties, tooth decay a hazard of the job. When the call flashed up on her screen Hannah had spat her half-chewed wine gum into the waiting tissue.

She tries again.

'Caller, can you hear me? Do you need police assistance?'

A hushed sound. A sob or a smothered laugh? Hannah's face contorts with concentration.

'Do you need help, caller?' Hannah hears a faint mewling like a kitten calling for its mother. Her brow furrows. She waits and listens. More silence.

She considers ending the call when a voice whispers.

'Please.'

Female, young. Her voice is muffled, her mouth too close to the phone. The word slurred but understandable. Is she drunk? It doesn't matter. There is no discernible background noise, but the clarity of sound presents Hannah with an overwhelming vision of a mortuary. Not an echo, but an emptiness, as if life has already slipped away.

'Caller, can you talk?'

'Please, help me.'

The voice trembles. This girl is scared. Hannah lowers the tone and volume of her own voice and speaks with purposeful calm.

'Where are you?'

'Don't know.'

'Can you tell me your name?'

'Tina.'

'What's your surname, Tina?'

'Cashen.'

Hannah keys the information into her computer.

'What's your home address?'

Tina gives an address in the south of the city. As she answers the routine questions, Hannah hears Tina's breathing settle, and her speech becomes clearer.

'Are you at home, Tina?'

'No.'

Hannah creates an incident log using Tina's home address to record the information.

'Can you tell me your date of birth?'

The computer identifies Tina. She has had no prior contact with the police force. Hannah calculates that Tina is nineteen years old. She tries again for a location.

'Where are you, Tina?'

'I don't know.'

There is a quiet whimper. Primitive, wounded.

'Are you injured, Tina? Do you need an ambulance?'

'I don't think so.'

Good.

'Are you in danger?' Hannah hears a sob and then a muffled panting. The girl on the phone is trying not to make a noise. Hannah is so attuned to listening, the noises paint a vivid picture in her mind. Tina is hiding, cowering somewhere with her mobile phone clutched in her shaking, sweating hand.

'I can't get out.'

Out of where?

'What's happened, Tina?'

'I don't remember. I can't remember anything after the bar. One minute I was there and the next I wasn't. I was, I was… here.'

Rohypnol. The date rape drug. Or at least something like it. Something to knock Tina out and erase her memory. Hannah's stomach knots. Her brain is exhuming unwanted memories. She bats away the nausea forming at the back of her throat. She knows about this. Only too well. Hannah must keep Tina calm. She remembers a bar. Her last known location might be a clue to where she is now.

'Which bar were you in, Tina?'

'The Grape and Glass.'

'What do you remember?'

'There was a man.'

Of course there was, there always is. He bought her a drink. Slipped in a pill.

'He paid for the drinks.'

Tina's voice has dropped to a mumble as if trying not to be overheard. Hannah guesses the man from the bar is close.

'Is the man there, Tina?'

'Next door.'

'You're doing well, Tina,' reassures Hannah. 'Really well. What happened after the drink?'

'My friends wanted to go. Not me.'

'So, did you stay, Tina?'

'Yeah.'

'Did your friends leave?'

'He promised me a taxi.'

Tina is avoiding the question. Hannah still has no idea what has happened, or why Tina has called for help. Or, more importantly, where she is.

'Told my friends to go.'

Quiet sobs fill Hannah's earpiece.

'Take some deep breaths, Tina.'

'I wasn't going to go with him. Not stupid. Just another drink.'

She stops talking and Hannah listens to sniffs and snivels. Tina sounds so young. Hannah's heart somersaults inside her rib cage.

'Tell me what happened after the drink, Tina.'

'Can't remember.'

'Do you remember leaving the bar?'

'No.'

'Do you remember the man's name?'

'Andrew.'

Probably false, thinks Hannah.

'How old was he?'

'Thirtyish.'

Too old for you.

'Can you describe him?'

'Tall. He was tall.'

'What colour was his hair?'

'Brown.'

'Can you remember anything else?'

'No.'

Hannah changes tack.

'Do you know what time you left the bar, or where you went?'

'No. Just woke up…'

She can't finish. Her tears smother her power of speech. Hannah is confident that she can finish the story, but this is Tina's narrative. She has to say the words. Hannah's scalp is tingling with dread and something much worse. A horrifying memory she has tried to bury in a place where she hoped it could never be dug up. Yet still the memory haunts her from the minute she wakes until the moment she falls asleep. A memory that imprisons her.

Focus on the call, she tells herself. *This isn't about you. Focus.* She adjusts her mouthpiece, presses the earpiece into her ear and returns her hands to the keyboard. The empty location box on the incident screen is burning Hannah's eyes.

'It's okay, Tina, you're going to be okay. Take a deep breath.'

Hannah takes one too.

'What happened when you woke up, Tina?'

Hannah feels that her words are irrelevant, meaningless, whipped away by the force of Tina's distress. But a human voice can be a lifeline for a person who is alone and afraid. Tina needs to know that someone hears her and is going to help. She needs to have hope.

Tina sniffs then whispers into the phone.

'I woke up on a bed. On my front. Him behind me. Inside me.' She pauses to sob and gulps in an effort to stifle the sound. 'Him banging away like an animal. Like I was an animal.'

Hannah screws her eyes shut as she feels Tina's experience. Her stomach muscles contract. Beads of sweat form at her hairline. Tina's voice is quieter, more controlled. She needs Hannah to understand.

Hannah wants to shout that she does. She knows what it's like to have your face pushed so hard into a duvet that you think you will suffocate. She knows what it's like to be used, defiled, and pummelled against your will. To be treated like nothing and left feeling like nothing.

'He was hurting me. I tried to say stop. I tried. My voice didn't work.'

Hannah absorbs the young woman's distress. She wants to say, I know Tina, I know. It's difficult for her to concentrate but she gathers every resource she possesses to follow this call through. She types 'rape' into the 'What's Happened' box on the computer. She senses the disturbance across the room as the inspector, sergeant, supervisor and dispatcher are alerted. Their questions jump onto Hannah's screen. They want a location. It's Hannah's job to provide it. For now, all she can type is 'unidentified'.

'Okay, Tina. You're doing well. Keep going.'

'I couldn't move. He finished and rolled away. I don't know how long it had been going on.'

Hannah's breath catches in her throat. *Focus*, she tells herself again.

'He kept shouting, you bitch, you bitch, over and over.'

Like you made him do it, Tina? Like it's your fault? That's what he wants you to believe.

'I don't know where my clothes are.'

Hannah's insides churn, and her hairline is damp with sweat. She pulls off her clip-on tie and undoes the top button of her uniform shirt.

'Where are you now, Tina?'

'In the bathroom. He's still on the bed. Asleep. I couldn't move for ages. When I got up, I tried to run but my legs wobbled, and the door wouldn't open. My fingers wouldn't work. I couldn't get out. I got my phone. Locked myself in the bathroom.'

Officers must be sent to assist this girl, but first Hannah needs to find out where she is.

'Have you any idea where you are?'

'No, I just woke up with him doing that.'

Hannah's mind races. Tina could be anywhere in the city. In any room. It will be like searching for an ear stud in a sack of rice. She wishes life could be like an American movie where the cops ping a phone and send squad cars rushing to the scene.

But there's nothing to stop Tina pinging herself.

'Tina, do you have Google Maps on your phone?'

When Tina speaks, her voice has the strength of a scrap of muslin flapping in the breeze.

'I don't have a signal.'

Hannah's legs jiggle under the desk.

'Nothing?'

'No. I don't know how I'm calling you.'

'You'll be camped on to another network. They all work together to support emergency calls.'

'Can't you track my phone?'

'The police are not allowed to do that without signed permission. But if you don't have a signal, it can't be done anyway.'

Tina falls quiet.

Hannah feels punctured. There must be another way to find this girl.

'Tina, can you hear anything?'

'No.'

'Can you see out of the window?'

'There's no window.'

'Can you tell me anything about the room and bathroom?'

'Um. I think it's a hotel.'

Hannah types 'unidentified hotel' in the location box on her screen.

'Did you see any logos or signs in the room?'

'No. I feel a bit dizzy, and my eyes are funny.'

Drugged for sure.

'What about the bathroom? Are there any toiletries with logos or names?'

The sound of Tina's breathing quietens as she moves the phone away from her mouth.

'There are tiny shampoos and stuff. Zephyr Spa.'

'Is the name of the hotel on the packaging?'

'No.'

Hannah is out of options. She has no way to locate Tina and no way to send help. If the man next door were to get up and leave, Tina would be safe. If he doesn't, she is still vulnerable. As far as Hannah can see, Tina has only two options. She can wait it out in the hotel bathroom and risk being attacked again, or she can try and get out.

'Okay, Tina. I need you to concentrate. Most hotels have key cards for the door, so if you couldn't open it, I'm guessing it was locked from the inside. Do you think you can leave the bathroom and try the bedroom door?'

Hannah's question elicits another small sob.

'I'm scared.'

'I'm going to send police officers to help you, Tina, but I need to know where you are. Have you got something to wear?'

'A robe.'

Hannah's pulse quickens.

'Is there a logo or name on the robe?'

There is the soft rustle of fabric as Tina takes it off.

'Nothing.'

Dammit.

'Tina. If it's safe to do so, I want you to try and get out of the room.'

The pitch of Tina's voice rises again. 'No! He might wake up.'

'I can't send help because I don't know where you are. Do you think you can try and leave?'

'But if he wakes up…'

'Then scream, Tina. Scream as long and loud as you can. You're in a hotel. Someone will hear you.'

'I can't.'

Tina is crying again.

'Tina, I must know where you are.'

Hannah knows it's a risk asking Tina to leave the safety of the bathroom, but she's out of options.

'No, I can't.'

Hannah has one final idea.

'Tina. Can you peep into the bedroom while he's asleep? Try to find something with the name of the hotel on.'

Silence.

'Tina?'

'Okay.'

'Okay. Keep your phone on, Tina. Tell me what's happening.'

'I'm going to open the door.'

'Okay, Tina. I'm here. I'm listening.'

The dispatchers are questioning Hannah again. 'Where is she?' *I don't bloody know*, thinks Hannah.

She can hear Tina's breath over the phone but there is no other discernible noise.

'It's open,' whispers Tina.

'Good girl. Tell me what you can see.'

'Just the room. He's on his back, asleep. The curtains are shut. It's dark.'

Hannah's brain is racing. She wants to ask Tina to make a run for it, but she knows it's too risky. If Tina fumbles at the door the man could wake and grab her. There has to be something in that room that will give them a clue.

'Can you see anything with the name of the hotel on?'

There is a short pause before Tina replies.

'I think there's a pen and pad by the bed.'

'Can you get it, Tina? Can you get it and take it back into the bathroom? It might have the hotel's name on it.'

I hope, thinks Hannah.

All she can hear is Tina's breathing. Hannah has no idea of the size of the room, nor the exact location of the pad and pen.

'His eyes are closed,' whispers Tina.

'Don't speak. Just get the pen and paper.'

There is a pause then a clatter. The noise of a pen dropping onto a hard surface. A male voice shouts.

Tina gasps. Her voice is a squeak.

'Let me go!'

There is a clunk as her phone lands on the floor.

'Tina! Can you hear me? Tina, pick up the phone.'

Sweat trickles down Hannah's back and gathers at the waistband of her trousers. Her neck and shoulder muscles tense. She must help Tina. Not just because it's her job; because she has a connection with this young woman. It's so much more than that. Helping Tina would be a recompense of sorts. To herself.

She focuses on Tina's whimpering. Hannah can hear only one word being repeated over and over.

'Please.'

'Tina, Tina!'

'Leave me alone. Please. Leave me alone.'

The cries assault Hannah's ears. Her eyes sting with threatening tears.

Tina screams, then stops. Hannah hears a cry like a stricken puppy. There is scratching and scrabbling as if someone is being dragged then a resounding smack. Tina is silent.

'You dirty fucking bitch.'

The man's voice is close to the phone. Unlike Tina's slurred words, his speech is enunciated with such clarity that Hannah freezes. He could be standing right next to her. He could be spitting those words into the back of her neck.

The phone is dead. Hannah sits with her headphones still

in place, the line open. Silence. She is frozen in her seat. She blows out a breath she didn't know she was holding.

She removes her headset with shaking hands. She types 'line cleared' and 'call ended' on her screen and marks herself as unavailable. She can't take another call. She can't speak.

The supervisor comes over and touches Hannah's shoulder. All the handlers know what it's like to take a tough call. But none of them will ever know what it was like for Hannah to take that call.

Because the man in Tina's hotel room is the man who raped Hannah.

2

*S*tupid bitch. Stupid, dirty fucking bitch.

 He looks down at the crumpled form lying on the floor and gives it a kick. He is the one in charge, he is the one who makes the rules. How dare she. Did he tell her she could call someone? Did he tell her she could leave the bed? He wants to stamp on her head but stamps on her mobile phone instead. No blood splatter that way.

The girl's arm twitches. He is still wearing his gloves, so he kneels beside her and places his hands around her neck. Even as he squeezes, he marvels at how slender it is. When her face is drained of colour he stands up and checks his watch. That part always takes longer than he would like. Five and a half minutes despite his strong hands. He needs to get it down to five.

He dresses quickly. His clothes and shoes are impressively clean. From the inside pocket of his jacket, he removes a packet of antiseptic wipes which he uses to scrub all the surfaces around the bed. Each wipe is placed inside a plastic bag that contains the used condom. His last action is to place the Do Not Disturb sign on the door and wipe the door handles.

He leaves the room satisfied that he is leaving no trace of himself behind. It's only when he removes the gloves that he notices the small tear at the side of his hand and the speck of blood from a graze. How the fuck did that happen? He hesitates, wondering if he should go back into the room. He has no memory of catching his hand on anything and the hole is tiny. Besides, he wiped down everything thoroughly. Didn't he? Yes, of course he did. He's good at this now.

The whine of an ascending lift makes up his mind. He takes the stairs to the lower car park and walks past the parked cars. There is one CCTV camera near the exit which he avoids easily by using the pedestrian door. He shoulders the door open to avoid leaving a fingerprint. His car is parked across the street.

As he takes the steering wheel he glances at his hand. The mark is barely more than a pinprick, but it makes him angry all the same. There is a scowl on his face as he drives away. He knows that one drop of blood is all it takes to identify an offender and even though he tries to reassure himself that he wiped everything down thoroughly, a germ of unease is niggling away inside his brain.

What the hell was that girl up to? What did she think she was doing? Who was she talking to?

Stupid bitch. Stupid, dirty fucking bitch.

3

Everything was the same.

The drugged drink, an anonymous hotel, the words, the voice. Especially the voice. Even when her useless body refused to move Hannah's hearing had remained crystal clear. She is certain that the man who attacked, is attacking Tina right now, is the same man who attacked her.

Hannah knows what he is capable of. She was terrified enough to run away and hide herself from him, from the world. But she did nothing. She was too weak, too scared, too ashamed. She told no-one.

I should have reported him, thinks Hannah. *I might have stopped him from hurting Tina.* The pressure of the supervisor's hand encourages Hannah to leave her desk.

'Let's have a debrief, Hannah.'

The supervisor has been in the job eighteen years. She doesn't need or expect a response. And Hannah has nothing to give. Colleagues' eyes swivel towards her as she leaves her desk and walks with exaggerated care towards the office. One foot must follow the other.

Even a toddler can do it.

Hannah's left shoulder bangs against the wall as her equilibrium shifts and the floor undulates around her.

She pushes herself away from the wall with her left hand and raises her right towards the colleague who is already half out of her chair ready to help.

I'm okay, she gestures, *I'll be fine.*

The debrief is not something that Hannah has had to do very often, and she's relieved when it's over.

She half staggers back past her desk, through the double doors into the corridor and heads for the break room. The compact space is over-heated but mercifully empty. Hannah falls onto a coffee-stained sofa. Her hands cover her eyes. She leans forward and supports her head, its weight almost too much to bear. She waits for the deluge of tears to arrive but when it doesn't, she slumps back and closes her eyes. They spring open as the break-room door opens. Angie's voice. Her confidante in all things job-related. She can't tell her this.

'Do you need anything, Hannah? Coffee? Company?'

A shake of Hannah's head is enough. Hannah loves her for not being pushy. Angie withdraws with a gentle smile and closes the door behind her. Hannah shuts her eyes again.

Devastating calls are part of the job. A baby found dead in its cot; a child's face torn apart by an unleashed dog; a mother killed by a drunken youth speeding across a pedestrian crossing; an arson attack on a family targeted because of the colour of their skin. Fortunately, those calls are few and far between. Even seasoned call handlers count them in single digits. But this one is different.

This one is personal.

Despite her head feeling as if excavators are rooting around in her brain matter, Hannah is aware that the shift is a handler down. Right at this minute, someone might be waiting for the police to answer their call. Someone like Tina. Perhaps the call is from the person who has found Tina and officers are on their way to rescue her. Perhaps she managed to scream, and someone heard her.

Already someone will be applying for permission to trace Tina's call, experts will be analysing its content and city hotels will be put on alert. *Please, God, let it be enough.* Hannah must get back to her desk and be in a fit state to work.

Hot, sweet tea is the enduring remedy for shock, but she opts for sugarless coffee. She leaves the sofa and crosses to the tired excuse for a kitchen. The kettle is half full and warm so boils quickly. Hannah's mug has been used by someone else and sits beneath the dripping tap. She washes it and rinses it out with boiling water before she fills the mug with strong, black, bulk-buy coffee. It's disgusting but the foul taste makes it feel like medicine and she gulps it down.

The clock tells her it's twenty past four. Where did the time go? How long was Tina's call? How long has she been in the break room? She needs to return to work. She can't do that with her head in this state.

She goes back over the phone call in her head. She heard one sentence. Can she be one hundred per cent certain it was the same voice? It wasn't the same name. Her attacker called himself Dan. Dan who? She doesn't know his surname, his address, or anything useful at all.

'You dirty fucking bitch.'

It *was* him. Wasn't it?

Hannah shakes her head as the memories of her own attack assault her brain. Over and over. The same words erupting from his mouth, droplets of saliva spattering her shoulders. His hand pressed against the back of her neck, pushing her face into the duvet with such force that she struggled to breathe. But even if she had wanted to fight, her physical ability to move had been sucked away like water swirling into a drain. Afterwards, she thought about people with locked-in syndrome, able to breathe and feel but not able to respond. She was this man's rag doll, tossed onto the bed to be abused until he was done. As the door closed behind him leaving her helpless and immobile, he spat out the words one last time.

'Dirty fucking bitch.'

Was it just that Hannah recognised the phrase? Or was it his voice? Her certainty is fading. If she does tell someone, how would he be found? All she has is his Christian name which is probably fake. Would she be in trouble for failing to report an incident that happened thirteen months ago? How could she explain why she didn't? That she couldn't face the disbelief of the police, the questions, the investigation. The sneers when she revealed that she was on a date, wore a short skirt, drank alcohol. That she went to a hotel room with a man she barely knew. That she doesn't trust the police and would be better off waving down a bus if she's in trouble.

Does that make it her fault that Tina has been hurt? Because she did nothing? All she has done since the attack is hide. From men, from the police, from everyone. She wants to go home and bury herself under her poppy duvet. Her safe place where no one can reach her.

But she can't. She can't let her colleagues down. She has to stay on duty if only to wait and see if a call comes in about Tina. She is still out there in some anonymous hotel room, frightened out of her wits and in fear for her life.

It's almost five before Hannah makes it back to her workstation, but no one glares. There must be a lull in calls because she sees several people chatting or relaxing in their chairs. A bar of chocolate is passed between colleagues, yesterday's newspaper waves in the air. She puts on her headset and focuses on the screen in front of her. She knows she won't be bothered. They're in this together and most of her colleagues are sensitive to the needs of others. Isn't that one of the reasons they do the job? To help others. God knows it's not for the pay and unsocial hours.

Hannah adjusts her mouthpiece and watches her screen. She is soon occupied with a handful of triple one calls, all mercifully dull. In between she pretends to read a book she has brought from home. She is not disturbed by her colleagues but the words on the page can't compete with those words ringing in her ears. The same four words repeated over and over.

'You dirty fucking bitch.'

Hannah's uncertainty is demolished.

It *was* the voice of her attacker.

She feels the weight of his body against her own, the suffocating feeling of her face pressed into the duvet, his fingers bruising the back of her neck as she struggles to breathe.

Hannah starts when her supervisor's hand appears beside her elbow. It takes Hannah's mouse and logs her off from the system.

'Go home, Hannah. I'll let you know if we hear anything.'

4

There is a particular feeling that only night workers experience and understand. It happens when they emerge, blinking into the morning light, and find themselves at odds with the rest of the world. All the daylight people, who are making their way to work after a night tucked up in bed, have the rise of the sun about them. Even when they hate their jobs, day workers have a freshness that you only really notice when you stand right next to them, wilting from your night shift. They smell of showers, shampoo, and satisfaction. It's a discomfiting disconnection for the person who has spent ten or more hours blinking away sleep.

Night workers swim against the tide of their biorhythms, with exhaustion making each day a struggle upstream. Emerging to squint at the morning sky, the light hurts their eyes, and their brain screams for bed. Their body clock has no idea which way to tick. Insides feel hollow, appetite is upside down and actions disordered. Is it better to drink coffee to stay awake on the way home or hot milk to aid sleep?

Most night workers develop their own habits and rituals. How to get home. Whether to stop at the shops. Whether to eat when they arrive home. Is it breakfast or dinner? Do they go straight to bed? Do they set the alarm? Do they wake up and stay up or wake up for a few hours then sleep again for a few hours? Do they have a meal before they go on shift, or take a meal to work to reheat in the microwave?

Everyone is different.

For Hannah, working nights used to be hateful and she would give anything not to have to do them. But that's the job.

That was before her attack.

Now she volunteers to swap from days to nights. It's easier to hide at night. There are fewer cars to conceal a rapist. Fewer tall, handsome men striding towards her, instilling a dread in her belly, only dissipating when they have passed by as strangers. Fewer voices to listen to in case one of them is familiar. Fewer shadows, fewer footsteps. Fewer expectations from those who know you. Hannah drives to work and drives home with her car doors locked. She eats, she sleeps, she goes to work.

She is always afraid.

Tonight, she drives too fast, anxious to be home, constantly checking her rear-view mirror. She is grateful for the quiet streets. Only when she turns into her road does she take a deep breath and feel her ribs and shoulders relax. When she removes her hands from the steering wheel, her fingers remain curled into claws.

The man that Hannah has been trying to banish from her consciousness for the last thirteen months might as well be sitting in the back seat of the car. Her knees are trembling as she leaves the car. She stumbles as she climbs the three steps to the front door. It takes two attempts to fit the key into the lock, step inside and shut the door with a quiet but firm thunk.

Hannah has been hiding, trying to keep herself safe. And it's worked. Nothing bad has happened to her since Dan. But something sickening happened to Tina last night. Which means that Dan is still around. What if Hannah bumps into him in the supermarket or in a queue at the post office?

She cannot continue to live with this fear. Not anymore. It's up to her to end it. If she can identify Dan as Tina's attacker, maybe it's not too late to get him arrested, to stop him. What if there are other women like her? Maybe if Hannah goes to the police, other victims will come forward. Maybe Dan will be sent to prison for a long time. Perhaps Tina's call is a nudge from fate to do the right thing. To face up to what happened to her and report it.

Hannah makes her way up the stairs to the first floor of the semi-detached house converted into three flats. Deborah has the top floor and despite her heavy feet, Hannah is often comforted by the sound of her stamping about to the melodies of Ed Sheeran.

No music this morning. Deborah is a secondary-school teacher and will already be in the staff room preparing to do battle with a chemistry lab full of unruly teenagers. The house is silent.

On the hour she switches on the radio and listens to the local news headlines. Nothing about a girl in a hotel. Hannah wants to believe that Tina is okay, that she got away. She turns off the radio at the end of the bulletin, gets undressed, wraps herself in her poppy duvet, and lies on top of the bed. She is too hot. She throws off the duvet and opens a window. She lies down again. She is too cold. She is thirsty so gets up to fetch a glass of water. Back to bed. She needs the loo. Back to bed? No point. She gets dressed and goes to the kitchen to make a mug of tea.

As she stares out of the window, the tenant from the ground-floor flat turns into the driveway. He has a newspaper and a brown paper bag in his hand. Hannah recognises the logo of the local bakery. It's a beautiful late summer morning and the sunshine is scattering golden highlights into his uncombed sandy hair. He's walking as if the world is wonderful. A stab of resentment catches Hannah in the gut and her hands shake just enough to spill her tea. She hears the front door close and the sound of her neighbour entering his flat.

Hannah doesn't know much about him. Since his arrival six months ago they have exchanged the occasional greeting but because Hannah doesn't go out except for work and essential appointments, there has not been much opportunity for them to get to know each other and that has suited Hannah just fine.

The exception was a weekend in July when the sun soaked the communal garden in a pool of light so startling Hannah felt compelled to go outside. All three tenants in the house are meant to keep the garden tidy but Deborah has no interest and the tenant before Gates was elderly and too frail to manage the steps down to the suburban jungle outside his kitchen window. So, when Gates appeared as Hannah was swinging a borrowed brush cutter through the two-foot-high grass, she almost sliced his leg in surprise.

'Careful!'

Hannah switched off the machine and blushed as she regarded her neighbour.

'Let me,' he said.

Hannah started to protest but he held out his hands and she passed him the brush cutter. While Gates uncovered the remnants of a lawn with precise sweeps through the undergrowth, Hannah tackled the hedge. She was too preoccupied to notice that the brush cutter had stopped, and it was only when Gates came into her line of sight that she swung round to see him holding two cold drinks and a picnic rug.

A wave of shyness and uncertainty passed through Hannah, but she managed somehow to capture it and tie it down with logic. This man was her neighbour. He was helping to clear the garden. He was not a threat.

'Break time,' he said. 'Can you put down the rug?'

Hannah laid the rug on the newly revealed grass which was yellow and scratchy but at least visible.

'Thank you,' she said, a wave of her arm indicating the cut grass.

'My pleasure. But it is the responsibility of all of us, isn't it?'

Hannah nodded and sat cross-legged on the rug. Gates handed her the cold drink and sprawled opposite her right at the edge of the rug.

'I'm Harry Gates, but I like to be called Gates.'

'I'm Hannah.'

Hannah wondered why he didn't offer a handshake and why he sipped his drink in silence, as if he knew somehow that she was afraid to be touched, that she didn't enjoy conversations with strangers. Did he notice that she found prolonged eye contact difficult? That she dropped her head and wrapped her free arm around her body? That her hands shook ever so slightly as she raised the glass to her mouth?

Working with the police has accustomed Hannah to physically strong men whose uniform gives some of them a swagger, often ill-deserved and usually exploited. She used to ignore the men who invaded her personal space, leaned over her while she was sitting at her desk and leered and nudged when their mates were around. Before the attack, Hannah rolled her eyes and moved away. Now she cowers and trembles. Her reaction seems to encourage them. Teasing the female staff is an office sport and no one stops them.

Away from work, men are a species to be avoided. Hannah is the mouse scurrying along the skirting board. On days when Hannah stands at her window watching life pass by, she sometimes spots Gates coming and going. Perhaps Gates watches her in return. They had met in the hall on only a handful of occasions before the gardening, all of which had passed with an innocuous greeting and a ghost of a smile from each of them.

What interested Hannah that day was that although almost any man made her feel extraordinarily shy, her neighbour did not. She thought about why this was, and she concluded that unlike many men, he didn't assume a right to her personal space. In fact, he respected it. He stepped back if she needed to pass. He never stood too close. He never asked her personal questions or made flippant or sexual remarks. She felt calm in his presence.

For the first time in over a year she had initiated a conversation with an almost unknown male.

'Do you like living here?'

By the time their glasses were empty they had discovered each other's jobs, Gates was into computers and worked from home in cyber security; their marital status, Hannah single, Gates dodged the question; and their views on the garden. They both wished it was tidier. Then Gates held out his hand for Hannah's glass, said 'see ya' and headed inside.

'Thanks for the help,' she called after him.

Gates raised a hand and replied, 'anytime' and then he was gone.

Hannah was surprised at how sorry she felt that he'd left.

Since then, Hannah has pottered in the garden two or three times, but Gates has not reappeared.

Thinking back to the day in the garden and remembering that Gates works with computers leaves Hannah with an urge to see him now. The feeling takes her by surprise and at first Hannah does her best to quell the idea of going downstairs and knocking on his door. This is not her. It's not what she does. But hasn't she decided to change? Didn't she just make up her mind that she wants to finally report her attack? To do something about Dan? Maybe Gates can help.

Hannah knows the police will be replaying the call and searching for Tina, but she also knows how hamstrung they are by lack of resources, by the paperwork, the need for written permission to track a phone, to search a house. If Tina is still in the hotel, she is in trouble right now and she needs to be found. Gates is an expert with computers. He might be able to track Tina down. He is also the only person that Hannah feels comfortable asking for help. Correction, he's the only person she knows that is accessible and a computer expert.

Tina's call wasn't just distressing, it was personal.

So, it's not enough to just sit and wait and watch the news.

5

*H*e needs to be at work early, so he goes straight home, lights the log burner to destroy the bag of waste, showers, dresses for work then settles into a chair to watch the evidence burn. He will doze for a little while, but he won't sleep deeply. He never does after a kill. He is not just hyper and agitated, he is euphoric. Payback is beatific and best enjoyed fresh while his pulse is still racing and his heart swelling against his ribs.

He is triumphant. If only she knew. The one who started it all. But he was too green and naïve in those days. He knew what he wanted to do to her, he just didn't know how to do it without getting caught. Even now he would be prime suspect number one if anything happened to her. He dare not touch her. At least not yet. But he watches and he waits. Who knows when he might get a chance? And if he does, he will make sure she gets what she deserves.

Meanwhile there is more than enough fodder to feed his appetites and hone his craft. The bitches are so stupid. Throw a few compliments around, buy a few drinks, add the powder to the alcohol and they are putty in his hands. They never learn. They have no idea how easy they make it for predators like him.

Predator. I am a predator. He likes that.

Of course, the first one was a bit of a cock-up. He never expected the blood. He is ashamed now at the way he panicked and ran away. He is more ashamed of the fact that he left her alive. He certainly hasn't made that mistake since, nor will he in the future.

6

Hannah dresses in jeans and a T-shirt, grabs her keys and patters down the stairs before she has a chance to change her mind. She knocks on the door of the ground-floor flat. Her thoughts make it impossible to smile.

Gates flings his door open with a flourish. 'Hannah, good morning. Shouldn't you be asleep?'

She blinks at the greeting. How does he know that?

She must be frowning because he seems to pick up on her thoughts and smiles. 'I hear the front door,' he explains. 'I know you try to close it quietly, unlike some.' At this he rolls his eyes upwards, and Hannah tries to smile at the thought of Deborah's comings and goings. Her lips twitch just a little.

'Especially when she drops the books,' Hannah says.

He slaps his hand to his forehead. 'The exercise books. What a racket they make when they splatter all over the tiles. Hasn't she heard of a bag?'

'Do you come out and help her pick them up?'

'Do you?'

Hannah shakes her head. 'Two flights of stairs.'

Gates glances at the stairs and nods. 'Fair point. I did come out the first few times and helped her gather them up. But then

I made the mistake of carrying them up to her flat for her. After that she seemed to drop things with a frequency that made me exceedingly suspicious.'

They look at each other again. Apart from their brief spell of gardening, this is the most intimate conversation they've had since he moved in. She judges that Gates is in his early thirties so a few years older than her. He is tall and slim and has the look of a rangy dog. Long-limbed, slightly untidy but with a calm, kind face. Hannah searches for a word to describe him. Unhurried comes to mind. Yes, he is an unhurried kind of guy. She needs a snippet of his calm right now. She takes a calming breath.

'I need some help,' she says, 'with a computer search. I remember you saying that you do that sort of thing.'

He steps aside and waves a hand towards his living room. 'Come on in. Can I make you a drink?'

Hannah is aware that her hands are trembling. She clasps them together.

'Your coffee always smells delicious.'

'Won't it keep you awake?'

'Not sleeping today.'

His grey eyes narrow and she is grateful that he turns away without comment. 'Make yourself at home,' he calls as he heads off to clatter around in the kitchen.

This is the first time Hannah has been inside his flat and her curiosity overcomes her nervousness. His living room is untidy but in a homely, comforting way. If a room can appear aggressive, it can also appear kind. Gates' room is kind and welcoming, helped by the aroma of good coffee wafting through the air. She sees two huge sofas buried underneath a muddle of throws and pillows, an alcove of bookshelves with the volumes scattered any which way and an empty fireplace that looks as if it could still be in use. Hannah wanders over to the bay window where three over-sized computer screens are set up amongst a variety of keyboards and a massive tangle of wires. The slatted window blinds are half closed so that a ladder of shadows shimmers and trembles across the long desk.

'Latte okay?'

Hannah jumps as Gates enters the room carrying a chunky mug. If he notices her nerves he doesn't comment. Hannah sits on one of the sofas and he passes her the mug of steaming, milky coffee.

'Sugar?'

'No thanks.'

He goes back to the kitchen and returns with his own coffee and a plate bearing two croissants.

'Breakfast?'

She shakes her head. With the sick feeling still inside her, she doesn't trust herself to eat and not throw up. 'But please, go ahead.'

Gates bites and chews with tidy precision. Hannah sits and thinks. Her brain buzzes with ways to start the conversation. Now and again, she takes a breath then expels it into the air without any words attached. Gates licks his lips and fingers with relish as he finishes.

'Don't you just love almonds?'

'My favourite,' Hannah says.

His face falls and he gestures towards the street. 'Oh, I could go…'

'No, please. Honestly. I'm really not hungry.'

At that precise moment Hannah's stomach gurgles. The edges of Gates mouth twitch but before he dares to speak Hannah challenges him with a glare of such intensity that he looks away.

'Okay then,' he says as he places his plate on the fireplace.

His gaze lingers on it for a moment as if he wishes it was still piled with almond pastry. Hannah has already decided that Gates is one of those annoying people who eats what he likes and never puts on an ounce of weight.

Her words are still stuck somewhere deep in her throat, fighting, and squabbling to escape. Despite her nerves, it's not an uncomfortable silence. The coffee is delicious, Gates is happy and relaxed after his simple breakfast, and Hannah realises with some surprise that she feels safe here in this room.

Gates sits back to regard her.

'So, how can I help?'

He smiles at her and for the first time she notices the deep lines around his eyes. Those grey eyes, waiting with sympathy and kindness. He can't know what's wrong, but he seems to know that something is. Hannah still hesitates. When she entered Gates' flat, she crossed a threshold. She physically and voluntarily handed herself over into the presence of this man. Now here she is settled into a comfortable sofa, drinking good coffee, and being invited to ask for help.

There is still time to run. She can make an excuse and leave, scuttle back upstairs to her flat and crawl into her shell. She can forget about Tina. She can leave Dan to wander around city bars and pick up young women to abuse and discard. Or she can do something. Something that no one else can.

She raises her eyes to his. Gates is smiling, willing and eager.

Where to start? At the beginning.

'You know that I'm a triple nine call handler?'

'I do know that. And I know that you work shifts.'

'Sorry, I must disturb you going in and out.'

'Never. Only the book lady does.'

'She's a teacher.'

'She's a menace.'

How has he been able to make her smile? Just a little. It doesn't matter. What matters is that she feels able to tell her story to this near stranger.

'I had a tough call last night.'

His nod says, *I thought so.*

'Tell me.'

So, she does. She tells him about the call as it happened. And she tells him how it ended. How inadequate it made her feel. How she's been listening to the news. How she can't settle for thinking about it.

'It's shaken you up quite badly,' he observes.

'It has.'

Her coffee is finished, and she leans forward to put the mug on the fireplace next to his abandoned plate. A tear falls onto her hand. She sits up and stares at it, wondering where it's come from. It's only when Gates hands her a box of tissues that she realises she's crying, and she can't stop. He moves to sit beside her, but he doesn't touch her. She relishes the close comfort of a warm, human body and lets the tears come. Their arms touch. Just. This is the first physical contact she has had with a man for thirteen months. It's nice.

It's a long time before the tears stop. Gates takes their mugs to the kitchen for a refill. He takes his time. When he returns, Hannah's blotchy face is dry and the torrent of tears is stemmed. He sits opposite her.

'I'm so sorry,' she says.

'Don't apologise for being human. So, what else?'

The 'there is nothing else' denial is already hanging off Hannah's tongue, but she swallows it down to drown in acid. She doesn't know why she feels that she can talk to this man. Maybe because he's a stranger, maybe it's because he's a sympathetic listener or maybe it's simply time that she unloaded on someone who has the time to listen.

She is all cried out, her eyes are dry.
It's time to tell her story.
She will tell it to Gates.

7

Hannah looks straight into Gates' grey eyes. As each word leaves her mouth the sense of relief and liberation grows inside her.

'Thirteen months ago, I went for a drink after work with some friends. I met a man. He was tall, dark, handsome, well-dressed, well-spoken, interested in me. He was the cliché. Too good to be true, and then some. Even though we were chatting away my friends stuck like glue. It was the arrangement we had. Never leave a woman behind, especially with a stranger. So, at the end of the night, I gave him my mobile number, we said goodnight and went our separate ways.

'I didn't expect him to call but he did. The very next morning. He said he hadn't been able to sleep, couldn't get me out of his head. Had never felt like this about anyone before, he needed to see me. I was flattered, excited. So, I agreed to meet him for a drink. In a bar, a public place, plenty of people around.

'He asked me to have dinner with him, but I refused. Although I'd been excited to see him again, I wasn't feeling great. I was tired from work, my period had started, I had a headache and painful cramps. I didn't tell him that, of course.

Far too embarrassing. I made an excuse about needing to be up early for work and said that I had to go. That's when things changed.'

Gates doesn't speak but he stiffens and sits more upright in his seat.

'He begged me to stay for one more drink. After all, we had both made the effort to come into town. He was having a great time, didn't want me to leave so soon. You get the picture?'

Gates nods, his expression serious and attentive. 'I do.'

'So, against my wishes, he fetched me another drink. When he came back, he seemed a bit off. Nothing I could put my finger on, but he had cooled. There was an edge to him that I hadn't noticed before, a brusqueness. I assumed he was hoping I'd go home with him, and he was disappointed. But it wasn't meant to be a brush-off, so I tried to be extra nice to him. Only I started to feel odd. I couldn't manage the drink and felt nauseous after just a few sips. It was only tonic water, so I decided to leave it and head home. He insisted I finish the drink.'

Gates scowls and his fists clench.

'He said it was wasteful to leave it. His tone changed and I felt as if I was being told off. I didn't like the feeling it gave me. As if he was trying to control me. So, I told him he was welcome to drink it himself if he felt like that.'

'Did he?'

'No. He seemed to get angrier to be honest. He offered to walk me to my car. I didn't want him to, but he insisted, and it was only around the corner. It seemed easier to let him escort me than have an argument. As we walked along the street, I began to feel more unwell and more and more uncomfortable with him. We had just got to the entrance to the car park when my legs gave way.'

Gates closes his eyes for a moment then opens them to examine Hannah's face.

'Do you know why?'

Hannah nods. 'I think he doctored my drink. I'd only had a few sips, so it wasn't enough to knock me out, but enough to render me unfit to drive.'

'So, he drove you home?'

Hannah shook her head. 'I still had wits enough to refuse to give him my address. I didn't want him to know where I lived. Just in case. I was feeling spooked and so unwell. Dizzy and sick. I just wanted him gone. He took my keys off me and drove my car. I thought we were going to his place. I had no intention of going inside with him. I just wanted to be out in the open so I could shout for help if I needed to.'

'But you didn't go to his place?'

'No. He took me to a hotel. I tried to say no, but he left me in the car while he got a room. I knew this wasn't right, but I couldn't think straight. I had a vague idea that I should telephone someone, but my arms wouldn't move. Then he was back. He bundled me inside the hotel and dragged me up the stairs. The reception was empty, so no one saw us. He was half carrying me. I was trying to say no, but he put his hand over my mouth. I remember not being able to breathe. I think I passed out.

'When I woke up, I was on the bed. He was undressing me. I couldn't do anything. I couldn't move or speak but I was aware what was happening. I kept my eyes shut and let him do what he wanted. I was afraid that if I fought back, he would hurt me. Or worse.'

Hannah stops then. She can't share the precise details of her ordeal with Gates. She's not sure she can share it with anyone. Ever. She can't tell him about the pain and the helplessness and the degradation. The horror of being abused and treated as if she were nothing more than a lump of meat.

Her vision is blurry with tears, but she refuses to let them fall, she refuses to blink. She presses a tissue to her closed lids.

'You did the right thing, Hannah. He could have killed you.'

Gates shifts on his seat as if he's going to come over and comfort her, but he sits back almost at once as if he's had second thoughts. Hannah is glad. She thinks that if he touches her right at this moment she will run. When he speaks his voice is gentle.

'Then what happened?'

'I'm not sure because I think I passed out again. When I woke up, I was alone in the bed. The sheets were covered in blood.'

'Had he hurt you?'

'No. It was just a heavy period which obviously hadn't stopped him. There was no sign of him, and I could move, after a fashion. I felt dizzy and wobbly, but I managed to clean myself up, then got dressed and caught a cab home. I went back to collect my car the next day.'

Hannah shrugs as if it were nothing and then stares at Gates, challenging him to tell her how stupid she was. Because that's how the incident had made her feel. It's how she still feels. Stupid and ashamed.

'And you didn't go to the police.'

She shakes her head.

'At first, I was too dizzy and sick to do anything except go to bed. I slept for sixteen hours straight. Then I imagined what the police would say. I went on a second date with this man. I let him walk me to my car. When I felt ill, he took me to a hotel room, and he did what he wanted.'

Gates is out of his chair, pacing the room.

'But you didn't consent.'

'I had passed out. He could argue that I consented. After all, I willingly went to a hotel room with him. It would have been his word against mine. And because I was drugged, there were no bruises because there was no struggle.'

'But what man has sex with a sick woman they've only just met?'

Hannah shrugs.

'The thought of the police and all the interviews and examinations was enough to put me off. I would have been gossip fodder at work for all eternity. And imagine a court case with my face plastered all over the media. I couldn't bear the thought of that. Especially knowing that he would probably get off. I know from work that most of them do. I just wanted to forget about it. It was bad enough having to go to a Sexual Health Clinic for a checkup.'

Hannah can hear her voice becoming shrill.

Gates eyebrows are raised so high there are creases in his forehead.

'It's okay,' says Gates. 'I hear what you're saying.'

'I'm saying that I made a stupid mistake. Now I need to put it right.'

'So that's why you hide,' Gates says.

It's a statement, not a question, and Hannah is surprised at the depth of his perception.

'I don't…' Hannah starts her denial, but the words tangle in her throat the way blackberry vines catch your sleeve when you try to reach the heart of the bush. Gates has speared the very core of her. The place where she shelters all the mistrust and hurt. The place she thinks she guards so well. She feels as if Gates can see her there. He can see the damaged parts of her.

He studies her without speaking. Only a slight twitch of his eyebrows indicates that he is waiting. Hannah senses that the wrong reply will close this thing down and Gates will show her out without a twinge of regret. He comes across as an intelligent and confident man. One who is not afraid to make tough decisions. Hannah feels as if she is about to be tested. She nods and meets Gates' eyes.

'Yes, I hide.'

He examines her before he nods in return. He rubs his chin before he speaks.

'Hannah, you must understand that I hardly know you, and you don't know me. Yet you knock on my door with a story about a perilous situation for this girl Tina and ask for help. I will help you, gladly. But first I have to trust you.'

Hannah wonders why he is getting on his high horse over a simple computer search and her legs are itching to stand up and carry her from the room, head held high. Instead, she pulls herself further into the sofa and forces a small smile. If she is going to help Tina, she needs this man.

'It's just a computer search.'

'Even so.'

Hannah wonders if she should have tried to do it herself. Gates seems to read her thoughts.

'I will be fast, and I'll be thorough. I can find things faster and more efficiently than the police are able to.'

'Ask me anything,' she says.

Gates regards her with a serious face.

'You have to answer with complete honesty.'

'Do we have to pinky swear?'

Gates' serious expression holds firm.

'Sorry,' says Hannah, feeling her cheeks flush with warmth. 'I can be a dork when I'm nervous.'

Gates relaxes his face. 'We can shake on it?'

Gates holds out his hand and they shake. It's a good shake. His skin is warm and dry, and when she looks down at their clasped hands Hannah sees that despite his firm grip his fingers are long and elegant. They are good fingers. Kind fingers. Not the sort that would hurt a woman. They are the sort that would make music, stroke a kitten.

'Do you play the piano?' she asks.

'I do. I play well. What about you?'

'School recorder.'

Finally, he smiles. 'Age?'

'Eleven.'

Gates snorts.

'I mean, how old are you now?'

'Twenty-eight. How is this relevant?'

'It's not. I'm interested in getting to know you.'

'How old are you?'

'Thirty-two.'

'Have you always worked with computers?'

'Since school. Tell me about your family.'

'Mum died when I was eighteen. Cancer.'

Hannah rubs at her forearm. It's something she does when she's uncomfortable. Gates has noticed and she clasps her hands together in her lap.

'That must have been tough.'

'Yes, it was. But I was at uni, so I kept busy studying and I had good friends to support me.'

'Your dad?'

'Remarried to an Italian countess and enjoying the life of Riley in Tuscany. We get on but I barely hear from him. No siblings to talk about either. I'm an only child. You?'

'No siblings,' says Gates. 'Both parents dead. I was a late-in-life baby.'

'Is that a thing?'

'It is. My mum was forty-four and my dad was fifty when I was born. The doctor told my mum I was a fibroid.'

Hannah clasps her hand to her mouth to stifle a giggle.

'It's okay, you can laugh,' says Gates. 'Just don't ever call me a fibroid.'

'Kids at school?' Hannah asks.

'Inevitably. How could they resist?'

'Do you know where they live? I could go and sort them out for you.'

Gates laughs, and Hannah feels herself grinning back. Gates resumes his inquisition.

'So, what did you do before your current job?'

'I was a language teacher, French and Italian. But I decided it wasn't for me.'

'Why?'

'I hate kids.'

'Do you hate all kids?'

'Definitely kids in classrooms. So, what is your job? I know you're a whizz with computers and you work for yourself in cyber security, but what do you actually do?'

There is a long silence while Gates examines his knuckles. When he lifts his eyes to Hannah's, his gaze is steadfast.

'I access information.'

'What sort of information?' Hannah is curious.

'Anything that's stored on a computer.'

'You mean anything on the internet?'

'Anything that can be accessed via the internet. I think of myself as an excavator.'

For the first time his eyes slide away and now it's his right thumbnail that seems to fascinate him. Hannah feels her lungs shrink inside her rib cage as realisation dawns.

'You're a hacker.'

Gates looks up and gives a small nod.

'Can you access anything?'

'Pretty much.'

'Can you access GCHQ?'

'I can, but I don't.'

'Why not?'

'Because I don't know how to do it without getting caught and I don't fancy being detained at His Majesty's

Pleasure. Besides, that's not the sort of thing I need to do to help people.'

'So, you help people?'

'If I can.'

'Isn't hacking illegal?'

'The Computer Misuse Act of 1990 says so.'

'Aren't you worried about getting caught and going to prison?'

'I'm comfortable with what I do. I never mine information to perpetrate harm and I won't get caught. If you can live with that, I can help you.'

'You trust me now then?'

There is a brief pause while Gates examines Hannah's face. She doesn't falter.

'I do.'

'That was a quick decision.'

Gates smiles. 'I have to trust my own judgement, and remember, I've lived here for six months.'

'Have you been watching me?'

'I see you come and go, Hannah. I wonder who or what you're hiding from but that's all. I can tell that you are a good person.'

Hannah slaps her hands onto her knees which are juddering with relief.

'Well, let's stop wasting time and get cracking. I need to help Tina.'

Gates gets up and moves over to his desk.

'So, what do you want to do, Hannah?'

'I want to try and find the hotel. It's not the same one that I was taken to. That place was old and creaky. I know the police will be looking but they can be so slow. If I can tell the police where she is, they can help her.'

'And will it help you?'

'Without a doubt. Whatever has happened to Tina is on me. I could have stopped this man, but I didn't because I was a coward. Oh, if you could only have heard her yourself, Gates. It was wretched taking that call. I need to do something before it happens to someone else.'

At this point, Hannah pauses to take a breath. 'Will you help me?'

'I will. Tell me what you need.'

8

Gates clears a space on his desk and fetches a kitchen chair for Hannah so she can sit beside him.

'Where do you want to start?'

'With the hotel. There hasn't been anything on the news so there's a chance Tina is still there.'

'You're sure it's not the hotel he took you to?'

'Tina couldn't give me much information, but I didn't pick up on any similarities. The place she was in sounded more like a modern, chain hotel. It was bland. The place he took me to was old.'

'More anonymity in a business hotel.'

'Unless he's just gone upmarket?'

'If he's a serial offender,' muses Gates, 'he'll be refining his behaviour, getting better at covering his tracks. Serial offenders become forensically aware and learn how to avoid detection.'

Hannah shivers at the thought that there may be other girls who have been hurt. Gates starts mapping the known locations. The bar where Tina was picked up by Andrew, the bar where Hannah met the mysterious Dan, the car park where she left her car and the hotel she was taken to. All three locations are within half a mile of each other, but it is a half square mile of dense city centre.

'What else do we know?' asks Gates.

Hannah smiles at his use of the word 'we'. Whatever happens, it feels liberating to have someone with her on this.

'The bathroom products. Zephyr Spa.'

'Ah, a soft gentle breeze.'

'What?'

'A zephyr is a soft, gentle breeze.'

'There's nothing soft or gentle about this.'

'True, but it's an unusual name. Let's see what I can find.'

Hannah watches the central screen for a while as Gates types and scrolls with determination. Despite the coffee, her head is nodding. Gates turns to her. 'Go and lie down on the sofa. I'll wake you if I find anything.'

Too exhausted to argue she sinks into the soft cushions with a sigh of pleasure. After what feels like no more than ten minutes Gates is shaking her awake.

'Hannah.'

She is instantly alert. Gates is leaning over her bristling with excitement. He reminds her of an over-eager puppy with a furiously wagging tail. Hannah sits up and tries to straighten her hair with her fingers while Gates shifts from one foot to the other in front of her. He can't keep still.

'You found something,' she says.

His grin says it all, but Gates speaks anyway. 'Come and look.'

'How long have I been asleep?'

'Not long enough but I'm guessing we don't have a lot of time.'

He goes over to the computer screens and sits down. Hannah takes the incongruous kitchen chair that Gates fetched for her earlier. The sun is high in the sky and the window blinds are fully closed. Even so, slivers of light peep through the slats and line both of their faces. Gates is beaming as he pushes aside three empty coffee cups so that Hannah can lean her elbows on the desk.

'I've found the hotel.'

'What? How?'

'Let's just say Zephyr Spa is not the most popular brand of toiletries. The hotel is part of a chain of low-budget rooms designed for overnight and short stays. There are three across the city but only one in the vicinity of the bars and the car park.'

Gates presses a key and the website for the hotel fills the centre screen. Hannah stares without blinking while Gates flicks through several screens of photographs and hotel blurb. She notes an ensuite bathroom and pictures Tina in there wearing the robe that was hanging on a hook behind the door.

'You're sure this is the one?'

'It has to be. It's the only hotel within our target area that stocks Zephyr Spa.'

Excitement gives Hannah a surge of energy.

'What are we waiting for?'

Hannah hurries upstairs to grab her bag and jacket and joins Gates at the front door. She has assumed that he will come with her and is relieved to find him waiting when she comes back downstairs.

'I'll drive,' he offers.

'You sure?'

He nods and points a finger at her. 'Sleep deprivation.'

Hannah shrugs.

'Fair.'

'But you have to navigate.'

'Also fair.'

Rather than fiddle with an unfamiliar satnav, Hannah opens Google Maps on her phone, and they head for the hotel on the outskirts of the city centre. Hannah's insides are involved in some crazy gymnastics, and she presses her fist hard into her abdomen to try and find some relief. Gates is a competent and skilful driver, and with the merciful absence of roadworks and accidents they reach the street they need in twelve minutes flat.

And stop.

The street where the hotel is situated is a non-descript jumble of mixed buildings. A collection of shops and a smattering of low-rise housing fill one side of the road and commercial buildings line the other. A handful of brave, indomitable trees push what's left of their tired, scrappy branches and limp leaves into the stonewashed sky. Parked cars line both sides of the road. There is no obvious sign of a hotel. What they do see is a police barricade preventing them from turning into the street.

'Oh shit,' Hannah says.

She cranes her neck as Gates drives slowly past the crime scene tape and the line of squad cars with their blue lights flashing and finds a place to park on the side of the road. He opens his boot and removes an overnight bag which he slings onto his shoulder. Hannah raises an eyebrow.

'Props,' he says.

'Really?'

'Okay, sports kit.'

Without another word to each other they stride back to the road where the hotel is located. Hannah finds it hard not to run. An officer is manning the barricade and it's clear from his actions that he is turning onlookers away. Hannah and Gates approach with what they hope is a purposeful demeanour. Gates is polite, calm, and respectful. *My unhurried companion,* thinks Hannah. *I need his calm right now.*

'Good afternoon, officer. We were hoping to reach the hotel,' says Gates.

'Sorry, sir. Due to an incident, there will be no access to the street for several hours.'

An incident, thinks Hannah. *In the hotel where Tina was attacked. They've found her.*

Gates points to his overnight bag and engages the officer in a conversation about a planned night at the hotel. Meanwhile Hannah moves forward as far as she dares and strains to look up the street. There are police cars scattered across the road and small clusters of personnel dotted about. Uniformed officers and people in plain clothes are engaged in a variety of activities. Some search the ground while a few Scene of Crime Officers in their white forensic suits huddle outside the hotel, shiny silver-coloured cases clutched in their hands.

The centre for all this activity is a characterless, concrete building. When Hannah stands on tiptoes and strains her neck, she can see an unlit neon Majestic Inn sign above the double glass doors. There is nothing majestic or welcoming about it. It's a depressing building in a depressing street. Hannah feels a lump form in the back of her throat as she thinks of Tina being carried inside to be abused and violated. Because this must be the place. And Hannah has seen enough episodes of *Silent Witness* to know that what she is looking at is a major crime scene.

Hannah's gut contracts and she presses both hands into her abdomen. *Please, God, no.* She stands on the street but is not there in person. She is an empty carcass supported by legs of soft clay. She sees a black van reverse up to the hotel's entrance. Two men in dark suits enter the hotel with a wheeled trolley between them.

She knows by his worried glances that Gates is watching her. When he catches her eye, she gives a brief, sad nod. They are too late. Hannah has no doubt that Tina has been hurt.

Gates chats to the police officer about the forthcoming football season. He is distracting the officer as a gift to Hannah.

As a thank you, she refuses to cry. She will not draw attention to herself in this anonymous street with its ugly commercial buildings and littered gutters. The lifeless windows that stare down at her don't care about a random young woman who has been manipulated and abused by an evil man.

Hannah waits for her clay legs to set and as she does, she watches the suited duo leave the hotel. The trolley is carrying a shape shrouded in black, followed by a white forensic suited man with several cameras around his neck.

She must have let a small sound of frustration escape from her mouth because the police officer looks at her then turns to follow her gaze. All three of them watch the trolley being loaded into the back of the discreet van before the doors are closed and it drives away. Gates thanks the police officer and comes towards Hannah. He takes her arm to lead her away.

'I'm sorry,' says Gates, and catches Hannah as she crumples.

He supports her the few metres back to his car. She stumbles once then pulls herself upright and walks with what she hopes is dignity. For Tina. Hannah hopes that someone will grieve for Tina. Her friends from the bar, her family, maybe her boss, perhaps some flat mates. Another part hopes that Tina's loved ones will be able to bear their grief because if they don't, that will be Hannah's burden too.

9

He loves his job because he can get out and about and sneak around. He makes up an excuse and slips away. He is never questioned. It's only what he deserves. He has spent years building up his persona, gaining the trust of work colleagues. Yes, he's had to work hard at times, put the hours in, deal with shit, keep his mouth shut. But it is so fucking worth it. He is accepted, respected and that means he can do what the hell he likes. He has a free pass.

Even without the address he could have picked up and identified the call on his police scanner from the selection of people and services sent out. SOCOs, of course, uniforms, murder squad detectives, and the mortuary van. It was lucky he was on his way into work, or he might have missed the call. As it was, he called his office, delivered an excuse, and made sure he had eyes on the activity on the street.

There are enough rubberneckers for him to blend in behind a small group of mums and pushchairs. He ignores their gawping and gossiping and stands watching. It is his next favourite thing after the actual event. He loves to watch the chaos created by his own actions. The excitement he feels at watching the corpse being loaded into the mortuary van brings him out in a sweat and his breathing became faster and harsher. He wishes, every time, that it is her corpse. It should be hers. She was the first after all. He won't be able to relax until he has squeezed every breath from her body. He is aware that one of the mums is staring at him. She looks as if she might speak to him, but he turns away to avoid her scrutiny. After all, he is just a casual passer-by, detached but curious.

He approaches the police constable standing at the crime scene tape, but the officer is engrossed in the scene down the street. He doesn't even turn around. So much for observation. Useless, the lot of them. Right now, he needs to get to his office, so he turns away and heads back to his car. This is a good day, he thinks. One of the best.

10

Inside the car Gates clutches the steering wheel and stares through the windscreen. Hannah shuts her eyes and tries not to imagine the closing scenes that ended Tina's life. She fails. Did he beat her, strangle her with his bare hands, or smother her with a pillow? She will know soon enough. The media are never far behind a juicy story. Will the journalists discover that Tina called for help, but it never arrived? Hannah opens her eyes and turns to Gates.

'Why did he kill her?'

Gates' eyes widen. He opens his mouth to speak but closes it again and shrugs.

'I mean, why did he kill Tina and not me? I know he drugged and raped her, but he drugged and raped me too, yet he left me to go home. Why? What did Tina do to make him so angry?'

Gates purses his lips and blows out a long whistle of air. 'That's the million-dollar question, isn't it? What makes a human being kill another person? If we knew the answer to that we could try and do something to stop it.'

Hannah thinks about this. She was submissive. She didn't scream or shout or fight back. Could it be as simple as that?

Could Tina's attempt to reach for the pencil and pad of paper have been enough for her to lose her life? *Did I cause this?* thinks Hannah. Even so, why *did* he kill Tina and not her? Gates interrupts her thoughts.

'What do you want to do?'

The sight of the body bag has clarified Hannah's thoughts. She has been in hiding for so long she has almost forgotten what life used to be like. But at least she has a life. Tina has lost hers, and whether or not her thoughts are justified, Hannah feels responsible. If her attacker had been reported and caught, he wouldn't have been walking the streets picking up girls. He wouldn't have picked up Tina. Despite her distress over Tina, Hannah's over-riding feeling is one of anger. She detests this man. She detests what he has done. He must think he can get away with anything.

Not if Hannah has anything to do with it. She sits up straight and stares ahead. She has made her decision. And even though that decision terrifies her, she knows it's the right one.

'I'm going to the police.' Her voice is strong, resolute.

Gates nods his agreement.

'I think you should.'

'Will you come with me?'

Gates leans across and takes her hand. Hannah suppresses the instinct to snatch it away. She feels the gentle pressure of a comforting squeeze. 'I'll take you there, but I'll wait outside.'

'You won't come in?'

He shakes his head. 'The police and I don't mix. I'm sorry.'

She feels a little let down although she has no right to be disappointed by someone who is already doing more than enough to help her. Someone she barely knows.

'Don't you trust them either?'

'It's more complicated than that.'

Hannah thinks, but not for long.

'I want to go.'

'Do you want to go straight there?'

Hannah shakes her head. 'I'm exhausted. Would it matter if I left it until tomorrow?'

'Not for Tina. But it might be an idea to wait until the news breaks in the media. Unless you can explain to the police how you managed to track down the hotel on your own?'

'I'm sure you can talk me through it. But I really need to sleep. I can't think straight.'

Gates starts the car and executes a confident U-turn to head back the way they have come. As they pass the end of the cordoned-off street Hannah glances across Gates towards the hotel, at the policeman guarding the end of the street, at the suited man standing behind him. Standing and staring at the hotel and surrounding activity. There is something familiar about the tall man in the suit. Maybe it's his profile. Hannah is not sure what it is, but she feels a bolt of recognition hit her. She knows this man. As they pass by, she glances back just as the man turns to walk away. A turn that reveals his face. Hannah screams and throws her head down onto her knees. She covers her ears with her hands and cries out.

'No, no, no, no!'

Gates starts to brake but the blare of a lorry's horn forces him to keep moving. He flicks on his indicator and slows to search for a parking space, but Hannah leans an arm across and switches the indicator off.

'Don't stop, keep driving.'

She squeezes the words out from the back of her throat as paralysis overtakes her. First her mouth sets as solid as stone, then her whole body retracts until she is immobile, her fingers digging into the sides of her head. From the corner of her eye, she sees Gates give her a worried glance as he presses his foot onto the accelerator. He drives in silence until they are well away from the hotel, and he turns into the car park of a suburban supermarket. He parks the car well away from the entrance and switches off the engine. He does not ask Hannah what's wrong. He rubs the space between her shoulder blades while she reanimates herself.

When she's ready to speak Hannah raises her head and says one word.

'Dan.'

'Dan?'

Hannah nods.

'He was there, on the corner, standing behind the police officer.'

Gates pulls himself upright in his seat and half turns towards Hannah. He studies her face as if he needs to assess the truthfulness of her words. 'Are you sure? Could you be mistaken?'

Hannah shakes her head. She has imagined her attacker's face hundreds of times over the last thirteen months. He has been the shape of her postman standing behind the glass of her front door with a parcel to deliver. He has been the profile of the man sitting in the car next to her at the traffic lights. She has seen him in the waiting room at the dentist; in front of a mirror at her hairdresser's; in the car park at work at the start of a moonless night shift. It's always the briefest of glances as an iron hammer swings into her abdomen expelling every breath of air. Then a second look and her diaphragm lifts because she sees that no, she's mistaken, it isn't him at all.

Until today.

The second glance crushed Hannah. Without a doubt the man she saw was Dan and even though she only saw him in profile, it felt as if his ice-blue eyes were looking straight at her.

Bile is rising at the back of her throat, and she scrabbles at the handle of the car door like a caged wild animal. Gates leans across and opens it for her. She stumbles out of the car onto the grass verge next to their parking space, where she drops to her knees and retches, spitting out acidic yellow bile. When she is able to stand upright on shaking legs, Gates is beside her offering a tissue.

'I'm sorry,' says Hannah.

'Don't be. Shock does that to you. Listen, I'll go and get you some water, will you be okay here?'

Hannah shakes her head and reaches towards him. 'No, don't leave me. Please.'

Gates nods and takes her hand. Together they walk to the supermarket where Gates buys water, sandwiches, and apples. After he has paid, he points out the toilets and waits outside while Hannah rinses out her mouth and washes her face and hands. When she emerges white-faced and trembling, Gates takes her hand again and leads her back to the car. They sit inside with the doors open and Hannah sips her water.

'Are you positive it was him?'

'One hundred per cent.'

'Did he see you?'

Hannah shakes her head. 'I can't be certain, but he wasn't looking at our car. He was looking down the street. He only turned as we drove away.'

'We passed quickly, and we were on the other side of the road. It's unlikely that he saw you.'

'But what if he saw me when I was standing at the barrier?'

Gates is silent.

'What if he saw me?' Hannah asks again, her voice strained.

'I didn't see anyone else near us. He couldn't have been behind us without us clocking him. And you were watching the hotel. You would've seen him if he came from that direction.'

Hannah wants to be reassured but a sudden chill has doused her body and she shivers.

'Hannah?' asks Gates. 'What is it?'

'What if he was watching us the whole time?'

'I think he was watching the crime scene.'

'But you don't know that, do you?'

Gates remains calm but Hannah wonders if he too is appalled at their situation and is trying not to show it.

'We need to get to the police station. I don't think I should wait.'

'Okay, but let's go via the flat. It's a small detour. You need to think through what you will tell the police and I need to get online. There's nothing we can do for Tina now.'

Hannah nods. It is the only movement available to her. She feels like a corpse herself.

11

Back at the house Gates leads Hannah into his flat and stands over her until her sandwich is eaten. Hannah is almost immobile from exhaustion and shock.

'You need to sleep,' says Gates.

Hannah shakes her head. 'I have to go to the police right away.'

'How so?'

'Because Dan was there. He was watching Tina's body being removed.'

'We don't know for sure that this man is her killer.'

'Of course we do.' Hannah is almost shouting. 'Dan was right there. The very same man who attacked me. He was watching and gloating. Why else would he suddenly appear at the scene? You can't possibly think his presence is some sort of coincidence?'

'You're right. It is weird that he was there.'

'Don't murderers often return to the scene of the crime, especially serial killers? They want to re-live the sensations they felt when they were committing the crime. Google it if you don't believe me.'

'I do believe you.'

'So, why don't you want me to go to the police?'

Despite Hannah's obvious agitation, Gates remains calm and measured.

'I'm not saying don't go, Hannah. I just want you to think things through first. This is not just a rape case now. This is murder and the investigation will be massive. You will be a key witness. Are you prepared to let this take over your life?'

Hannah replies without hesitation.

'I'm involved. I answered Tina's call. The police will have been listening to it and analysing it for hours.'

'Exactly,' interrupts Gates. 'And if there's anything on there to help catch this man, the police will find it.'

What is it that he's not telling her? One minute he's saying that she should go to the police and now he's backing off. Hannah is too tired and upset to make sense of anything.

'But it's not only about the call, Gates. It's about the fact that I can identify Dan.'

Gates sits down next to Hannah. He studies her face.

'It's everything about the call,' he says. 'The call *is* everything. You can identify this man from your attack but the 999 call can also identify you. I'm worried about what that means for you and your safety.'

'But Dan won't know that it was me who took the call. How can he? It's not possible. Call handlers are anonymous. We're just a voice. We might as well be a satnav speaking.'

'You must protect yourself, Hannah. I'm asking you to slow down and think before you act, that's all. In this world of technology, no-one has privacy, no-one is anonymous, and anyone can be traced and tracked. And dealt with if needs be.'

'Dealt with? Are you saying this man will come and get me? That's preposterous.'

Gates is fidgeting. Hannah guesses he is anxious to return

to the internet, yet his face shows his ongoing concern. He holds up his hands, his palms open to Hannah.

'Okay, I've got a proposal,' he says.

Hannah meets his gaze, but she is too shaken to speak.

'You go and get some sleep. I'm going to do some research. Based on what I find, we'll have a discussion in the morning and then you can decide what you want to do. Whatever it is, I'll support you.'

Hannah remains subdued but she nods in agreement and gets up to return to her own flat.

'Wait,' says Gates, 'give me your phone.' Hannah hands it over without question and Gates enters his number. 'If you need anything, call or text. I'll be right here, all night.'

Hannah manages the ghost of a smile. 'Thank you. I am grateful for all your help.'

'Go and get some sleep. I don't know how you're still standing.'

Hannah drags herself up the stairs.

Inside her flat she throws her clothes on the floor, slips under the poppy duvet, and allows sleep to carry her away.

***

The next morning Hannah wakes with a start. She has three days off before her next early shift on Sunday, so it's the thought of Tina and not work that propels her from her bed and into the shower. She's knocking on Gates' door a few minutes after seven. He throws open the door and ushers her inside. Hannah can see that he too has showered, shaved, and changed.

'Did you get some sleep?' he asks.

'Yes, I did. Even though I wasn't expecting to. Did you?'

'I did.'

Gates sits at his desk, and he beckons Hannah towards what she now considers her chair. She examines the screens and recognises the logos and headers. What she sees impresses, rather than surprises her.

'You hacked the police.' It's a statement, not a question.

'I did.'

'And?'

'Well, first, you must understand that I can only monitor the information that is recorded on the police systems. I have no access to briefings, discussions, chats etc., other than notes taken and entered onto the system. A few of the officers are a bit shoddy on that front but there appears to be a very competent DI in charge of the case. His name is Neil Waterhouse. He is very experienced by the look of things, and his notes are meticulous and timely. I've checked the records of as many of the officers involved on the case as I can, and our DI Waterhouse seems to be the man of the moment. For us, at least. He is also the Senior Investigating Officer, so he's a decision-maker.'

'Why does that matter?'

'Because I want to know that you are going to be protected from this Dan and DI Waterhouse is experienced and thorough.'

'That's great. I'll see him. I want to go today.'

Hannah wishes Gates would go with her, but she can't ask. Gates lives with risk and he has learned to manage that risk. It's not Hannah's place to disrupt that. He examines her face before he speaks.

'I can't come, Hannah.'

'I know.'

'I'm sorry, but I can't bring myself into line of sight. I've told you I live under the radar.'

'What does that even mean?'

'It means that nothing is in my name. It means that as far as possible I earn cash and pay cash. It means I keep away from authorities, I avoid social media, I keep my head down. I don't relax, ever. It means that no-one will ever steal my identity because I don't have one.'

'How does that work?'

'There are two of us. Olly lives in Scotland. Not his real name by the way. We help each other to live without leaving a trail.'

'If there's no trail, why can't you go to the police with me?'

Gates leans across to hold Hannah's hand where it's rubbing her forearm. 'I just can't, Hannah. There will be too many questions and I'll get dragged into the case. I'm much more use to you in front of a computer screen.'

Hannah manages a wobbly smile and nods in acknowledgement.

'So, tell me. Are you some kind of villain?'

Gates laughs and shakes his head.

'Not quite.'

'I don't really understand.'

Gates leans back in his chair.

'Much of my work is totally legit. I work for companies who want their systems tested. If I can get in, then I can show them how to stop other people doing the same.'

'Yes, but…'

Gates holds his hand up to stop Hannah interrupting.

'But I also work for people who need help with problems when the authorities let them down. I can trace people, and money. I can follow paper trails, unearth documents, find evidence and signatures, and I can do it quickly.'

'Though not always legally.'

'Precisely.'

'Why are you telling me all this? Isn't it a risk?'

Gates gives a slight shake of his head.

'You need my help, Hannah. I trust that you want that help badly enough to keep me out of the spotlight.'

'I do. I will.'

'That's good enough. Shake?'

Gates holds out his hand and Hannah shakes it.

'Deal. So, this someone I need to see. You said his name's DI Waterhouse? Do you know him?'

'Not personally. But from his work he comes across as a good, safe copper.'

'So, you're fully behind me going to the police.'

'I am,' says Gates.

Hannah hears the words, but she has already spent enough hours with Gates to pick up on the slight hesitation in his voice.

'What are you not telling me?'

Gates starts to scroll and click through a myriad of screens pointing out information to Hannah and explaining its significance. After twenty minutes of this Hannah has learned several things. The most important of these is that examination of the crime scene has revealed no forensic evidence.

'Nothing at all?' asks Hannah.

'Nada. No fingerprints, no fibres, no skin or hair, no semen. According to the SOCOs, there was no one in the hotel room with Tina.'

'How is that possible? What does this mean?'

'It means that Tina's attacker is forensically aware. An expert.'

'Like a professional expert?'

'Could be, but not necessarily. These days the information is all out there for anyone that is interested enough to look. It does suggest that this guy either knows what he's doing professionally or else he has studied forensic techniques. He knows what SOCOs and the police look for and he knows how to avoid leaving anything behind.'

'So, he's done this before.'

'He must have done. This man has no intention of getting caught, so unless the forensics team get a lucky break, this attacker could already be home free. The police can't prosecute without evidence.'

Gates returns to his screens and starts clicking and scrolling again. He explains to Hannah that despite the presence of CCTV cameras, there is no evidence of the man that Hannah has identified, or any man come to that. He is either a master of disguise or he has managed to evade the cameras.

'So, he's local,' surmises Hannah.

'Not just local,' says Gates. 'He knows the area so well that he knows where the cameras are and how to avoid them. He knows how to conceal whatever form of transport he uses. He managed to get Tina into the hotel without being seen, perhaps by going in through the rear entrance. He's a ghost, Hannah.'

'A ghost?'

'This crime has been meticulously planned. The attacker must have staked out the area, checked for cameras, car parking, identified a non-descript hotel in a quiet backstreet. It's like he's set out to play the system and he plans to win. Whoever the attacker is, he stands a good chance of getting away with this.'

'What?'

Hannah swings round to look Gates in the eye. She needs to check that he is serious.

'Are you sure?'

'The evidence coming in is crazy, Hannah. This guy has raped and murdered a young woman and left no trace. The case has already hit the morning news.'

'How was she murdered?' asks Hannah.

Gates draws in a breath. 'She was strangled. The full post-mortem is happening today, but the pathologist thinks she was knocked unconscious by a blow to the head then strangled.'

'So, she didn't suffer?'

Hannah is studying Gates with an intensity that makes him fidget. His words are delivered with truthfulness.

'No, not at the end.'

Hannah's eyes are wet with tears but today she is in control. She knew yesterday that Tina was dead and there is nothing she can do to change that. But she can still fight for justice for her. She can help the police catch the man who is hurting women and who has killed at least one of them. She can stop him doing it to anyone else. Hannah is so deep in thought that it's only when Gates comes into the room with a tray of coffee and toast that she is aware he had left in the first place.

Her brain is a mass of tangled vines with too many facts for her to extract a reasonable narrative from the mess, too many questions to unravel from the tendrils, too many secrets concealed in the roots. She sips her coffee in silence.

'You're quiet,' observes Gates.

'It's too much to take in. What does all this mean?'

Gates cradles his mug of coffee as if he's warming his hands. Hannah finds herself studying his fingers again. He has the most beautiful hands. He works his way through a slice of toast and swallows. She comes to attention as he speaks.

'It means we have to do what we can, as well as we can, and leave the rest to the police.'

'Which means I have to start by reporting my attack.'

Gates nods.

'I know it's the right thing to do but I still don't feel that I can trust the police. How do I know they will even listen to me? Rape cases are so often dismissed, and the rapists get away while the women are blamed for encouraging them. The conviction rate is appalling.'

'DI Waterhouse seems to be a good guy. His record is squeaky clean, no complaints, no disciplinaries, good clean-up rate, a few commendations. And they can't ignore the 999 call.

It's on record. And remember this is not just rape. This guy has escalated to murder. That's a whole different ball game.'

'So, when am I going to see him?'

Gates grins. 'I'm glad you're up early. You're in his diary for nine thirty this morning.'

'How…'

'Don't ask,' says Gates.

12

Despite being a call handler, Hannah isn't familiar with her local police station, and she's surprised to find it housed in a modern purpose-built building with a curved façade and floor-to-ceiling glass frontage. It makes Hannah think of an upmarket lawyer's office or a trendy advertising agency. Inside a single policeman sits behind a desk surrounded by a protective screen. He looks so young Hannah thinks his uniform should be from the local grammar school rather than the police force. The reception is bare of any accoutrements, no doubt to avoid loose items being used as weapons. Hannah gives her name to the youngster and asks for DI Neil Waterhouse.

During a brief wait Hannah is entertained by a scruffy middle-aged man who discovered a bunch of keys under a bench while walking his dog that morning. He's happy to hand them in to lost property but expects a reward for his efforts. A substantial one at that. At one point fifty quid is mentioned. Watching the scene unfold calms Hannah's nerves. She is happy to be distracted. While the young constable's cheeks turn pink with frustration, DI Waterhouse bangs through a side door, dispatches the finder of the keys and then approaches Hannah with his hand held out.

He is somewhere in his mid to late fifties. A little under six feet in height, he has the beginnings of a paunch that suggests too much desk work and junk food. Without his physical bulk he would fill the space in front of Hannah with his firm voice and strong handshake. When he smiles, an attractive crinkle of laughter lines appears at the outer corners of his eyes. Hannah warms to him straight away. Gates has chosen well.

'Come through,' says DI Waterhouse as he swipes his key card and holds open the door.

The DI strides down a long corridor to the interview room. Hannah hurries to keep up. After watching too many cop shows, she's expecting a bare room with a table, two chairs and a murky two-way mirror on the wall. Instead, she finds herself in a small, pleasant room with a window, a two-seater settee, a coffee table and two semi-comfortable-looking chairs.

'Can I get you anything?' asks the DI. 'Coffee, tea?'

'Just some water, please.'

The DI disappears for a few minutes and returns with two styrofoam cups of water. Hannah is settled on the sofa and waits while the DI makes himself comfortable in the chair opposite her.

'I understand you want to talk to me about the Tina Cashen case.'

Hannah nods. 'At least, it's something that I think might be related.'

'In what way?'

'I work as a triple nine call handler,' begins Hannah. 'I took the call made by Tina in the early hours of yesterday morning.'

'We have access to the recording of the call,' says the DI. 'It's being analysed as we speak.'

Hannah nods.

'Yes, I realise that. But thirteen months ago, I was attacked in the same way as Tina, and I recognised the attacker's voice. It was the same man.'

DI Waterhouse shifts forward in his seat.

'You're sure?'

'Absolutely.'

He holds up his hand. 'Wait, just a moment.'

He gets up and leaves the room. Hannah wonders what's going on, but she doesn't have to wonder for long. He returns in a matter of minutes accompanied by a young female officer who smiles at Hannah before taking the second vacant chair.

'This is Sergeant Ann Flynn. I've asked her to join us so she can take a statement as we talk. I believe you're an important witness in this case, and I'd like to take a formal statement if that's okay with you?'

Hannah nods, grateful to be taken seriously.

'Anything I can do to help.'

The statement takes a long time. There's a break for coffee and biscuits, and DI Waterhouse is called out of the room twice to take urgent calls. In between all this, Hannah tells her story.

The questions are easy at first, name, age, address, occupation. Then come the details of the call. It is clear to Hannah that the DI has listened to the call with great care and attention but all the same, he wants to hear Hannah's words. He dissects her thoughts and feelings, and shares her horror as the situation escalates, Tina's attacker wakes, and then there is only silence.

'That must have been tough to hear,' he says.

He asks Hannah about her own attack.

'I haven't told anyone this before,' she says, blushing as she delivers the lie. *Gates doesn't count*, she tells herself.

'That's okay, tell it to me now,' says the DI. 'Take your time.'

Hannah is hesitant at first. She still feels like a fool for meeting the man, for allowing herself to be drugged, for going to the hotel room without a struggle. She is awkward and self-conscious when she talks about the attack and the blood afterwards and her cheeks burn with embarrassment. Yet despite this, she also hears her voice growing stronger as she relates her story. She feels the weight of the events from that night lift away from her shoulders. They aren't eliminated. Not at all. But they are eased a little, just as they had been when she talked to Gates. The horror of that night is still with Hannah but at the same time she experiences a liberation of sorts. The load lifts with every re-telling.

'You are positive that this is the same man who killed Tina?'

'Positive,' she replies. 'Same voice, same words, same actions. I'm one hundred per cent positive.'

'So, you could identify him in a line-up?'

'Without a doubt.'

The DI almost smiles when she says this. He is silent for some time after Hannah has finished but when he does finally speak his voice is kind.

'Can I ask you why you didn't report your own attack at the time?'

Hannah pauses as she struggles to wrangle her thoughts into coherent sentences.

'There were so many reasons not to,' she finally manages. 'The embarrassment of the investigation, the examination and questioning. The feeling that I might not be believed or that I might be accused of leading him on. The fear of my name being made public. Knowing how few men get arrested and charged. And even when they are, how few are convicted. But most of all…'

Hannah pauses. The anger she felt when she learnt that Tina was dead has taken root inside her. It has become part of her and drives her on now.

'…I don't want to cause offence.'

'Say it.'

'All the stuff in the press about police corruption, their attitude towards women, the crimes they commit.'

Hannah compresses her lips together, afraid that she has gone too far. Her face feels hot, and her palms are damp. The DI takes a breath before he speaks.

'I understand what you're saying and I'm very grateful that you've come forward now. It's a brave thing to do. But I want you to understand that while there have been cases of police officers abusing their position to target people, both men and women, it's a very small minority.'

Hannah opens her mouth to speak but once again the DI holds up a hand to stop her.

'Even one case is one too many. I want you to know that the police force is working hard to root this out. The fact that these cases have been in the press is because the officers in question have been discovered, charged, and convicted. They have been caught and will continue to be caught. Meanwhile we are doing our best to put systems and procedures in place that will prevent these things happening in the future.'

'But they will still happen, won't they?'

The DI puffs out a stream of air.

'It's possible, of course. There are over 135,000 police officers in England and Wales and almost every one of them is in the job to do some good and help people. Almost everyone. Most of us can be trusted and Hannah, if you help us, I promise you I will do everything in my power to make sure we earn your trust and we keep it.'

Hannah is not sure she is entirely convinced but her need to do something for Tina and help catch Dan overrides her concerns.

'Thank you.'

'Are you still happy to proceed?'

Hannah hears the determination in her own voice when

she replies. She wants to get the bastard.

'Yes, I am.'

The DI smiles.

'Hannah, thank you for this. Sergeant Flynn is going to produce your statement and I want you to read it carefully before signing it. If there's anything that you disagree with or are not sure about, it's important that you tell her.' He fishes in his pocket and withdraws a business card. He scribbles something on the back and hands the card to Hannah. 'This is my private number. If you think of anything else, anything at all, or you're worried, you call me at any time.'

'Why would I be worried?'

'I'm sure you won't be but keep it with you at all times.'

Hannah wants to repeat her question, but the DI is talking again.

'Your statement has been incredibly useful, Hannah, and I can't thank you enough for coming in. Someone will contact you within the next twenty-four hours to help us construct a facial composite of the attacker.'

'Like an identikit?'

'Exactly like that. And I suspect we may ask you to come in again as we start to look at things in more detail. If that does happen, please don't worry. It will just be routine. Even though you can identify the attacker, we can't prosecute without evidence and this man is very good at hiding it. But when we do catch him, we'll ask you to come in and identify him. Do you have any questions for me?'

Hannah has only one burning question. 'Yes. I don't understand why he didn't kill me.'

Waterhouse nods and runs a hand through his hair. He suddenly looks exhausted.

'Honestly, Hannah? I think your period saved your life.'

This is not the answer Hannah is expecting.

'How?'

'I think the blood made him panic and he ran. We have two other cases linked to this man. If it is the same attacker, you could be his first victim and the only survivor. By the time Tina was attacked, he had become an accomplished and professional killer. None of us have ever seen a crime scene as spotless as this one. He covers up and cleans up. I can only imagine that your blood taught him a lesson.'

'How?'

'Cleaning up that sort of mess would have taken a long time and been difficult. I suspect he panicked and wanted to get out of the room before the domestic staff arrived and started asking questions. Slipping away during the night shift, gave him a better chance of leaving without being seen. The timing of a crime often means the difference between getting away and being arrested. This man has learned with each attack. He is thoughtful and clever. We're dealing with a highly intelligent, motivated, and methodical criminal.'

'You're saying my period saved my life?'

'It contaminated the crime scene, so he ran. This man leaves everything spotless. It's part of his MO. The bloody sheets would have impacted his process and he couldn't carry on with the way he wanted to do things. Date rape drugs are known to cause memory loss. I imagine he gambled that you wouldn't remember anything about the attack. So, no reason for you to report the crime. And as you've pointed out yourself, it would have been his word against yours if he was caught. The bottom line is that unless we can catch him, this is all speculation. We just don't know.'

'So, in a way, I was the lucky one?'

The DI sighs.

'Hannah, the other two cases involve girls who were given Rohypnol, probably in a drink, followed by Midazolam administered intravenously. Given in the right dose, it causes complete loss of memory. They were killed anyway. If you were his first victim, he's escalated from rape to murder. We honestly don't know at this stage. We need evidence.'

The DI gets up to leave then turns to look at Hannah. 'Listen to me carefully, Hannah. I want you to know that what happened to you and what happened to Tina is not down to you. None of this is your fault.'

Tears prick her eyes. 'Thank you.'

13

When Hannah is woken by Gates' knock on her door the following morning her bleary eyes register nothing more than the bakery bag in one hand and the two coffee mugs in the other.

'Breakfast,' declares Gates with a smile.

'This is getting to be a habit.'

'A nice one, I hope.'

'Of course.'

Hannah fetches plates from the kitchen. When she returns Gates is examining her lounge with interest. It is light and contemporary, with any potential harshness softened by cushions, throws and accent lamps. But it's cold and otherwise empty, not a place to linger.

Hannah invites Gates to sit down. After just two days in his company, she knows that eating will be his priority, so she sips her coffee and nibbles an almond croissant while he devours his breakfast. When he has finished, he comes straight to the point.

'I've been doing an awful lot of thinking about this situation.'

'And?' asks Hannah with trepidation.

'This is not over for us. I think we need to try and identify this Dan guy ourselves so that we can get him arrested.'

'Why not leave it to the police?'

'They're too slow. Hamstrung by all their rules and procedures. They even have to get permission to track a mobile phone these days. I can get into any system and leave without a trace. And I can do it fast. All we need is his name and he's off the streets.'

Hannah smiles.

'I couldn't have put it better myself.'

Gates throws his hands open as if the deal has already been agreed. Hannah doesn't tell him that she's spent several hours during the night coming to the same conclusion.

'How?'

'We find him.'

Hannah agrees with the sentiment but is not so impressed with the confidence in Gates' voice.

'It's a big job.'

'We use the tech. That's my job and there's nothing I like better than a challenge. I'll see you downstairs.'

***

Gates has left his door ajar and by the time Hannah knocks and slips inside he is already engrossed in his screens. He lifts a hand to acknowledge her presence but remains focused on the task in hand. Hannah sits on the settee and waits. In the confusion of the last two days, Gates has been the eye of Hannah's storm, her calm centre amongst the turmoil of Tina's attack and the resurrection of Hannah's own memories.

'What was the date and time of your attack?'

Details of Hannah's own attack have been pushed as far away from her present as she can manage to shove them, but they never fade. She gives Gates the date but struggles with the time.

'I was so fuzzy from the drugs. I can't be sure.'

'Do you know what time you went into the bar?'

That's easy. It was a day off. Hannah used to meet her girlfriends regularly, always in the same bar, always at the same time. Gates gives no acknowledgement but returns to his tapping and scrolling. Hannah lets her mind wander over the events of her last shift. After thirteen months trying to forget her attack, she is now hauling it into the present so she can remember every detail of the man she now knows is a killer.

'Over here, Hannah.'

Hannah goes over to the desk and sits in her chair next to Gates.

'I'm going to check for CCTV around the bar, car park and hotel on the date of your abduction, although it's so long ago I think it's unlikely I'll find anything. Most CCTV records over old footage which gets wiped. It's only more modern systems that download directly to a computer. I'm going to put you to work on available footage from Tina's case.'

'Won't the police be doing that?'

'They will. But without a solid description, they don't know who they're looking for. You know this guy's face. I need to get hold of a screen shot so I've pulled all relevant CCTV. I've got one camera from the hotel lobby that I want you to go through. There's nothing outside or behind the hotel but I've got two cameras from nearby streets which may give us his approach. Police witness statements say that Tina left the bar around nine-thirty on Friday night and the triple nine call came in at two forty-five a.m. See if you can spot this guy entering the hotel with Tina. If you have no luck there, we'll start on the surrounding streets. He must have taken Tina to the hotel in a car which means we might catch him parking nearby.'

Gates clicks to enlarge a photo labelled Tina Cashen on his second screen.

'She was nineteen,' says Gates, 'shared a flat with two friends and worked as a beauty therapist.'

Hannah finds herself looking at a pretty heart-shaped face framed by a cloud of soft white-blonde hair. She is smiling, her face perfectly made up. The sound of her sobs and cries as she is grabbed by her attacker echo in Hannah's ears. Hannah grips the edge of the desk with both hands and bites down hard on the inside of her cheek.

'She doesn't look old enough to be out drinking,' she says.

Gates demonstrates how to scroll through the footage then leaves her to stare at the computer screen while he prepares her second latte of the day. By lunchtime Hannah can feel herself going cross-eyed and, at Gates' insistence, she takes a break to eat the lunch that he has prepared.

'What have you been working on?' she asks him. She's been aware of him occupied at the other end of the desk but has not taken her eyes from the grainy pictures of a tired hotel lobby that sees about as much life as an Egyptian tomb.

'I've been going through the police records. There's nothing new about Tina and still no useful forensic evidence. There must be a clue to his identity somewhere. I just need to find it.'

They are interrupted by Hannah's mobile phone.

'I have to go to the police station,' she informs Gates as she ends the call. 'They want me to do a facial composite.'

'Right now?'

'They're threatening to come to my flat so that I won't be too inconvenienced. I said it would suit me to drop by as I'm going into town.'

Gates rises to his feet, but Hannah taps his arm to stop him. 'It's okay, I can do this.'

'Are you sure?' Gates voice offers concern, but his eyes slide toward his screens. He seems torn between his urge to find Tina and his need to protect Hannah.

'Yes, I'm sure. There's so much to do here. It's crazy for you to waste time sitting waiting for me.'

Gates' face looks doubtful, but Hannah is confident she can manage without an escort. Gates' assistance has made her feel part of something. She wants so much to do her bit. More than anything else on earth she wants to nail this man. Nothing and no-one will stop her.

'Come straight back.'

'Yes, Dad,' teases Hannah. As she turns to go Gates rests a hand on her shoulder.

'I'm serious, Hannah. I want you to be careful. At least for the next few days.'

She is touched by his concern. 'I will. I promise.'

<hr>

***

At the police station the same youth is manning the reception desk and DI Waterhouse bursts through the door just as he did before. Hannah is taken to the same room she was in yesterday and is introduced to Beverley, who will construct the composite.

It doesn't take long.

Hannah is a good subject to work with, confident and helpful. Apart from the fact that Dan's face is chiselled into her memory, the recent sighting of him at the police barricade has reinforced his features in her mind. She is shown screens of complete faces and features, and as she makes her selections Dan's face evolves in front of her.

Hannah remembers Dan as tall and muscular. He exuded strength and was classically handsome. Planed cheekbones, piercing blue eyes, a straight, symmetric nose, and a well-formed jaw. His good looks, however, were secondary to his charming personality. It was the way he engaged with Hannah that sparked her interest. The way he held eye contact, his smile, his attentiveness. The way he made her feel interesting and special. Right up until the point where she refused her drink and the façade started to wither.

With a short tea and toilet break Hannah is finished in ninety minutes. She is satisfied with the image on the screen. It's as good as a photograph. Yes, she is happy. No, she does not want to add anything else. She wants him caught, that's all.

She leaves the police station with a swing in her step. She has finally been able to do something that might help the police catch Dan. She knows arrest is only the first step, but if Hannah can help to get him off the streets, perhaps she can forgive herself for her cowardice after her own attack. And even better, maybe she can stop him attacking someone else.

As she heads towards her car, she texts Gates to tell him she is on her way back.

All done. Quick stop at the shops then heading home.

She can't claim to feel happy at this moment, but she feels lighter, hopeful. Most of all, she feels satisfied. Hannah would never have described herself as a vengeful person, but right now the thought of helping to get Dan arrested, to see him off the streets, to see him punished is at the forefront of her mind. Nothing else matters. It's like pushing hard to close a door that is wedged open and finally it's starting to inch forwards.

As Hannah reaches the car, her skin begins to prickle. She glances at her forearms half expecting to find a ladybird but there is nothing there. The trace of a shiver brushes Hannah's skin as she presses the key to open the car. She reaches for the door handle and stops, frozen. She is certain that someone is watching her. She can feel eyes boring into her back and her ears hum with a sudden and uncertain fear. She swings round and scans the car park. There's no-one there. Hannah moves to the rear of the car and opens the boot, pretends to rummage inside. It's just an excuse to check the passenger side of the car.

Still nothing.

She stands up and shuts the boot. Her eyes tell her that she is alone, but her body is vibrating with the certainty that she is being watched. *Now, I'm getting paranoid,* she tells herself. She gets into the car and locks the door, takes a final look around and drives away with shaking hands.

14

*S*tupid bitch.

He smirks as he watches her cowering behind the opened boot of her car. What the hell good does she think that will do? Does she seriously think she can swan across a public car park in full view of the world and then suddenly disappear if she stands behind the boot of her car? He watches her hurry into the driving seat and fumble with her seat belt, all the time scanning the car park. She even looks straight at the laurel hedge that he is hiding behind, but she is too frantic to see him through the thick foliage.

He smiles to himself as she drives away. Perhaps smile is the wrong word. It's more of a full-on self-satisfied smirk. Half a million people in the city and who should he almost bump into? Okay, so he got a tip-off. We all need a break.

He recognised her straight away. He never forgets any of them. Why would he? He plays the movie of their last hours in his head night after night. It's only when the movie gets stale that he refreshes his catalogue with fresh blood. Literally. This one though is his one and only mistake. Hannah. The one that got away. Not the ending that he wanted to write. More a debacle than anything else. Her story demands a new ending. Directors do that all the time, don't they? Change the ending. Some even film two endings and let the preview audience select the one they like best.

He can do that.

He knows how Hannah's story should finish. He knows he should tie up loose ends. Especially if she's paying visits to the local nick.

Yes, there needs to be a new finale. He will see to it.

He hurries to his car.

15

ates is waiting for her in the hallway and something about his rigid stance and serious face frightens her. He has so quickly become her oasis that his obvious disquiet unnerves her. He grabs her arm and draws her inside his flat.

'What is it?'

Gates pushes her down into her chair in front of the screens and at once Hannah sees the facial composite of Dan that she has created.

'What do you think?' she asks.

'I think I shouldn't be seeing this.'

'What?'

'It's already been released.'

Hannah is bewildered. She doesn't understand Gates' concern. 'That's good, isn't it?'

In reply Gates scrolls down. The composite is part of an alert that has gone around the police force. 'Read it,' says Gates. Hannah reads, stopping when she sees her own name. She turns to Gates with an expression of shock.

'They've named me?'

Gates points at the screen. The evidence is in front of her eyes.

'DI Waterhouse said my name wouldn't be mentioned. Why did he lie?'

'I'm not sure that he did.'

'What do you mean?'

Gates clicks back through some documents. 'As soon as I saw this, I checked the DI's drafts folder. I told you, he's meticulous. Your name is not in the draft.'

'So, someone else put it in?'

'Almost certainly.'

'But who would do that? How would they do that? And why?'

'I think perhaps someone wants you to distrust the police, so you stop helping them.'

Gates is still working the keyboard and mouse. Hannah tries to follow the different documents he is showing her. When her eyes start to ache, she stops following the flashing screens and listens instead.

'From what I can see, the memo was intercepted somewhere between the DI's computer and the communications team. Any member of the administrative staff could have made the change.'

'But why? I still don't understand.'

Gates releases his fingers from the keyboard and faces Hannah. 'Someone told them to.'

'Someone being?'

'I'm guessing it's someone who knows your attacker.'

'You're saying he has a friend on the force?'

'Friend, relative, girlfriend. Someone is helping him and that someone must work in the police station that you've just left.'

Hannah's gut churns.

'But it's not that long since I left.'

'It only takes a text or a phone call. The leak is deliberate. Someone in the building knows your attacker and is trying to disrupt the case.'

'I need some water.'

Gates rushes to the kitchen and comes back with a glass, which he hands to Hannah. She gulps several mouthfuls, her hands trembling. She wipes her mouth with the back of her hand.

'What does this mean?'

Gates is solemn. 'I don't know for sure why you've been named, Hannah, but I believe it's a message. They're trying to frighten you.'

'They're succeeding.'

'This is what I was worried about. As a living witness, you are vulnerable. What concerns me most is how quickly this has happened. I think you and I should take a short break.'

'Are you serious? The DI said I would be safe if I helped the police.'

'The DI probably doesn't know about this. I think he's been by-passed. We'll be able to tell by the way he reacts to the leaking of your name. Come on. Let's go upstairs. There's something else I need to show you.'

Hannah is confused and bewildered. She's not sure what she's feeling and has even less idea of what she ought to be feeling but she leads Gates up to her flat. Inside the living room Gates walks to the window. He keeps close to the wall and indicates that Hannah should do the same. At the window he stops and peers around the edge of the curtain. He glances at the street outside then pulls back and steers Hannah forward to take his place.

'Look left, across the road. See the blue saloon?'

Hannah squeezes one eye around the curtain and sees the car. She also sees the man in the passenger seat. He has a baseball cap pulled over his eyes and he's reading a newspaper. They move back against the wall and sit on Hannah's sofa.

'I was watching from my window, waiting for you to get back. He followed you down the road and parked when you parked. He hasn't left his car. I think he followed you.'

Hannah's stomach has dropped.

'What's going on, Gates?'

'Honestly? I don't know. What I do know is that someone is very interested in you right now.'

The trill of Hannah's phone interrupts them. It's DI Waterhouse. She puts the DI on speaker. He is a very angry man. He has just discovered that Hannah's name, as well as her status as a previous victim of Tina's murderer, has been released across the local constabulary. He is effusive with his apologies and promises a full investigation. Hannah would love to tell him not to bother because Gates has already done that, but she makes noises of acknowledgement and ends the call as soon as she can.

After the call is over, they both sit and think. Gates is ahead of Hannah, so it's Gates who breaks the silence.

'Hannah, I need you to pack. Do you have a rucksack?'

'Yes.'

'Pack it with essentials. Clothes, toiletries, that sort of thing. Take only what you can carry. Put on sturdy footwear and good socks. Don't worry about food but take a water canister if you have it. You also need to get released from work. Phone in sick or take leave. We don't want them looking for you. Is there anyone else that might notice you're missing?'

Hannah shakes her head. Her friends stopped worrying about her not long after she refused to see them. People only have a limited supply of patience when you don't tell them the reason for your withdrawal.

'I'm going to be out for a while.'

'Where are you going?'

'To move my car. This guy will already know yours so we can't use it. I'm going over the fence at the back and I'll double back. I'll move my car and we'll go to it on foot after dark.'

'Is that why you never park outside the flat?'

Gates gives a small nod.

'It pays to not be too obvious about some things.'

Gates sidles along the wall for another peep past the curtain. 'When you're packed, I want you to show yourself at the window. Don't look directly at the car. Maybe look in the other direction as if you're waiting for someone. Then close the curtains. Put on your table lamps in here and in your bedroom. Close the bedroom curtains too. Leave your phone on charge and switched on, then go downstairs and wait in my flat. Don't come back up here under any circumstances. Don't answer the door and don't answer the phone.'

'Gates, you're scaring me.'

He comes over to Hannah and holds her hands. 'I don't want to scare you, but I want you to understand that you must be careful. This Dan knows your identity, and someone is watching the house. I don't think that's a coincidence. They may just want to talk to you, but who knows?'

'I can't believe we have to run.'

Gates smiles. 'Let's just call it a bit of a trot.'

'Should we tell DI Waterhouse?'

'No, Hannah. We don't tell anyone, and no-one can see us leave.'

'I thought you trusted him?'

Gates pauses for a moment. 'Looking at his work record, I think we can trust him. But the truth is that's an informed assessment. I don't personally know the man. I certainly don't think we can trust all his colleagues though. That worries me. Until we know who leaked your identity, we need to be careful. I want you out of sight. Go and pack.'

It feels like Gates is gone forever. Hannah tries not to worry. Caution is the watchword for Gates' life and Hannah has no reason to believe that he will drop his guard now. Even so, she feels restless and agitated. She longs to open the blinds and check on the watching car, but she knows it will still be there and she risks drawing attention to Gates' flat and herself. Instead, she paces.

She will not invade Gates' privacy. He values trust above all else so she ignores the closed bedroom door, she does not open the bathroom cabinet after she has used the toilet and she stays away from the computers spread across the long desk in the bay window. She simply clasps her hands together and walks a circuit around the living room, into the kitchen and back again.

She is on the way back towards the kitchen as dusk is falling when she hears a key in the back door and Gates appears with a carrier bag that smells of Chinese food. Hannah is so pleased to see him that she puts her hands behind her back to stop herself from throwing her arms around him. Her own reaction shocks her. She doesn't touch anybody these days. What the hell is happening to her?

'Thought you might be hungry,' Gates says, as he starts to unpack the containers.

Hannah's stomach says yes.

'It should still be warm.' He feels the base of each container as he unpacks them.

'You must stop feeding me like this. I'll put on weight.'

'You eat like a bird. I don't think one takeaway will make much difference to you.'

As Gates removes the lids, the kitchen fills with the aromas of the food. He fetches plates and Hannah goes to the cutlery drawer for utensils. Cans of Diet Coke appear from the fridge.

'I do have chopsticks somewhere,' says Gates.

'Much too hungry,' answers Hannah. 'I'd prefer a small shovel to be honest.'

Gates laughs and when they sit down and tuck in, Hannah feels as if she's known this calm, unusual man forever. Then she remembers why she's here and that this is a last supper of sorts. Gates senses the change in her mood, and he leans across the table so she is forced to meet his gaze.

'Are you okay?'

'Yes, of course. This is lovely. It's just the circumstances, I guess. The thought of leaving the flat is weird. I'm feeling a bit disjointed.'

'Or even discombobulated?'

'What's the difference?'

'Disjointed is a bit confused, discombobulated is very confused.'

Hannah chews her chicken to give herself time to think.

'Not confused so much. I understand what's happening and why, but I feel completely out of control. It's as if I've climbed onto a sled and hit an icy patch. I can't slow down, and I can't get off. I can only sit here and let things happen.'

'Disordered then,' offers Gates.

'I'll take the word,' says Hannah. 'But it doesn't help with the feelings.'

Hannah starts to eat again, aware that Gates is examining her.

He puts his fork down and regards her with that lovely unhurried gaze of his. As always, it comforts her.

'This will get sorted, Hannah. It may take a little while and it's probably going to be bloody tough at times, but we will get Dan arrested and I'll bring you home.'

'You make it sound very simple.'

'I won't lie to you and pretend I'm not concerned about things. I don't like the fact that there's a rapist and murderer out there. I'm concerned that you're the one person that can identify him, and I'm bloody angry that our local nick leaks like a sieve.' He pauses to take a breath and run both hands through his hair. 'But when it comes to information, I'm better than the lot of them put together and that is our advantage. I can sort this.'

Hannah conjures a smile. 'Thank you. I'm so glad I have you as a neighbour.'

'I hope I'm your friend, too.'

16

Trying to doze on Gates' settee is a bit of an ask regardless of how comfortable it is. Hannah's body is too tense to relax, too fidgety to lie still and rest. Her nerve endings are buzzing, and it's impossible to keep her legs still. She doesn't yet know where Gates is taking her or how long for. She wonders if they can evade the watcher across the road. She wonders where Dan is at this very moment.

'Urgh.'

She tosses the throw to one side and sits up.

'Can't sleep?' asks Gates from his desk.

'Can't even doze. I'm too wound up.'

'That's okay, we can go.'

As soon as she hears the words she has been waiting for, Hannah regrets not taking a nap. Too late now.

'Just a quick trip up to your flat,' says Gates.

Inside Gates stands back while he instructs Hannah to go to the window, check the curtains, and switch off the table lamps. She does the same in the bedroom.

'Let's hope he believes you're heading to bed,' says Gates.

Back downstairs Gates' computer screens are in darkness. He shrugs his rucksack and laptop bag onto his shoulders.

Hannah glances at her watch. Midnight. She slips on walking boots, a warm jacket and rucksack, and heads for the back door where Gates is waiting. It feels strange leaving the flat that she has only known for a matter of days because somehow it feels more familiar to her than her own. She had been so nervous about coming to Gates for help, stressed about entering his flat, and now, it feels like a place of safety. She doesn't want to leave.

Gates turns off the lights and checks the door is securely locked before they cross the garden and slip through the gate into the park. Hannah follows as Gates jogs across the grass, skirting the duck pond, and exits via the furthest gate from their flats. They emerge onto a hill and Gates sets off at a brisk pace. Hannah finds herself trotting to keep up with his long-legged stride. This leaves no spare breath for conversation, so Hannah puts her head down and eases into a steady and bearable pace.

Their suburb is quiet and there are few people on the streets. A young couple strolling arm in arm after what looks like a successful date, an elderly man putting off bedtime by walking his dog and a young dad pushing a pram with a squalling baby inside. The dad exchanges a rueful grin with Gates and looks disappointed when Gates strides onwards without a pause.

Hannah likes the subdued air of the local streets. It's been so long since she's been out walking at night that she's forgotten the pleasure of wandering along spacious pavements, with only the thrum of the occasional passing car and the peace and quiet of slumbering suburbia for company. And Gates, of course. She glances at him, thankful for his reassuring presence. Even though Hannah is scared, he seems to make things better. That makes Hannah want to be better. Better at bringing a criminal to justice. At righting her wrongs.

Their route takes them through drowsy streets, avoiding high streets, shops, and pubs. They cross streets to the darker side, cut corners to avoid pools of lamplight, watch for, and avoid, cameras.

'Here's the car. Eighteen minutes,' says Gates. 'Not bad with a backpack. Well done, Hannah.'

Hannah grins with relief at the realisation that she has managed to keep up, even though her back is hot and sweaty, and her feet are sore. The perils of a desk job, she supposes. How does Gates keep so fit? She files the question away for now. She removes her backpack and jacket and slips into the passenger seat. Her legs are throbbing. Gates wastes no time getting the car started and turns south to head towards the motorway via another tortuous route through the back streets.

'Why did we walk so far?' asks Hannah.

'To make sure the police don't pick us up if they do a CCTV search. It meant we had to go the long way round.'

'That makes sense.'

'I suggest you try and get some sleep. The journey will take about three hours and there won't be much to see in the dark.'

'What about you?' asks Hannah. 'Shouldn't I help you stay awake?'

'I'll go to bed when we get there.'

Hannah means to ask where they're going but she makes the mistake of closing her eyes first.

She is woken by the noise and sensation of the car rumbling over a cattle grid. When its tyres hit pasture, the car starts to bump and roll as it sways over a rutted field. Hannah sits up and opens her window. The scent of the countryside rushes to invade the car: grass, baled hay, and the unmistakable odour of sheep poo.

'We're here,' says Gates.

It's still dark and the sky is washed with thick cloud, the world clothed in velvety darkness. The lurching headlights bounce over an uneven, grassy field, catching the bright eyes of startled sheep. One of the sheep is running ahead of them, too frightened to veer away from the car, its creamy woollen rump acting as a shit-stained pathfinder. Hannah turns her aching neck from side to side, searching for signs of light. Perhaps a streetlight or an illuminated window. There is nothing. Nowhere for Dan to hide.

'Where are we?' she asks.

'Somerset.'

Gates pulls the car to a halt next to a solitary caravan sitting squat and pale in the moonlight. Hannah spots two Calor gas bottles under a window but there is nothing else to be seen. Once the engine is cut, only the snuffles of the sheep break the silence.

'We shouldn't be bothered here,' says Gates. 'But if we are, just remember to call me Rick.'

'Rick?'

'Under the radar, remember.'

'So, who knows you here, Rick?'

He smiles. 'The farmer, his wife and a couple of his workers. They won't bother us. Come on, let's get inside.'

They step from the car towards the caravan and a handful of curious woolly faces shuffle forward to examine the interlopers. One or two of the brave ones baa a few times but they stay out of reach. Hannah steps forward with her hand outstretched but the sheep skitter away, their tiny hooves thudding on the ground. Gates unlocks the door to the caravan and reaches inside to extract a metal step which he pushes into the ground beneath the door.

'You might want to check your shoes for sheep poo,' he suggests, as he slips off his own boots and hops inside in one graceful movement. By the time Hannah has done the same and stepped into her new, musty-smelling home, Gates has closed the curtains and lit some gas lamps.

'I'll fetch the bags,' he says. While he unloads and locks the car, Hannah explores. It doesn't take long. A sitting/dining area at one end, a galley kitchen with a bathroom containing a chemical toilet, tiny sink, and shower opposite take up the middle, and a bedroom fills the far end. Every surface she touches feels cold. She hears Gates dropping their bags on the dining table and turns to face him.

'It's not much, I'm afraid, but it's safe and out of sight,' he says. Disappointment only comes with expectations and Hannah doesn't have any. She is happy to be anywhere that Dan isn't.

'It's cosy,' she says.

'It's also late and I'm knackered. You take the bed and I'll make up the one in here.' Gates waves at the table and two upholstered bench seats on either side. He is stooped with weariness.

'Don't be silly, we can share the bed.' The words slip out before Hannah is aware that they had formed in her brain. 'As friends,' she adds.

Gates hands drop to his sides. He looks wary, as if it's not a good idea. *Who is scared of who?* thinks Hannah.

'You sure?'

'Absolutely.'

'Thanks, Hannah.'

His boots are already off and have been brought inside to sit with their toes pointing at the locked door. He shrugs off his coat, throws it on the table then takes three steps to the bedroom where he drops himself onto the bed.

'Gates?' says Hannah.

Silence.

Hannah turns off the gas lights and joins him fully clothed on top of the ever so slightly damp bed.

17

He is angry and uncomfortable. There are few disadvantages to being tall but trying to get comfortable in a car is one of them. He is sitting on the back seat slumped down in an attempt to avoid detection from any potential passers-by. His legs are cramped and his back aches. Stupid bitch, it's all her fault. Stupid fucking bitch.

He really doesn't want to be here. His mind wanders to the city bars, to the dozens of fresh, young girls giggling and pouting in their short skirts and low-cut tops. They have the right. Of course they do. They have the right to do what the hell they like. And he has the right to be tempted. To flirt back. Hell, they make it so easy. Pay them some attention, flatter them, drown them with compliments, buy the drinks, slip in the Rohypnol, separate them from their friends. Get them back to the car just before their legs go.

He's been doing it for over a decade without a care in the world. It's only in the last year that the killing started. After that Hannah bitch and her stinking, disgusting bleeding. He was shaken after that one. Thought he might get caught. There was too much mess to be sure that he had cleaned and wiped everything. Leave just one speck of DNA these days and you are collared.

It's her fault that he is forced to finish them off. He can't risk leaving a witness. And now she's hanging around the local nick, for God's sake. He followed her to the shops and while he was waiting for her to emerge, he called Rachel at the station. Hannah had reported a rape and come in to do a composite. It looks like you, Rachel said. So like you.

Leak it, he told her. Expose her. Let her suffer some humiliation before she dies.

His rage is incandescent. He is going to deal with her. When she next leaves her flat it will be for the last time.

18

annah wakes to an empty caravan and a note from Gates. 'Gone to fetch supplies.' She looks out of the window to find the car gone and a cluster of sheep watching the caravan with anxious eyes. As she pushes open the door they bleat and baa and show her their woolly rumps as they run away. The sun is already high, and she can smell the countryside. Yes, sheep shit alright, but also a particular freshness that makes her think they might be near the sea.

Only now, in daylight, can Hannah appreciate how isolated they are. Beyond the field that houses the caravan, the ground rolls away into a distant vista of hills and valleys. The hills smooth and green and the valleys studded with thick, dark woodland. For a moment Hannah finds herself hoping that the weather holds and that she can stay here with Gates for as long as it takes to get her life back on track.

Whatever that will look like.

Her musings are interrupted by the sound of Gates' car and within seconds it is bouncing across the grass. He emerges with an incongruous-looking wicker basket and a self-effacing smile.

'Morning. Sleep well?'

'Yes. You?'

'Until my grumbling stomach woke me up. Why does Chinese food make you so hungry the next day?'

'One of life's mysteries.'

'Something to do with digestion of carbs, I think.' Gates raises the basket. 'Let's have some more.'

He has brought bread, butter, cheese, eggs, bacon, tomatoes, mushrooms, milk, tea, and marmalade. He refuses Hannah's offer to cook and sets to work on the double gas burner and tiny worktop.

'Is there a shop close by?'

Gates laughs. 'There's a farmhouse three miles away. The farmer there owns this land. If I let him know I'm coming, his wife gets me a few basics. There's a little gas fridge next to the sink. It will keep everything fresh.'

Hannah waits until Gates has almost finished his breakfast before she starts to question him. There are so many things she wants to ask.

'Where are we exactly?'

'Exmoor.'

'Is this your caravan?'

'One of them.'

'Er, how many do you have?'

'Five, dotted around.'

'Wow.' Hannah is surprised. 'Do you often have to hide?'

Is Gates blushing?

'Not hide so much as step back.'

'What does that mean?'

'You've heard the saying, out of sight, out of mind?'

Hannah is trying to read between the lines of Gates' somewhat inadequate explanation.

'Not sure I get it.'

Gates pops his last mushroom into his mouth and leans back.

'Sometimes I really need to be off grid.'

'So you're not caught?'

Gates raises his palms and lets his hands fall onto the table. Hannah recognises the gesture of unspoken agreement.

'How does that work?'

'You'll see later. It's not difficult these days. A mobile broadband router with 4G connectivity. It gives me off-the-grid internet speeds similar to home telephone wires. If I'm static I can get 5G in some places.'

'What about power?'

'Battery pack. Even touring caravans carry their own kit these days.'

Hannah had no idea.

'I need to contact my guy today.'

'Your guy?'

'Olly. I told you we've helped each other out over the years. I've already briefed him and asked him to look at CCTV.'

'I thought we'd looked at all that?'

To Hannah, it feels as if she has viewed every centimetre of dark, grainy footage available in the world.

'We've looked at the accessible, prime locations but there are private cameras scattered everywhere these days. Some of them, small businesses especially, archive all their CCTV footage. Olly is tracking down cameras to see what he can get hold of.'

Hannah wrinkles her nose. She remembers Angie saying that makes her look cute and quickly straightens her face. 'That sounds like a long shot.'

'It is, but it's one worth pursuing. I know the police do it themselves from time to time. It's resource-intensive but sometimes the result is a lottery win. This Dan guy is skilled, but he is human and I'm damn sure the invisibility cloak hasn't been invented yet. We'll get him. Even if it means chasing down every camera in the country.'

'Is there anything I can do?'

'I want you to make a very short telephone call to DI Waterhouse. Tell him you think someone is watching your flat and you've gone to stay with a friend. You can't say where you are, but you're safe, and you'll be in touch. It should keep him off our backs for a few days. I've got a box of burners in the boot, so you can use one of those and then destroy it.'

'You have a box of burner phones in your boot?'

'Tools of the trade.'

Hannah shakes her head. 'I feel like there's a whole world out there that I know nothing about.'

Gates gets up from the table. 'Fortunately, it's a very small one.'

Hannah clears the plates and washes up while Gates sets up his equipment and begins his clicking and scrolling. For Hannah, observing Gates is like watching a musician playing a beautiful melody. His long fingers dance over the keyboard, his eyes flit across the screen and his relaxed face says quite clearly that this is his happy place.

'You like it, don't you? What you do.'

He glances up at her.

'I feel lucky. And privileged.'

'Why?'

'I've found something I love. And I'm good at it. That makes me love it even more. I love the chase for information. For facts, for data, for images. And when I find one tiny detail that will help someone I feel, well, epic.'

'But it's illegal.'

Gates shrugs. 'Not everything is accessed illegally but you're right, some is. Some days I break the law. Technically. But it eases my conscience to only do as much as I need to do to help people. I would never do anything to help another person break the law, but I hate when law breakers get away with what they've done because the police are constrained by lack of resources or data protection rules.'

'But why are you helping me? You've left your flat and your work to take me on the run even though you barely know me. And I am so, so grateful to you. But why? Why are you helping *me*?'

Gates hesitates. Is he considering whether to reply or what to tell her?

'You deserve an answer to that,' he says. 'But it requires coffee.'

19

With two steaming mugs of instant coffee on the table between them Gates begins to speak. The formality of sitting down with coffee has unnerved Hannah. Their knees are close to touching beneath the table and Hannah pulls herself to the back of the bench seat to avoid physical contact with Gates. It's too distracting. His beautiful fingers are wrapped around his mug beneath the words Dunster Castle. His palms cover a photo of the castle.

'At the beginning of all this, when we were getting to know each other,' he says, 'I omitted something.'

Hannah is intrigued.

'You lied?' Her voice is teasing.

'No, I didn't lie. I left something out. I told you that I didn't have any living family. That is true. What I didn't tell you is that I had a sister.'

Hannah jumps on the past tense.

'Had?'

Gates avoids her eyes, staring into his Dunster Castle mug. His fingers intertwined around the body of the mug as if he's trying to warm them.

He lifts his gaze and fixes his eyes on a point beyond

Hannah's left shoulder. Hannah sips her coffee mechanically. She registers the warm fluid in her mouth before she swallows but tastes nothing. Her instinct is to ask Gates to stop. To tell him that she wants to take back her question, doesn't want to hear what he has to say.

'Her name was Ruth,' he says, his voice flat and devoid of emotion. 'I told you I was a late-in-life baby so when I was born, she was fourteen years old.

'In theory we shouldn't have been close. By the time I started school she was working full-time and living with her boyfriend. Unfortunately, my mum developed breast cancer. At that point I was already crazy about computers and working towards my GCSEs. Dad was working full-time so while Mum was in and out of hospital getting treatment, Ruth came back home to look after Dad and me. She was good at it. A born mother. Which was just as well because my mum fought to stay alive for three years.'

Hannah is sipping from an empty mug, transfixed not so much by Gates' words, but by the way they fall from his lips, resolute, unwavering. It occurs to her that Gates could be articulating his story for the first time. She could be the first person to hear this. She places her mug down on the table and the sound makes her jump.

'By the time Mum died, I depended on Ruth for everything. Her boyfriend had fallen by the wayside and Ruth decided to stay at home with me and Dad. She did everything for us. A year later, Dad died of a heart attack. There was no warning. I was on my computer in the bedroom at the front of the house. I heard Dad's car pull up on the drive, but he didn't come inside the house. I could smell the dinner Ruth was cooking, and my stomach was grumbling so I went outside to call him in. I expected to find him on his phone or something, but he was slumped over the steering wheel. I knew he was dead.'

'Oh my God, Gates.'

'I screamed for Ruth. She called an ambulance, but the paramedics certified him dead when they arrived.

'At the time I was eighteen and Ruth was thirty-two. Dad had a chain of launderettes and dry cleaners. Ruth took over the business when Dad died. It wasn't a career choice for her, but it was a good living and with competent managers, not a huge amount of work. She was happy.'

Hannah's heart aches for Ruth, who sacrificed so much for her family yet never got to grow old.

'Did you help her?' asked Hannah.

'In the holidays, a bit. I was off to uni and soon immersed in computing. You could say I'd found the love of my life. I was also young, selfish, ungrateful.'

Gates finally puts down his coffee mug and pushes it away. It's still full and coffee splashes onto the tabletop. They both ignore it. Hannah senses an approaching climax.

'That doesn't sound like you.'

'I was a teenager. Discovering myself and the world. Life was exciting. Thoughts of home, when I had them, were boring.'

'So, what happened?'

'Ruth went in one evening to close up one of the businesses. It wasn't something that she would do under normal circumstances. All the stores had a manager who ran things on a day-to-day basis. But Ron's wife was expecting a baby. She went into labour three weeks early and he was desperate to get to the hospital. Ruth offered to cover for him and secure the store. It wasn't a big deal. It was something she did when she needed to. She must have done it dozens of times a year.'

Hannah wants to stop Gates. She can already sense horror in the ending.

'Her car broke down on the way home. She managed to cruise to the side of the road and park safely. She could have called a breakdown service or a taxi to take her home, but she didn't. It wasn't even eight o'clock. It was getting dark, but the weather was mild, so she decided to walk home and deal with the car the following morning.'

Gates pauses and wipes his eyes. He meets Hannah's gaze for the first time. She can see the suffering in his expression. Her throat contracts. Tears are close. The caravan and its contents have dissolved. Hannah's world has contracted to this man and his loss.

'She took a short cut by the canal. It was a couple of hundred yards, well-lit at each end of the tow path but with a stretch of shrubbery halfway along. She was mugged. Some young guy came out of the bushes and tried to grab her bag. We'd talked about things like that in the family. Dad had always told us to let go of whatever the muggers wanted. Our life was worth more than a wallet or phone. But Ruth said her instinct was to hang on to her bag. She said he was just a young kid, and her bag held her phone, house keys, and her purse with all her cards. She just didn't want him to have it. Ruth was fighting for the bag and screaming at the lad to sod off, or worse.'

There was the ghost of a smile from Gates.

'He didn't like the noise she was making. He lunged at her and knocked her off her feet before running away with the bag. It was only when he'd gone that Ruth realised, she was bleeding.'

'Had he stabbed her?'

Gates nods.

'The police said it was a tiny knife, but it was a dirty one and she was unlucky. It perforated her bowel.'

Hannah's hand goes to her mouth, but Gates hasn't finished. He covers his face with his hands so that his voice is muffled.

'She lost the baby she was carrying.'

It's the anguish in Gates' voice that releases Hannah's tears. She wants him to stop now. She's heard enough. Her throat is clogged. Gates is still talking. The floodgates have opened, and he must finish.

'That devastated her more than the attack.'

Hannah is horrified. How could this lovely man have lived through such a brutal nightmare?

'Gates, I am so sorry.'

Hannah was beginning to understand so much about him. 'Did Ruth recover from the attack?'

Gates uncovers his face and looks at Hannah. He has aged a decade.

'No, she didn't. She died. She got septicaemia and she died a week later.'

Gates covers his face again and Hannah sees his ribs heave as he struggles to control his sobs. At first Hannah hesitates. She can only begin to imagine Gates' feelings but even with his grief openly on display, her body is rooted to the seat. It's only when his torso begins to rattle with grief that Hannah's reluctance to touch another person is overcome by compassion for a human in distress.

She goes round to Gates' side of the table so that she can sit next to him and put her arms around him. She holds him as tight as she can while his body shakes and her own tears mingle with his. He bends towards her so that her chin rests on his head. His hair smells of the countryside, woody and green. Hannah savours the scent of him. She can see the promontories of his spine beneath the fabric of his shirt. She feels his warmth.

So, she thinks, *it's tragedy that made this man.* His kindness and compassion and thoughtfulness grew from a devastating catastrophe. Hannah's heart aches.

It feels like a long time before Gates extricates himself. Hannah gets up to fetch the roll of kitchen paper from besides the sink and returns to her own seat opposite Gates. Her body feels cold without his warmth, and it surprises her to realise this is the first time she has held a man since her attack. Gates meets Hannah's eyes with a rueful smile.

'Thank you.'

Hannah inclines her head. She is scratching around for the right words. There are none.

Gates wipes his face with sheets of kitchen roll and shakes himself.

'I had told her so many times not to walk around alone at night. There were any number of people she could have called to go with her.'

'I guess eight wasn't exactly late.'

Gates hits the table with his fist and coffee from his still full cup splatters onto the table.

'The worst thing is the guy was never caught.'

'What?' Hannah's jaw drops in shock.

'The police think either he came in from outside the area or else he left after the attack. There were no witnesses, no CCTV, and Ruth didn't see his face. Someone must have helped him to hide.'

'But what about DNA?' asks Hannah.

'Oh, he left DNA. He left the knife stuck in Ruth's abdomen. But he wasn't on the national database so there was nothing to match it to.'

Things were finally beginning to make sense to Hannah.

'Now I see why you do what you do.'

Gates nods.

'I couldn't help Ruth. I didn't have enough knowledge then. You could say it's been my life's work to gather it. I sold the business, invested the money, and started to help people find justice. Most of my clients pay me well, so I make a good living.'

'Gates, I can pay you.'

'Don't do that, Hannah.'

The sudden and unexpected change in Gates' mood takes Hannah by surprise.

'Do what?'

'Project meaning onto words. Meaning that isn't there.'

'I don't know what you're talking about.'

'I told you why I do what I do. Selling the family business provided the funds I needed to set up. I didn't tell you all this because I was angling for some form of payment from you. If that was the deal, I would have said something up front. It's a female trait and it annoys me.'

'What is?' Hannah's mood sharpens, ready to defend herself.

'Reading between the lines when there isn't a gap. Imagining meaning that doesn't exist.'

'That's sounds very sexist.'

'It's an opinion based on observation. We agreed to be truthful with each other. That means if you have something to say then say it.'

'Isn't that what I just did?'

'What you just did was assume I was angling for money from you. I wasn't. You misinterpreted. Imagined I was saying one thing when I said another. I won't do that with you. I will say what's on my mind or I'll stay silent.'

'Silence sounds annoying.'

'Then ask the questions. Don't fill in the silence yourself. It's too easy to get it wrong.'

Hearing about Ruth has left Hannah shaky and unbalanced. She understands that bringing up the past has upset Gates deeply. Maybe he already regrets exposing his vulnerable side to her. Whatever the reason for this sudden downturn in his mood, she doesn't have the strength or desire to engage in an argument with Gates. She swiftly changes the subject.

'So, does it help, your work?'

'Every victory, however small, is a win for Ruth.'

'You were lucky to have her,' says Hannah.

***

For the rest of the day Gates keeps his headphones on and his head down. From time to time Hannah can hear him talking to Olly, discussing potential sources of CCTV footage and ways to find Dan. He gives Hannah an iPad with hours of CCTV footage to study. Her job is to scroll through and try and spot Dan.

'This will take hours.'

'Now you know why it takes the police so long. Do it in batches for twenty-minute periods then take a break from the screen otherwise you'll be frazzled.'

Hannah goes through to the bedroom to lie on the bed. She gets to work. Dan's face is imprinted on her memory, but she is fearful of flicking past and missing him. She takes her time. If Dan is here, she will find him.

20

The following morning Gates hunches over his computer as soon as they have finished breakfast. His concentration anchors him to the keyboard and screen. Hannah stays quiet. He may as well have a *Do Not Disturb* sign stamped on his forehead. He must find a face shot of the mystery Dan and with the help of Olly he is tracking down every frame of potentially useful CCTV from the area around the Majestic Inn.

Hannah clears away the breakfast remnants, washes up and wipes around the cramped space. The tiny caravan kitchen is tidy in less than ten minutes and the bed straightened in less than two. After opening the door to say hello to the startled sheep and taking a breath of fresh air, Hannah decides it's time she unpacks her rucksack and makes herself at home in the caravan.

She drops her rucksack onto the bed. With few belongings to stow away, and little space to stow them in, it isn't going to be a long job. Her head is already considering her tasks for the day and persuading Gates to take her grocery shopping is top of her list. Living on farm fare for the foreseeable future is a delicious thought but daily bacon is not her first choice for breakfast.

Distracted by her mental shopping list, Hannah has tipped up her rucksack without taking much notice of the contents. She is surprised to see her mobile phone on the duvet. She had no idea she had it with her. Gates had told her to leave it and she had forgotten about it. She must have picked it up without thinking. She sits down on the bed and switches it on. The signal is not bad for the middle of nowhere and a string of pings heralds the arrival of waiting messages.

Before Hannah can read the first one the phone flies from her hand. Momentarily confused she thinks she has dropped it as it skids and clatters through the bedroom door, but the sting across her hand and the looming presence of Gates in front of her tells her otherwise. She rubs the back of her hand but before she has a chance to vocalise the protest that is forming, Gates turns his back and stamps on her phone over and over. Hannah can only stare in horror. She is too shocked to react.

When the phone is in pieces, Gates kneels on the floor and retrieves what is left of the SIM card. He places it beneath the heel of his boot, stands up and crushes it repeatedly. Then he turns to face Hannah. She has not moved from her position at the end of the bed. She has no idea what is happening.

'What the fuck, Hannah?'

His voice is controlled. Too controlled. His diction is perfect, every syllable given even weight. In a way, his control is worse than a burst of temper. His disappointment fills the caravan. Hannah is mortified. She is crushed that she could have done something so wrong. Yet she still can't work out what it is she's done.

'What the fucking hell are you playing at?'

'I… I…'

Now it comes. The real anger. Hannah's silence and stutters seem to have stoked the fire of Gates' anger and disappointment.

He may as well have put on a mask taken from the shelf marked 'incandescent rage'. His gentle unhurried demeanour is gone, and his hands are balled into tight fists as he looms over her. Hannah imagines the bones of his knuckles breaking through the skin. A muscle is twitching at the hinge of his jaw. She feels her eyes prick with tears. She tries to stop them, but they start to roll down her cheeks.

'Really, Hannah. Tell me. Which part of leave your phone in your flat did you not understand? Are you just fucking messing with me? Because I've brought you down here to try and save your backside and you've just pinned a great fucking flag in the middle of the killer's satnav. And waved it back and forth. And, by the way, this is the killer that wants to stop you identifying him.'

'Gates, I… '

Gates is breathing heavily, but the volume of his voice is still set to low. That, more than his words, unnerves Hannah.

'You nothing, Hannah. You can't put this right with excuses and apologies. You've put yourself smack bang in front of the crosshairs and I'm standing right behind you. I'm the one who will cop the ricochet if the bullet hits. You fucking idiot.'

Gates turns to walk away from Hannah, then seems to realise there is nowhere to go in the tiny space. He swings back to face her again.

'Why didn't you listen? Tell me. Because right now you're just as bad as Ruth. You didn't listen, you ignored my advice. And you not only brought your phone, you also fucking *switched it on.* Jesus, Hannah. You might not care about your own safety, but I care about mine. Did you consider that?'

Hannah is horrified and devastated in equal parts.

'I only switched it on for a few seconds.'

'I heard messages coming through. That means you were connected to the grid. You are now visible. *We* are visible.'

Gates still hasn't raised his voice. Hannah almost wishes that he would because this cold, controlled anger is somehow worse than an uncontrolled flare-up. This is anger with intent. Hannah has let Gates down and by doing so, she has torn a gaping hole in the fabric of their relationship. This is bad and Hannah is aware that their friendship may never recover. She reaches for a tissue to mop at her tears which Gates ignores. His body vibrates with rage. He swings away with a final stamp at the SIM.

'I need to see if there's a RIPA.'

'What's a ripper?'

Gates is already at his computer and is typing frantically. His beautiful fingers stab at the keys. 'RIPA, the Regulatory Investigatory Powers Act. It governs the use of covert surveillance by public bodies. It allows the police to intercept private communications. Like your mobile phone.'

'Why would they do that?'

'To locate you, Hannah. To fucking find you. You're a missing witness. If your phone was in the flat and switched on, they would think you're there. Even if they realised you weren't there, they'd have no idea where to look. But like I said, you have just waved one enormous fucking flag in their faces saying, here I am, come to Exmoor.'

The enormity of what she has done is sinking into Hannah's brain, but she has no idea what to do with this knowledge. Neither does she have a clue how to assuage Gates' anger which is gusting around the caravan's interior like a winter squall. Part of her is aware that she is now in real danger of being discovered by Dan but her shock at Gates' reaction prevents her from addressing any other emotion right now.

Hannah fetches a dustpan and brush from under the sink and starts sweeping up the remnants of her phone. Her hands shake, and her tears fall onto the floor as she sweeps. She is crushed by her own stupidity and petrified that Gates will dump her in the mire that she has created. Most of all, she will never forgive herself for letting him down.

'Fuck, fuck, fuck!'

Hannah wishes Gates would stop speaking, but the words pour out. 'There's a RIPA application. A fucking RIPA.'

Gates gets to his feet and stamps backwards and forwards in the confined space. Hannah can feel the caravan rocking with each angry step. Even the sheep have run away to huddle in a corner of the field. Gates tugs at his hair with such force Hannah expects to see handfuls come away. He stops at the doorway, one hand on either side of the doorframe. He sucks in great lungfuls of air before turning to Hannah. He is stony-faced.

'Right, get packed. We need to clear out.'

'But…'

'Now!'

Hannah is too stunned and shocked to say anything else, too devastated to do anything other than obey. The remains of her phone are in the rubbish bag which she ties off and leaves by the door. She shoves her few belongings back into the rucksack and packs the remains of their food into the wicker basket. Hannah recalls the grin on Gates' face as he raised the basket of breakfast goodies. Was that only yesterday? She has ruined everything.

Gates is silent as he packs his rucksack and laptop bag. He hands Hannah the car keys and she loads everything into the boot of the car. Gates disconnects the fridge and the batteries, closes the curtains, and locks the door of the caravan. He climbs into the car next to Hannah and drives away fast enough to scatter the huddle of cowering sheep in every direction. They judder over the cattle grid and speed down a narrow lane squeezed between high hedgerows. Gates is focused on his driving, but he lets out one huge sigh.

Hannah shrivels. Just like Tina's death, this is on her.

There is a brief stop to return the wicker basket to the farmhouse and deposit their bag of rubbish before they race across Exmoor. In silence. On an ordinary day Hannah would gaze across the rolling countryside, enjoying the wide-open vistas dotted with Highland cattle and bunches of wild ponies. Today her insides ache with misery and not even the late summer sun beaming from a cloud-free sky can raise her spirits.

They stop for fuel at a petrol station in Bridgwater and Gates returns to the car with Costa coffees and hot sausage rolls. When he has eaten, Gates finally speaks.

'I don't know how long it will take the RIPA application to be processed but we can't have more than a couple of days.'

'What happens then?' Hannah is surprised at how small her voice sounds.

'They'll ping the last location of your phone and head to the caravan. Which they will rip apart, of course.'

'Gates, I'm so sorry.'

Gates closes his eyes. 'Hannah, if we're going to get through this you can stop apologising. I know that you're sorry and I appreciate you saying so, but constant repetition does nothing to help our situation.'

Hannah is about to say, yes, I'm sorry when she stops herself. Even though she is sorry, deeply sorry. Not just for forgetting to leave her phone behind, but for losing the kind, gentle Gates and unleashing this angry, unkind version of him.

'Get rid of your rubbish and go to the loo if you need to. We have to hit the road.'

As she settles back into the passenger seat, Gates is setting up a new burner phone. When he's finished, he removes the SIM from his current phone and disappears into the gents. They head north on the M5 then turn west to cross the Severn Bridge into Monmouthshire. The sun has brushed the wave tops with silver, but Hannah turns her head away and closes her eyes. The beautiful day is hurting her heart. She won't ask Gates their destination. She knows it's a long, long drive.

21

There is one more stop for fuel at a petrol station with a Tesco Express. Gates fills four Bags for Life with food that he can prepare with a knife, a spoon, and a gas ring. He also buys a bottle of gas. They both use the toilets and Hannah strips off as far as she can in the confined space and washes herself down. How she longs for a hot shower. They leave with their fugitive diet of hot coffee and pastries.

The atmosphere in the car remains oppressive and Hannah is miserable. She feels like a child that has had a row with her best friend and now they are no longer speaking to each other. Gates' presence in the car feels unwilling and resentful. Hannah misses him.

After leaving the main roads they drive through an expanse of stunning wilderness. On a good day Hannah would be hanging out of the car window, drinking in the scenery. Today it feels deserted and barren. She longs for the safety and familiarity of her flat.

They follow a forest track for several miles, the car bumping and grinding over ruts and tree roots. Gates drives slowly in an attempt to spare the car too much damage which makes this section of the journey last a lifetime. Finally, he stops in a clearing and pulls on the handbrake.

'Now we walk.'

Walking means carrying a backpack each, Gates' laptop bag and the four bags of groceries they picked up at the service station. At least Hannah managed to follow Gates' instruction to wear good footwear.

They leave the car in the clearing and head into the trees. There is no discernible path to follow but Gates strides ahead with confidence. Hannah finds herself hurrying behind him, breathless and sweaty, but determined not to complain.

When the caravan comes into sight, Hannah's relief is tempered by its isolation. There are no friendly farmers here and not a woolly sheep butt in sight. There is however a beautiful, bubbling stream below the caravan, accessible via a flattened mud beach.

'You can drink the water,' says Gates, 'but don't piss in it. Go in amongst the trees. And don't get lost.'

Hannah keeps her face expressionless. She still wants to shrink to invisibility. If he can't see her, he can't be reminded of her stupidity.

Gates unlocks the door to the caravan. It is smaller and in a worse state than the previous one. No bedroom or bathroom, just a strip of kitchen and a table and two benches that convert to a double bed. It smells damp and unused. Hannah shivers.

Hannah's curiosity overrides her initial desire to stay quiet.

'How did you even get this out here?'

'In pieces. I carried it.'

'Is this your land?'

'Eighteen acres is.'

The caravan smells musty and mouldy. Hannah goes down to the stream to fill the kettle. She boils the water while she retrieves a cleaning cloth and bottle of Flash from one of the shopping bags.

'Go easy on the gas,' says Gates. 'I'll fetch the new bottle from the car later, but lugging gas canisters is not something I plan to do a lot of.'

'Okay,' Hannah agrees. *Is this how things are going to be from now on?*

Hannah occupies herself wiping every possible surface of the caravan so that it smells better even if it still looks like the inside of a battered dustbin. She hangs the bed linen from the lower branches of nearby trees to air it as best she can and drags the seat cushions that make up the mattress outside, where she props them against the side of the caravan. Then she sits on the grass, puts her head in her hands and cries.

She waits for Gates to come out and sit beside her. She waits for comfort and reconciliation. Instead, she listens to him cursing inside the caravan because even with his fancy kit and batteries, the signal is too weak for him to work.

Difficulty with his tech has done nothing to improve Gates' mood. Unable to get online he prepares a meal of salad, new potatoes, and fried steak. They eat in silence. Hannah's throat is lumpy, and she forces herself to swallow the food.

'Thank you,' says Hannah, as she finishes.

'You're welcome,' replies Gates.

The following silence is stretching into discomfort when Gates takes a deep breath in and blows it out with a faint whistle.

'I want to apologise.'

Hannah's face grows hot.

'Bringing the phone was thoughtless and stupid. I know how much damage I've caused.'

'I was still upset after talking about Ruth but I overreacted and I was rude. I'm sorry.'

'I hate that I've ruined our friendship.'

'That's not true,' says Gates.

'Yes, it is,' says Hannah. And she knows it is because Gates doesn't meet her eyes. He doesn't change the architecture of his face, which remains passive and grim. He doesn't say anything else either. He clears the table and boils water for the washing up while Hannah sits and stares at his rigid back.

***

The following morning Gates wakes her with a mug of coffee.

'Are you up for a walk this morning?'

'Yes.' Hannah can think of nothing better than getting out into the fresh air with Gates.

'I'll carry my gear and try and get a signal. I need to contact Olly to see how he's getting on. If I can't work, we'll probably have to move again.'

Hannah bites back 'I'm sorry' and busies herself pulling on socks and boots.

Gates has already made sandwiches and filled their water canisters. Hannah puts them in her backpack with some fruit. She stuffs a sweater and waterproof on top because although September is upon them and the weather is holding, the woods are cool from the shade of the trees. Gates has his computer and kit packed into his own rucksack. It's nine thirty when they step onto the track and Hannah is looking forward to the day.

Gates sets off with a powerful stride through the undergrowth. The forest is a mix of oak, ash, and field maple with a number of trees that Hannah doesn't recognise. In several places she wades through thigh-high ferns and dodges the holly that tries to catch her jeans as she pushes past.

Gates is several strides ahead, making conversation impossible, but Hannah is enthralled by the bird song. She has no idea which species are emitting the trills and whistles but there is something about the sounds that lifts her spirits. Nature always has this effect on her, and she has missed being outdoors during her thirteen months of enforced isolation. It's exactly what she needs right now. She soaks it up.

By the time they reach the tree line Hannah is tired and sweaty, but she has composed herself. She made a mistake and Gates lost his temper. Why is she so shocked that he even has a temper? Doesn't everyone? She barely knows the man, and this is her getting to know him.

Just below the ridge Gates sets up his equipment within the shelter of a rock formation. Hannah continues right up to the ridge line where she stands and turns a slow three-hundred-and-sixty-degree circle. The views are stunning, and she drinks in the sight of the mountains and valleys laid out around her. She can even see a lake or two. She retrieves her lunch from her rucksack and props her back against a rock so that she can eat and admire the view at the same time.

An hour slips away before Gates joins her. His forehead is creased, and his lips pressed tightly together.

'Problem?'

Although the sun is warm, an early autumnal wind is tugging at their hair and buffeting their ears. Gates indicates with a turn of his head that she should move to the other side of the rock where they will be sheltered.

'Several problems.'

'What?'

'Olly has tracked down some CCTV from an independent house renovation business near the hotel where Tina was found. They do kitchens, bathrooms, conservatories, that sort of thing, so they have a lot of expensive stock. They have three cameras, and they archive all their CCTV. They've got a man walking past their showroom with an intoxicated-looking girl around ten pm on the night Tina was murdered.'

Hannah's spirits soar. 'That's them. It must be. Can I see it?'

'That's one of the problems. I managed a crackly call but I'm struggling to hold a signal long enough to download anything. We're in the middle of nowhere and I'm dependent on what's available in the area. Not much, is the answer.'

'But we can use it, can't we?'

'We need to see it first. At least, you need to see it. It's risky opening ourselves up to scrutiny and I'll only do so if you're sure it's our guy.'

'So, we're going to have to go and find a better signal.'

'Yes, we are.'

Hannah wants to smile because Gates is talking with her and not at her. She doesn't think for a minute that the incident with the phone is forgotten, but it's been shoved into a filing cabinet and the drawer slammed shut. At least, she hopes that's the case.

'Eat your sandwich,' she suggests, 'and we can decide what to do.'

22

They make plans, good plans. A return to the car and a trip to Crickhowell for Wi-Fi. After Gates has eaten his lunch, they pack up the computer gear and set off down the mountain. With few clouds to mar the sky they hurry to reach the welcoming shade of the trees. Hannah's hurried footsteps fail to disperse the thoughts clattering inside her head and she finds her attention wandering from the narrow, rugged path they are following.

Gates pauses once they reach the shade of the trees and they both drink some water. Without speaking they hoist their backpacks and set off. Hannah is relieved they're travelling down the mountain and not up as Gates sets a brisk pace. She's anxious to get back to the caravan, to get back on track with the job in hand. If they have solid evidence of Dan taking Tina it will mean their ordeal might soon be over. That means returning home, going to work, finding normal.

When Gates told Hannah about his sister's death, he revealed a huge and complicated part of himself. It was a brave thing to do, and she understands that by telling her what happened, he has exposed himself to her, exposed his vulnerabilities.

Knowing that Gates told his sister to be careful and knowing that she shrugged off his warnings also goes a long way to explaining his anger when he discovered that Hannah had ignored him by bringing her phone. Hannah is still upset with herself for letting Gates down, but she feels that his apology to her has recalibrated their relationship. They're probably not yet back to the warm if slightly cautious friendship they had before, but things feel stable at least.

Nothing lasts.

They are almost within sight of the caravan when Gates comes to a sudden stop. Hannah is moving so fast she grabs a tree branch to prevent herself bowling into his back. He turns and puts a finger to his lips. They listen to the bird song, to the trills and whistles, and to the sound of a man climbing the track below. A man shoving his way through the undergrowth towards them.

'Fuck,' Gates mouths.

He twirls his hand to indicate that Hannah should turn around and retrace her steps. She heads back up the hill with quiet, swift steps. Her heart thuds in her chest and her legs shake. After a few hundred metres Gates taps her back and she halts. He turns sideways off the path skirting a tumble of rock. He bends to swish the long grass back over the indentations made by their footsteps, so they are invisible to the untrained eye.

Gates hands her his car keys and his latest burner phone and whispers, 'Walk straight ahead until you come to a large clearing. It should take you about half an hour. If you can see the sun ahead of you through the trees, you're going the wrong way. It should be behind you. Keep your shadow in front of you. When you get to the clearing turn right and head back down the hill. You should find the track that we came in on and see the car. Get in the car and get out of the forest. Don't drive fast. Satnav to Crickhowell. Do you know how to spell that?'

Hannah nods. She has never been there, but she has seen the name before.

'Park somewhere out of sight and dial the number on the phone. There's only one. You'll get Olly. He knows who you are. Tell him what's happened, and he'll give you further instructions. Do you understand?'

'Perfectly.' Hannah will never fail to follow his instructions again. Ever. 'What about you?'

'I'll catch up with you. I need you to be safe and that means getting you out of here. I'll see you in Crickhowell.'

'What about the man?'

'He's not a tracker, he's following the path. There's very little chance that he'll follow you, but I'll watch to make sure. If you keep moving and don't make any loud noises, he won't find you. You'll be safe.'

He meets her eyes and lifts the corners of his mouth. That's all the encouragement Hannah needs. She turns and strides into the forest. She's a woman with something to prove and she feels a burst of adrenaline surge through her. Her heart beats faster, her breathing quickens, and Hannah feels strong and powerful. She is prepared to fight. Excitement at the challenge ahead propels her forward. She glances back but Gates has already vanished.

Hannah moves as fast as she is able given the density of the vegetation and the need to move with muted precision. She can't give away her position or indeed her presence in the forest, and she can't fall. Her steps are confident and purposeful, her feet placed with accuracy.

Knee-high ferns grasp her legs and despite the sunny day, the base of the forest is cool and damp. Hannah smells fungus and leaf mould and in the small patches where the ground clears her boots sink into the soft undergrowth. She steps with care over exposed roots that are slippery with damp moss. Moisture starts to penetrate the legs of her jeans.

Without a clearly defined path she must concentrate on her route through the trees. When the sun squeezes through the overhead canopy, she checks that her shadow is in front of her. She is accompanied by glorious birdsong and chides herself for responding to the distraction. Birdsong is for normal days, for normal life. Hannah is on a mission, and she will not let herself be distracted. She's not afraid of the man on the mountain. She's eluding him and while the thought brings a sense of satisfaction, this is not the time for over-confidence. Her concentration must be absolute.

She refuses to allow herself to even consider the possibility that she could get lost or even worse, that she might get caught. The route that she and Gates took up and then down the mountain earlier that day is well trodden and easy to follow. It makes sense that the man will follow the obvious path. Why would he look for signs that someone has deviated from the evident route? Hannah is confident that her diversion from the path will not be spotted. And if it were? So what? Gates is on the case. He has her back.

She's safe for a while. At least until the man reaches the mountain top and realises that she and Gates have flown the coop. Hannah wonders who he is. She has a horrible feeling it's Dan, but there was no voice to enable her to confirm that.

Hannah can imagine the man cursing and stamping and hurrying back down the path. She wonders where he has parked his car. It's probably near Gates' car. She must be careful when she gets there. She steps into the promised clearing and stops. Hannah checks the position of the sun and turns right to descend towards the main track. She is confident that she's not being followed so she increases her pace.

Her brain is whirling. Where did Gates go? What is he up to? What's his plan? Because he's sure to have one. How will he get out of the forest if Hannah has the car? And the mobile phone.

Hannah has shut out the birdsong. She hears only Gates' voice and his instructions. She's so determined to get this right and not let him down again. She sees only the way ahead and there, below her and to her right, she glimpses a glint of blue metal caught by a ray of sunshine.

Instinctively she drops to the ground and shuffles towards a tree with a broad trunk. She forces herself to remain still while her breathing returns to normal and she watches the car. There is no sign of a second vehicle. No sign of a man. No sounds other than the rustle of leaves in the breeze and the songs of the birds.

After several minutes Hannah moves forward with caution. She uses the larger tree trunks to hide behind while she pauses and checks the area around the car. Still no movement and no sound. Even so, she is afraid there might be someone hiding near the car ready to pounce. Her heart is thudding in her ears and her eyelids twitch with tension.

The closer she gets to the vehicle, the quieter Hannah tries to be. When she's near enough to have a clear view of the car, she removes her backpack and lowers it to the ground in case she needs to run. She takes a final look around.

Her heart sinks to her boots and she stifles a cry of despair. There are no hidden men guarding the vehicle. There are none required because all four of the car's tyres have been slashed.

Oh shit, oh shit, oh shit.

Now what? Don't cry, Hannah. Don't cry.

She grabs her backpack and hurries to the car. She unlocks the boot and takes four of the burner phones from the box before relocking the car and hurrying back to the safety of the trees. What now? Gates was insistent that she leave the forest.

She was to drive out. But she can't. The car is stuffed. Her feet aren't, so she will walk.

Hannah checks the area is still clear before she returns to the car. She takes a torch from the glovebox and a blanket from the back seat, re-locks the car and hides herself in the trees. Now that she has located the car, she can find her way out of the forest without getting lost. All she needs to do is follow the track. She'll stay in the trees, out of sight. The minute she has a phone signal, she'll call Olly. She can do this. She will do this.

She soon discovers that walking through the trees is slow and cumbersome. When she and Gates heard the man approaching them on the hill above the caravan, it was because he was traipsing through the trees and ferns without a care in the world. He was noisy, and that's how she and Gates were able to avoid him. Hannah concludes that if she's quiet, she can risk travelling at the side of the track that she and Gates drove down. If she hears anything she can dive into the trees and hide. Even so, it's going to be a long walk.

Hannah took little notice of their journey into the forest. She was far too busy feeling miserable and sorry for herself to take any note of their route. So, she has no sense of direction, apart from following the track, no idea at all how long it might take her to find civilisation and, apart from telephoning Olly, no clue what to do once she gets to Crickhowell.

One step at a time, Hannah. One foot in front of the other. Keep walking.

She's determined to stay alert to the sound of cars or humans, but it's difficult to prevent her mind from wandering back to Gates. She's thankful that he's helping her through a tough time. But she hates that she let him down, that he lost his temper, that she disappointed him. Hannah feels diminished in his eyes. Does the fact that she cares so much mean she has feelings for him? Feelings beyond friendship, tenderness, and gratitude.

Tenderness. Christ, where did that come from?
Keep walking, Hannah.

From time to time Hannah checks the phone Gates has given her for a signal. She's determined to follow his instructions but as a plan B she decides that if she can't make it to Crickhowell, she will phone DI Waterhouse. Didn't Gates say that he believes the DI is a good guy? She still has his card in her wallet, so Hannah can call him, and he will come and rescue her and take her home. Then what? She remembers the car parked outside her flat. The car that started this chase. Can she really trust the DI? Does she have a choice?

It occurs to Hannah that the man she and Gates heard could have been an innocent hiker enjoying the Welsh countryside. Honestly, how likely is that? How likely is it that he would find the caravan and follow Gates and Hannah's trail? Christ. Her head is hurting. She can hear a stream gurgling below her and she steps off the track towards it. Once beside the water she drinks, fills her water bottle, and splashes her face.

Even though the forest is deserted, Hannah moves behind a tree to pull down her jeans and squat amongst the ferns. She has barely finished when she hears a car engine. She fastens her jeans and pulls her rucksack towards her. The engine is roaring and the vehicle moving fast. As it surges past her hiding place Hannah peeps out to see the back of a large SUV disappearing along the track.

She remains immobile until her breathing slows, and the pounding of her heart subsides. She has no idea where the SUV has been parked but it came from the direction of the caravan and seemed to be in a hurry to leave the forest. There was no opportunity to see who was driving the vehicle. Hannah assumes it was the man from the mountain. She hopes that Gates wasn't bundled up on the back seat.

Even though the vehicle has gone, Hannah continues with caution.

She keeps walking.

In the shade of the forest the light starts to fade early, and as soft twilight blankets the trees, Hannah can feel the temperature drop as the faintest autumnal chill touches the air. Her legs are aching, and she is hungry and thirsty. She knows it's time to rest for the night.

Without a bedroom and bathroom there can be no routine of tooth-brushing and washing. Hannah leaves the path and searches the ground until she finds a thick patch of ferns which she tamps down like a dog turning circles to make her bed. She tries to break off some ferns to cover herself, but the soft fronds are attached to stalks that feel as strong as wire. Hannah settles for pulling on her sweater and wrapping herself in the car blanket. She makes sure that she covers her head, makes a pillow from her rucksack, and lies down. Within minutes she can feel damp seeping into her bones, but stress and exhaustion overcome her, and she falls asleep to the call of tawny owls.

23

In the past, if anyone mentioned the idea of spending a night sleeping in the open or even in a tent, Hannah hummed and hawed and changed the subject. The thought of being without a bathroom was deeply unattractive. It never occurred to her that it would be the noise, and not the lack of plumbing, that would keep her awake. The minute the moon nestled into the night sky the forest came alive with rustles and hoots. Hannah's initial reaction was fear and shakes but when she found herself uninterrupted and ignored, she relaxed just enough to fall back into a light if disturbed sleep.

Her alarm call is the deafening symphony of birds and she's surprised to find that it's almost six. She has done it. She's survived a night alone in the forest and she's feeling very pleased with herself. Until she tries to move and discovers her limbs have stiffened from the damp cold that has invaded her joints. Even her fingers are reluctant to move.

Once she's on her feet, she squats behind a tree then rummages in the rucksack for the remains of yesterday's lunch. She is starving. She finds two apples and two bananas. She selects an apple and eats slowly, relishing every bite. When she's finished only the stalk and pips are left. She leaves them in a tiny pile to mark the spot where she slept and is soon on her way. Although her memory of the distance and terrain are almost non-existent, she feels confident that she can make it out of the forest today.

The initial soreness in her legs eases as she walks and with little weight in her backpack Hannah strides out. She wonders how long her endorphins will last.

After a couple of hours, she has a break at a stream to freshen up and refill her water bottle, then marches on. Spending last night under the sky was a unique experience for Hannah and she feels changed by it. She senses a new vitality within her as if her spirit has been lifted by a surge of energy.

It comes to her with a start that her feeling is confidence. She did something that she thought was beyond her. What's more, she did it alone, without any help.

While the thought of inflicting vengeance on Dan is still her driving force, the very act of working towards that goal, albeit with the assistance of Gates, is changing Hannah in ways that she would never have even considered before the call. The last call that Tina made before her life was cut short. Hannah sees it as her personal quest to ensure Dan is not left free to end another young life.

When the forest falls away, she stops so abruptly she almost falls over her own feet.

Before her is a breathtaking view across Central Wales. The scent in the air has changed from the thick, dense atmosphere of mature trees and decaying undergrowth to the fresh breeze of open pasture. The sound of birds is overtaken by baaing sheep and the green-leaf-canopy is now a vast open sky. The beauty of the countryside does something physical to Hannah's body. She feels lighter and brighter.

Look at this.

Hannah pulls out the phone. Still no signal. No compass

either. And not a chance in hell of Google Maps. But she has the sun, and it sets in the west. If she keeps it behind her as she walks, she should be able to keep herself orientated east.

She finds herself energised by the realisation that she has made it through the forest without getting lost or caught. The issue now is the lack of cover. Hannah feels vulnerable and exposed out in the open and is aware that she'll have to find some sort of protection before night falls. It's soon lunchtime and despite her determination to ration her pieces of fruit, Hannah's willpower crashes around her ankles. She eats the remaining banana before continuing her trek.

As the afternoon slides away, Hannah's rests become more frequent. Her legs ache and her feet are sore. She begins to worry about where she will spend the night in this open country.

Salvation appears with the twinkling of a light. At first Hannah thinks it's a trick of the setting sun but as she approaches it gets larger. It becomes square. It's a window. A farmhouse window. Hannah is euphoric and picks up her pace. But Gates has taught her well. By the time she raises her hand to knock on the door she has her story prepared.

A frenzy of barking erupts from inside the house followed by a sharp reprimand then silence. The door opens and two hazel eyes appraise Hannah. They belong to a woman in her sixties, tall and lean with toned arms and an erect, no-nonsense posture. She is not the least fazed by the sight of Hannah on her doorstep. Two sheepdogs wind around the woman's ankles, their tails wagging like helicopter rotors.

'I'm sorry to disturb you…' Hannah begins.

'Come in,' says the woman, stepping back and holding the door open.

Though a little taken aback by the unexpected invitation, Hannah steps inside. She removes her rucksack and drops it by the front door but keeps hold of the mobile phone clutched in her hand.

'I'm Glenn,' says the woman as she indicates that Hannah should follow her down a flagstone hallway to a spacious kitchen.

'Cup of tea?' she asks.

'Please. That would be lovely.'

'What's your name?'

'Sarah,' says Hannah. Just to be on the safe side.

'Are you lost, or are you running?'

The question is direct. Hannah raises her eyebrows.

'Don't look surprised,' says Glenn as she deftly fills the teapot and lays out mugs and spoons. 'There aren't many reasons why a young woman would be out here on her own with night falling. I've heard them all over the years. You hungry?'

Hannah nods, possibly a little too vigorously. Glenn is already carving thick slices of bread from a home-baked loaf which she slathers with butter.

'Cheese or jam?'

Hannah hesitates, overcome by the house, the welcome, the food, and a sudden awareness that she probably smells.

'I'll do both,' says Glenn. Hannah watches and rehearses what she's going to say to this kind and capable woman. As soon as she has found her voice.

Glenn places a laden plate in front of Hannah and pours the tea.

'Help yourself to milk and sugar.'

It takes all Hannah's self-control to eat with a little decorum and not stuff slice after slice into her mouth and swallow without chewing.

'So, which is it?' asks Glenn.

Between mouthfuls Hannah shares her carefully rehearsed story. A hiking trip with her boyfriend, an argument, his unexpected aggression, and Hannah's flight. She has taken their phone but there's no signal. She wants to get back to Crickhowell, but she doesn't want him to find her. She's frightened of him. If he doesn't get his own way with her, she's afraid of what he might do. Hannah thinks of Dan and what he did do to her. Tears are waiting. They always are. Hannah makes good use of them.

Glenn listens in silence to Hannah's story.

'Well,' she says.

She pours them both another cup of tea then examines Hannah. It's an open and unashamed appraisal. She points a finger at Hannah to indicate that her decision is made.

'I can drive you to Crickhowell but not until the morning. My husband's away in Cardiff and won't be back until tomorrow. I don't like to leave the place unattended for too long.'

'How far is it to walk?'

'Too far in the dark. The bryn is pocked with rabbit burrows and you'll likely break a bone.'

'Bryn?'

'The hillside. There's a proper track that takes you to the road but that's the long way round. Too far in the dark.'

The combination of good food, hot tea and kindness has allowed last night's aches to seep into Hannah's bones. She still has no idea what's ahead. The long way round, in the dark, is not going to be it.

'I'll pay you, of course.'

Glenn waves a hand. 'I'll be glad of the company with the old fogey away. He's nothing but work and nuisance but I miss him when he's not here.'

Hannah chuckles. 'What's his name?'

'It's Rhys.' Glenn smiles as she says the name and Hannah envies the happiness that she sees in Glenn's face.

Hannah is about to offer to help with the dishes when the dogs begin growling deep within their throats. Glenn leaps to her feet and hurries to the window. When she turns to face Hannah, her face is grim.

'Upstairs,' she hisses. 'Now.'

Glenn grabs Hannah's rucksack from the hallway and clatters up the stairs. Hannah hurries behind, slightly bewildered but not really in a position to argue. Glenn leads the way into a bedroom with a large window overlooking the front of the house. She beckons Hannah to join her and Glenn points to the land that rises from the front garden.

'Is that your man?'

The dark figure striding towards the farmhouse is tall. It can't be Dan. It's impossible. As he nears the house, moonlight illuminates his features. Hannah turns to stone at the sight of him. The dogs' growls have developed into the same frenzy of barking that greeted Hannah when she arrived.

'It's him.'

'Quick, follow me.'

Hannah forces her legs to follow Glenn into a bedroom at the back of the house. The walls are panelled in dark wood. Glenn pulls on a section of the panel nearest the window and a door opens. 'In here.'

Hannah is too scared to refuse. She steps inside the empty wardrobe and huddles into the corner. Glenn hands over the rucksack.

'Make sure that phone is switched off.'

Hannah turns off her phone and rests her head on her bent knees as Glenn shuts her into darkness. She hears Glenn's footsteps hurrying down the stairs. Hannah's raggedy breathing fills the space around her, and she tightens her arms around her legs to stop them jiggling.

Bang, bang, bang, bang.

The dogs bark even louder. There is a short delay, a sharp command for the dogs then Glenn must be opening the door.

Hannah strains her ears but although she catches the occasional word, she can't hear enough to follow the conversation. It's a short exchange and the front door bangs shut. Hannah sits where she is and waits. Pins and needles are beginning in her foot when she hears Glenn's footsteps and the light from the bedroom makes her squint as the door to the cupboard opens.

'He's gone.'

Hannah hasn't moved.

'You're sure.'

'I'm sure.'

Glenn helps Hannah out of the wardrobe, and she sits on the bed rubbing her foot until the feeling has returned.

'He likes to throw his weight around, doesn't he?' says Glenn.

'And then some…'

'He's a nasty little shit.'

Hannah's head snaps up. The eyes of the two women meet and they laugh, Glenn with a derogatory snort, Hannah's giggle close to hysteria.

'Not too much noise,' says Glenn, 'he's probably a lurker.'

'How did you get rid of him?'

'I had the shotgun tucked under my arm. He played the I'm a policeman card and I told him my nephew is Chief Constable of the South Wales Police so let's phone him, shall we?'

'And is he?'

'He is. Bright little thing. He's grown up into a clever, handsome man. My sister is rightfully proud. Now, I think you should sleep in here tonight. I want you to stay upstairs because if I start closing all the curtains downstairs, Sergeant Lurker might get suspicious. There's a bathroom next door and a robe on the back of the door. You take a bath or shower and I'll fix some supper. Leave your clothes outside the bathroom door and I'll wash them for you.'

'Thank you so much, Glenn.'

'No need for thanks,' says Glenn. 'If this guy is a policeman, I know from my nephew's stories what some of these guys are like. Pompous, blown-up bullies. And those are the better ones. Unfortunately, you seem to be tangled up with something else altogether.'

Something else altogether, thinks Hannah. *Is that what Dan is? Yes, he is something else. He's a rapist and a killer.*

Hannah pours bath foam into the stream of water plunging from the taps. She strips off her clothes and leaves them outside the bathroom door as instructed. The scent of jasmine rises in the steam, and she lowers herself into the water with a deep, calming breath.

She leans forward to turn off the taps, then moves to ease herself back into the water. She doesn't make it. She feels something break inside her. Little pieces of calm and control are cracking and snapping until all Hannah can do is rest her forehead on her bent knees and sob. Great, hacking sobs that make her bones rattle.

After everything, and despite Gates' best efforts, Dan has still managed to find her. He is somewhere outside the farmhouse, watching and waiting. He is a predator stalking his prey. Hannah is his target.

It's only when the water begins to cool that she lies back and submerges herself in the dying bubbles. Crying underwater is not an easy feat and Hannah sits up to wash herself and rinse her hair. By the time she is dry and wrapped in a bathrobe she is calmer, but the dull weight of fear and uncertainty has settled inside her. She climbs into the comfort of a real bed with feather pillows. Her eyes are open, but she sees nothing.

***

Glenn returns with a tray loaded with buttered crumpets and hot chocolate. She hands the tray to Hannah before closing the curtains and turning on a table lamp. Her competent actions remind Hannah of an old-fashioned hospital matron bustling around the wards. Glenn sits on the bed and takes a crumpet.

'Tuck in, Sarah.'

Hannah reaches for a mug of hot chocolate with a shaky hand and takes a tentative sip.

'This is heaven. Thank you.'

'I've been thinking about Sergeant Lurk-a-lot,' says Glenn.

'What about him?'

'The old fogey doesn't leave me very often,' she says, 'so, when he does go, I keep a good watch. I know who's out and about and it's usually no-one. Then you turn up, followed an hour later by your creepy stalker.'

Hannah is sipping her hot chocolate, waiting for the punch line.

'How the hell did he do that?'

'Do what?'

'How did he follow you so exactly? He came down that mountain step for step behind you.'

'I followed the light in the window. I expect he did the same.'

'Were his ancestors Indian trackers or something?'

Hannah shakes her head. 'Not that I'm aware of.' She doesn't say that she knows very little about the man other than the fact he is a rapist and killer.

Glenn pauses. Hannah can see her choosing her words.

'Is it at all possible,' asks Glenn, 'that your boyfriend could be tracking you?'

'What? No, it's not possible.'

How could he? thinks Hannah. *He hasn't been near me.*

'It's amazing what gadgets you can get on the internet these days.'

Hannah can't tell Glenn that Dan isn't really her boyfriend or that she has had no recent physical contact with him. Nor can she tell her about Gates.

'By the way, he was asking for Hannah.'

Hannah blushes. 'I'm sorry. I didn't know if I could trust you.'

Glenn waves a hand. 'You need to be clever with a partner like that. Good for you.'

'Are you sure he's gone?'

Glenn nods. 'The dogs will tell me if he comes back. And I shall take the gun to bed.'

Glenn slides off the bed. Just before she lifts the tray, she puts her hand in her pocket and offers Hannah a toothbrush, a small tube of toothpaste and a plastic comb. 'Take them,' she offers. 'And think about that tracker. I want you to make sure you check your stuff before we leave tomorrow.'

24

Oh, she's a clever one. She probably thinks he admires her, but he doesn't. He hates her even more than he thought possible. First, she drags him out into the middle of fucking Wales, forces him to climb a fucking mountain and then gets away. Bitch! A wily bitch at that. At least he managed to immobilise her car. Hope she enjoyed her walk.

He has hidden himself behind the farmhouse. The curtains are drawn and it's not too long before the lights go out. He is tempted to give things a try here, out in the wilds, but those bastard dogs are a problem, not to mention the fact the old biddy has a shotgun. She looks ugly enough to use it too. Nah, impatience leads to mistakes. One thing he is exceptionally good at is planning. He knows how to cover his tracks and even though he made a mistake leaving Hannah alive, he has still not been caught. He will bide his time.

He does what he needs to do at the back of the house then steals away towards the track and his concealed car. He will sleep in the car tonight. He'll be able to pick up her trail tomorrow. He's seen to that. He also wants to eyeball her. If his suspicions are correct, she has company. Why would a call handler have two caravans available in the middle of nowhere? How did she manage to sneak *away from her flat without him seeing? It took him forty-eight hours to realise she was gone. She had to have had help.*

It's not just curiosity that's nagging at his thoughts. If someone is with her, someone is helping her, then she must have confided in them. This might turn out to be his first double. That will be a challenge. He grins at the thought. Two for the price of one.

That will be a great challenge.

25

Despite the comfortable bed, Hannah does not sleep well that night. Perhaps it's because she's waiting to hear Dan's fist return to bang on the front door. Or her concern for Gates and worry about what's happened to him. Most of all, Glenn's questions about tracking are going over and over in her head until her brain feels as if it's been tumble-dried. More than that, there is something nagging at the edge of her consciousness. Something that's important, that she should be paying attention to, yet every time she thinks it's within her grasp, it slides away.

Hannah showers before she ventures downstairs to the kitchen in her borrowed robe. She pushes open the door and is engulfed in a blast of warm air scented with coffee, freshly baked bread, and the bacon that she can hear sizzling in a pan on top of the Aga.

'How do you like your eggs?' asks Glenn. 'Poached, scrambled, or fried?'

'Good morning. Scrambled, please.'

'Take a seat,' says Glenn as she breaks eggs into a large enamel bowl and starts to whisk. 'How did you sleep?'

'Fine, thanks,' lies Hannah.

Glenn raises one eyebrow.

'Really. It was the best night's sleep I've had for days.'

That is the truth. Glenn nods but her eyebrow doesn't settle down completely.

'The dogs have been out on patrol. There's no sign of him.'

'He's gone?'

'It looks like it. Help yourself to fruit juice and coffee. There's toast and butter on the table. And please ignore the dogs. Their pleading eyes may try to convince you that they're starving but they deserve a doggie Oscar for their acting.'

Hannah chuckles and sits down to demolish a mouth-watering breakfast of bacon, scrambled eggs, and mushrooms. The juice is freshly squeezed and the coffee creamy. There is homemade marmalade for the home-baked bread. She feels relaxed and secure for the first time in a long time.

'This is delicious. You should do bed and breakfast,' Hannah says.

'I do,' Glenn replies with a smile. 'I do laundry too,' and she points to Hannah's freshly laundered clothes. Hannah swallows a lump that has formed in her throat.

'Thank you so much, Glenn.'

Glenn shrugs. 'All part of the service.'

After breakfast, Hannah goes upstairs to dress. She tips out her rucksack onto the bed, shuddering from the memory of doing the same thing in the caravan on Exmoor. Why do bad memories always chase away the good ones?

Hannah brought very little from the flat and the few spare items of clothing and toiletries that she did bring were left behind in the caravan. She has the torch and blanket from the car, the spare burner phones, one apple, slightly bruised, her water canister and her wallet. In the front pocket are the bunch of keys which she hasn't touched since she left the flat. She examines every item.

She empties her wallet. Driving licence, bank card, DI Waterhouse's business card, thirty pounds in fivers and a small assortment of coins. She refills the wallet and puts it back into the pocket of the rucksack. She picks up her keys and pauses.

What the hell?

Hannah has several keys. Two keys for the flat, car key, locker key, all attached to a pretty key ring decorated with a stainless steel panda bear. It's a mummy panda with her arms folded around a baby panda. But there appears to be a tumour growing from the mummy's back. Cold fingers slide up and down Hannah's spine. She rushes down the stairs with the keys held out in front of her as if they are a bomb about to go off.

Glenn looks at Hannah's face and then at the keys. Hannah points to the panda. Glenn takes the key ring and holds the panda bear to the light. She looks at Hannah.

'Sorry, love. I don't always like to be right.'

Glenn disappears through a door to a utility room and reappears with a pair of pliers. She prises a black disc from the back of the panda and hands it to Hannah.

'It's a tracker all right.'

'Are you sure?'

'Let's just say there was a time when I didn't trust his nibs the way I do now. The internet is a wonderful thing when you need something.'

Icy fingers grip Hannah's neck, and she shivers. How could this have happened? She hasn't been anywhere without her keys apart from visiting the police station to do the visual composite. She drove herself. She had her keys and her phone in her hand. She put them on the coffee table. Did she leave the room? *Think, Hannah.* Did she? Hell, there was a tea break, and she popped to the toilet. She left her keys on the table. Did Beverley the facial compositor plant a tracker on her keys? Did someone else? Could Beverley be the person who tampered with the police records? Could she be the one that's helping Dan?

'Should we smash it?' she asks, thinking of Gates' boots grinding her phone into the floor.

'Let's not,' says Glenn. 'Let's have some fun with it instead. You don't have to let the bastards of this world get the upper hand.'

'What do you mean?'

Glenn grins.

'Use brain not brawn. Be clever. Fight back.'

Hannah passes the tracker to Glenn. 'I get scared,' she admits.

'We all get scared,' says Glenn. 'You can't change that. But you can change the way that you react to being scared.'

'How?'

'Don't let men take away your power. There's always something you can do to fight back. Even if it's only a small thing. It will give you back some control and make you feel better. If you let things like fear take over, you risk becoming a victim and that's a hard thing to shake off. Be strong. Kill the fear.'

'But how can I do that?'

Glenn smiles again.

'For example,' she says, 'your creepy-crawly stalker might think he's on to you, but tomorrow he'll be taking an afternoon drive to Brecon. I know a nice little hotel where I can leave this.'

She holds the tracker between her finger and thumb.

Hannah's own face breaks into a smile.

'That's too much to ask, Glenn.'

'You're not asking, I'm offering. It should buy you time enough to get away. Go and grab your things. Do you want to use the landline before you go? Your mobile won't be any good until we get to town.'

'Thank you, yes.'

Hannah fetches her bag. She dials the number from the mobile that Gates left her.

'Yeah,' says a voice. Male. Indeterminate age. No discernible accent.

'It's Hannah.'

'Where are you?'

'On my way to Crickhowell.'

She hears computer keys tapping.

'Go to the Kings House Hotel at three pm and take tea. Use the name Jane Cartland.'

'Okay, and…'

The line is dead. Hannah replaces the receiver. Given that Olly is supposed to be Gates' best friend, she is perturbed at his officious and off-hand manner. He didn't even ask her if she was okay. So while she is relieved to know where she is going next, her encounter with Olly leaves her unsettled.

'Sorted?' asks Glenn.

Hannah nods. 'Yes, thank you.'

'Let's go then.'

Hannah grabs her bag and follows Glenn outside. They use the back door which is screened from the hillside by a solid bank of mature hedging and trees. Glenn leads the way into the garage where a sturdy mud-spattered Land Rover is parked. Hannah can't help straining her neck to peer through the trees.

'Don't worry about the nasty one,' says Glenn. 'He'll be monitoring the tracker. That's why he's not here in person.'

'Small mercies.'

'I'll need you to keep your head down for the first part of the journey so sit where you'll be most comfortable,' says Glenn. 'The back seat might be best. There's a bag of food there for you too.'

Hannah throws her rucksack into the vehicle but hesitates before she climbs in.

'What is it?' asks Glenn.

'If Dan followed me here last night, why did he disappear when you told him I wasn't in the house? If he had been tracking me, he would have known you were lying.'

'The dogs? The shotgun? I suspect he's going to carry on using it. Maybe he wants to follow you to see if you're having an affair? That's why I'm taking it on a little jaunt after I've dropped you off.'

Hannah is still thinking. She closes the car door and steps back.

'In the movies,' she says, 'the trackers are always put on the vehicles.'

'Dammit, you're right. Here, take these.'

Glenn hands Hannah a pair of gardening gloves from a bench and puts on a pair herself. Between them they start to feel around the wheel arches.

'Nothing,' says Hannah, after checking the back.

'Nothing on the front either. Hang on a minute.'

Glenn lies on the ground on her back and pulls herself part way underneath the vehicle. There's a gleeful 'aha' and she pulls herself out. She hands Hannah a small black box the size of a pack of playing cards.

'Well done. It's clean too so probably put there last night before he slipped away.'

'Another tracker?'

Glenn nods and tosses it onto the bench. 'It can join the other one. That'll keep Sir Stalk-a-Lot busy. Come on. Let's get you out of here.'

Hannah lies down on the back seat and covers herself with a hairy plaid blanket. It smells of wet dog and Hannah is glad to sit up when Glenn gives her the all-clear. She admires the beautiful Welsh countryside and wishes she were here under better circumstances.

'I'll drop you off on the High Street,' says Glenn as they approach the town. 'You should hop out as quick as you can. No long farewells. You never know who's watching. Is someone coming for you?'

'This afternoon,' replies Hannah with more confidence than she feels.

'Well, keep out of sight if you can.'

Glenn reaches over her shoulder to hand Hannah a slip of paper.

'Call me if you run into any difficulty. If I'm not around the old fogey will help.'

'Rhys.'

'Yes, my Rhys.' That smile again.

Hannah swallows an enormous lump wedged at the back of her throat. The urge to linger or refuse to leave the car is overwhelming. Glenn forestalls the possibility of any weakness with a hearty farewell.

'Goodbye, Hannah. You take care. And let me know how you get on.'

'I will, I promise. Thank you. You have literally saved my life.'

'Well, just make sure you go and enjoy it.'

Hannah hops out clutching the rucksack and bag of food and Glenn drives away. Hannah looks along the High Street where people are going about their business with a relaxed confidence and purpose that Hannah finds utterly alienating. A mother pushes a pram and leans forward to cluck at her baby, two middle-aged women stare at a display of cakes in a bakery window, an elderly man with a walking stick enters a pharmacy.

She feels more alone than she did in the isolated forest. She had a purpose when she was in the forest but now, she has nothing to occupy her except worry. Worry about Gates. Worry about Dan. Worry about what she will do if she comes face to face with the wrong man.

Hannah swings the backpack onto her shoulders and sets off to find the Kings House Hotel. The main street is not crowded, and she makes sure she scans every approaching male face. Knowing that Dan will be on his way to Brecon soon, Hannah is wary rather than afraid, but her nerves remain on edge, and she grips her rucksack straps so tightly her palms are marked.

She finds the Kings House Hotel within minutes. It's far too early to go in so instead, Hannah turns away to look for a café. She selects a combined bookshop and teashop where she occupies a corner table with a clear view of the shop doorway in front of her and a customer toilet and backdoor behind her. She keeps her backpack within easy reach. Just in case.

At ten to three Hannah returns to the Kings House Hotel. Gates' phone is clutched in her hand. She climbs the steps to the hotel. They are worn and hollowed by decades of feet. She imagines Gates' feet walking beside hers. She's not expecting him to be here, but deep down she hopes desperately that he will be.

The hotel lobby is old-fashioned and over-decorated with burgundy walls and embossed light fittings. Chairs upholstered in deep jewel colours overflow with tasselled cushions and nearby console tables are decorated with extravagant flower arrangements. The scent of furniture polish mixes with the aroma of lilies and roses.

Hannah likes it. It's a place she would have liked to play hide and seek when she was a child. The nostalgia suits her mood of isolation. For a microsecond she wishes her clothes were smarter but then remembers that Glenn laundered them yesterday so at least they're clean. In any case, she doesn't care very much.

She is greeted by a receptionist who asks if she can help in a lilting Welsh accent.

'I've come to take tea,' says Hannah. She delivers her words without inflection because there is no hope or certainty packaged around them. Hannah is simply following an instruction from an impersonal voice. She's not convinced that current events have anything to do with her at all.

'Your name, please?'

'Jane Cartland.'

The receptionist consults a computer screen.

'Yes, I have your afternoon tea booking here. I'm afraid your room won't be ready until four, but I can take your bag if you would like.'

Room? What room?

Before Hannah can ask the question, she is presented with a registration form and a pen. Yep, that says Jane Cartland all right. A double room, bed and breakfast, all paid for.

Hannah sighs to herself. She has no transport, no alternative accommodation and not a huge amount of money. She has no plans of any kind. She is bone-tired, and her joints ache. She feels bereft. She signs the form in what she hopes is an illegible scrawl, refuses to hand over her rucksack and follows the smart-suited rear of the young woman as her heeled court shoes trip across the entrance hall, through a set of double doors and into the tearoom.

The tearoom makes Hannah think of *Downtown Abbey*. She half expects to see sharply bobbed hair and headbands. A waitress shows her to a pair of low-armed upholstered chairs placed each side of a polished table. The two chairs are covered in a black and white fabric with a charming depiction of dogs and foxes. Hannah pushes her chair back to sit down and it gives an agonised squeak. Piped piano music tinkles in the background and tall potted ferns rustle as waitresses sweep by.

Hannah is handed a menu. After a quick glance at the selection of teas she studies the room.

A handful of other places are occupied. Five middle-aged women in the far corner who laugh uproariously, possibly a result of the three empty Prosecco bottles in the middle of the table. In the centre of the room sits an elderly couple who have been together long enough to run out of things to say to each other and there is a young couple tucked against the wall. They are not talking much either, but they are holding hands and can't take their eyes off each other. Hannah feels an unaccustomed stab of jealousy.

She starts when a cork pops out of another Prosecco bottle and two of the five women shriek in tandem. The elderly couple turn their heads and stare. The young couple ignore everyone but each other. Hannah slumps back in her chair and closes her eyes. She has never felt more lost and alone. She is displaced from everything she knows and has no plan beyond breakfast tomorrow morning.

Hannah's thoughts are interrupted by the waitress who comes to take her order. She chooses Lady Grey with orange slices and says yes to the standard afternoon tea. No, she won't have Prosecco, thank you. It's hard enough keeping her wits about her in this crazy world without mussing up her brain cells with a wash of alcoholic bubbles.

It occurs to her that to an outsider she must look like someone with a life. The reality is that she is alone, unloved, and running for her life. She's a coward who failed to report a devastating attack and now another woman is dead. All she has done is hide and when she did get the chance to do something useful, she switched on her bloody phone. She waved the flag as Gates said and he doesn't even know about the tracker yet. What if he doesn't come and find her? What if he's gone?

Hannah fights tears and stares down at the tangled fingers in her lap as if surprised to see them there. She wonders how long she will have to endure this. She wonders how many sips of tea she will have to swallow and how many sandwiches and cakes she will have to nibble before she can leave. A room at four, the receptionist said. Surely, she can leave at four. One hour, that's all. Just one hour.

There is a disturbance in the atmosphere, a movement beside her, and air hisses from the cushion of the chair opposite. A familiar scent. A presence. Hannah lifts her head. Slowly. Cautiously.

There he is.

Gates sits opposite with his gentle gaze focused on her. He smiles. Her throat constricts and her eyes sting. The oxygen has been sucked from the room. Two tears roll down her cheeks.

'Hello, Hannah,' he says.

26

Multi-tiered stands are lowered between them followed by an enormous teapot and a plate of orange slices. Cups, saucers, and tea plates are laid out with cutlery and napkins. Hannah's crumbling world has been fortified. She wipes the tears away.

'Would you like sugar?' asks the waitress, and they both shake their heads without breaking eye contact. The waitress melts away.

'You're here,' says Hannah.

Gates smiles. 'Here and hungry.'

Of course he is. Hannah returns his smile. 'Then eat.'

Gates does as he's told and attacks the tempting array of sandwiches, scones, and cakes with such gusto that she wants to ask when he last ate, where he's been, what he's been doing. Instead, she helps herself to a cucumber sandwich. She can't take her eyes off him.

It's forty-eight hours since they separated on the mountain above the caravan and Gates has arrived unwashed, unshaved, and dressed in the same clothes that he was wearing on Monday. He is spreading clotted cream onto a fruit scone but pauses, aware of her scrutiny.

'Apologies for my appearance. No access to bathroom facilities.'

Hannah just smiles. She would accept him with a dressing of farmyard manure if she had to. Anything. Just to have him here with her. Her tilted world is upright again. She leans forward to pour the tea and the scent of orange blossom rises from the teacup. It's clean and refreshing and makes Hannah think of springtime and new beginnings.

She is anxious to hear how Gates has spent the last forty-eight hours, but she knows him well enough to allow him time to enjoy his afternoon tea. She eats another sandwich and then a scone but leaves the cakes untouched. Her appetite has dissolved. She sips her tea while drinking in the sight of the man that she has come to depend upon more than she thought possible.

At last Gates is done.

'Are you okay?' he asks.

'I am now. I've been so worried about you. Tell me what happened.'

Gates tells his story in his usual calm manner, without fuss and drama. He hid himself amongst the trees, kept his distance and watched the man. As Hannah had anticipated, the stranger followed the track to the top of the mountain then turned around and headed back to the caravan.

Gates had followed him back down past their caravan to the car which was concealed amongst the trees.

'An SUV?' asks Hannah.

'You saw it?'

'I did.'

Gates spotted the slashed tyres on his own car. He guessed and hoped that Hannah had headed out anyway. He returned to the caravan which had been ransacked but he managed to grab a few of their clothes before he left.

'How did I not see you?' asks Hannah.

'I went south of your route. I thought it would be safer if we separated and it got me down off the mountain more quickly. Plus, I yomped.'

'Yomped?'

'I moved fast with my pack on my back. I made it to Ebbw Vale yesterday after a night in the forest and I found my way to a park. Actually, it was mostly a bloody great lake, but I set up camp and got online. I worked until my battery died and it was getting dark then found a bed in a bunkhouse. This morning I hitched a ride to Abergavenny. Olly had a hire car sorted for me, but I had to charge my batteries and sort out a few things before I got here. I was so relieved when Olly told me you were on your way.'

'What was the work?'

'That can wait. Tell me what happened to you.'

They are interrupted by the waitress offering more tea which they both refuse.

Hannah relates her own journey. When she describes the arrival of Dan, Gates' lips tighten.

'And he was alone?'

'Apparently. He arrived on foot and there was a clear view up the hill. There was no one with him.'

Hannah also explains about the keyring and the tiny tracker plus her theory about it being attached when she went to the police station to construct the facial composite.

'Which is how he found us so easily at the second caravan,' observes Gates.

'I should have seen it. I'm sorry.'

'No, Hannah.' Gates shifts forward in his chair. 'This is not on you. Why would you have seen it? How could you have seen something that you didn't know was there and you weren't looking for?'

'But if I had…'

'If you had we might still be in the forest, but in terms of what we're trying to achieve, we'd be exactly where we are now. Without the delicious food.'

Hannah smiles. 'Thank you for being so nice about it.'

Gates leans forward and reaches towards Hannah's hand which she offers with a shy smile. She is surprised to find herself relishing the gentle squeeze that he bestows before sitting back.

'Hannah, I'm so sorry for the way I lost it on Exmoor. I had no right to speak to you like that and I can't tell you how ashamed and mortified I feel. In my defence, I can only tell you that right then I thought squad cars were going to come screaming into the field to take us both away. I thought everything was over. I was genuinely terrified. I haven't felt like that since Ruth. I hate not being in control. I let my emotions get the better of me. It was wrong.'

Hannah smiles. 'Can we just forget it ever happened and not talk about it anymore?'

Gates holds out his hand. 'Shake on it?'

They shake hands. 'But if I ever start to shout or swear at you in the future, shout Exmoor straight back.'

Hannah smiles at the thought that they now have their own special word. A tiny seal on their friendship.

'But back to you,' says Gates. 'How did you get here?'

'Glenn gave me a lift. She smuggled me out on the back seat of her Land Rover but not before she removed a tracker from the wheel rim.'

Gates whistles. 'This is one determined guy. What did Glenn do with the trackers?'

'She took them for a nice hotel break in Brecon. I'm sure they're having a lovely time.'

'I owe her big time,' says Gates. 'When this is over, we'll have to come back together and thank her.'

'I'd like that,' agrees Hannah.

And she does. She likes the idea of thanking Glenn properly, but she likes the idea of coming back with Gates even more. It suggests that when their current situation comes to an end, they'll still be friends. They'll return to Wales together.

'Why are you smiling?' asks Gates.

Hannah straightens her face. 'Just thinking how great it'll be when this is over.'

'On that score, I need to update you on where I am. Shall we go to the room?'

They fetch their key from reception and carry their rucksacks up the stairs to the first floor. Their spacious room is at the back of the hotel and overlooks a sweeping lawn bordered with shrubs and the last of the summer perennials. The room has two double beds and an ensuite bathroom. Gates looks around and nods.

'Good man, Olly.'

Hannah wonders if she should mention her feeling of disquiet at Olly's abrupt attitude on the phone but decides not to. What does she know about the relationship between the two men? Olly is helping them after all.

'Did he book this?'

'He did.'

'You're going to owe him, aren't you?'

Gates kicks off his boots and throws himself back onto the nearest bed with a sigh.

'We don't keep score. We don't need to. Right now, he's helping me, but I've helped him in the past and I have no doubt I will do the same in the future. It's a cycle. We both get it. We're the same.'

'It must be nice having a friend like that. Someone you can trust and depend on.'

Gates pushes himself up into a sitting position. 'He's my family, Hannah.'

He reaches for his laptop bag and logs on while Hannah divests herself of her own boots and gets comfortable on the other bed.

Gates moves over to Hannah's bed and sits next to her so they can both see the laptop.

'My boy has done me proud,' says Gates.

Their upper arms are just touching, and Hannah feels a shiver of pleasure. For a woman who has not been within hand-shaking distance of any other man for thirteen months, this is progress. She is thawing, and the thought both frightens and thrills her.

Gates has brought up CCTV footage and Hannah concentrates on the car that's pulling onto the forecourt of a light industrial unit. The car's headlights go off. The driver gets out, walks around to the passenger door, and opens it. The man speaks to the passenger and then reaches into the car to pull out a young woman with blonde hair, a short dress, and stiletto heels. The woman's head hangs down, but Hannah doesn't need to see her face to know that this is Tina. She staggers as if she's drunk or drugged, maybe both, but at this point in time, she's alive.

Without warning her knees appear to give way and the man grabs her. He hauls her to her feet and as he does so, he looks up and across the street. Hannah's skin burns with heat as she stares at the man who ruined her life and ended Tina's.

Gates rewinds the footage, freezes the frame, and enlarges the shot. There's some pixelation, so the shot is fuzzy, but it's clear enough for Hannah to feel her body fizz with distress. Will he always haunt her?

'Is that your attacker?' asks Gates.

'Yes.'

'One hundred per cent?'

'One hundred per cent.'

Gates nudges her shoulder with his own. 'I was hoping you'd say that.' He lets the footage run and they watch as Dan crosses the road towards the hotel. He has one arm around the staggering Tina's waist, and he stretches out the other to lock his car behind him.

'We've had no luck identifying the car so I'm assuming the plates are false. Now, we still need a name for this guy and that means accessing facial recognition software.'

'And you can do that?'

Gates smiles. 'I can. But facial recognition is a category of biometric security, and the best systems are well-protected. I need specialist software and given that my flat is not the best place to be right now, we will have to go to Olly's and use his kit.'

'And this special software can give us Dan's real name?'

'Should do. And… there is more good news.'

Hannah feels a shift in Gates' body as excitement causes his arm to twitch. His enthusiasm is infectious.

'Tell me.'

'Olly went back to the date of your attack.'

'Went back where?'

'In the police database.'

'But I didn't report it.'

'I know that. But what you don't know is that the hotel did.'

'What?'

Hannah sits up so that she can turn and face Gates. She doesn't understand exactly what this might mean but her insides churn with excitement.

'You must have left a lot of blood, Hannah. Housekeeping went straight to the hotel manager when they saw the sheets. The hotel manager called it in, and SOCA retrieved partial male and female DNA.'

Hannah gasps. Male DNA. Dan's DNA. They have it. Hannah can't speak. She knows how important this is. She takes a deep breath.

'This is a breakthrough, isn't it?'

'It could be. Providing it's Dan's DNA at the scene. And only Dan's. But it is a partial profile.'

'What does that mean?'

'A partial profile can match with more than one person so there's a likelihood of a false positive identification. However, in your case, you can give a positive identification as a living witness to your attack. It could be enough to nail him for your rape. Hotel rooms are normally cleaned by women so unless there was any maintenance in the room, the DNA should all be female. Olly is checking that now.'

'What about DNA from Tina's crime scene?'

'Tina's crime scene is clean. The lab's working on her clothing and her bag, but this guy knew how to protect himself and he cleaned up. We might be out of luck.'

Hannah's slump does not go unnoticed.

'Don't underestimate how much trouble the investigation into your case could cause this guy.'

Hannah is a little mollified.

'So, if you have his DNA, and a mug shot of him with Tina, why can't we get him arrested?'

'He still doesn't have a name. Without a name we can't find him. That's why we must go to Olly's place in Scotland. Even then, without DNA evidence from Tina's crime scene the police may not have enough evidence to prosecute.'

Hannah sighs. It all seems so complicated. 'So when do we go?'

'Tomorrow, we head for Cardiff Airport. Olly will fly down to pick us up and take us to Scotland.'

'Olly can fly a plane?'

'It's one of his many skills, alongside mountain climbing, scuba diving and extreme kayaking.'

'And I thought computer nerds were all pasty-faced hermits.'

Gates arches an eyebrow.

'I'm not sure what offends me the most, Hannah. Nerd, pasty-faced or hermit.'

Hannah giggles. 'Present company excepted, of course. How did you meet Olly?'

'On the dark web.'

'Is that real?'

'Oh yes, it's real. And it's not to be messed with. There's some nasty stuff on there.'

'So why were you on it?'

'If you know what you're doing, you can exchange information with total anonymity. In fact, it was created by the US Government to do just that. But if you don't know what you're doing you can end up in all sorts of shit. Stay away.'

'I wouldn't know where to start.'

'Keep it that way. There are things on there that you never want to see.'

'But you went on and found Olly?'

'Yes. Like I say, I consider him family.'

Hannah shakes her head. She is suddenly overwhelmed with tiredness and is not sure she can absorb any more information tonight.

'Do you mind if I go to bed? I'm feeling shattered.'

The truth is Hannah feels weighed down by the events of the last few days. Despite Gates' optimism, she's not convinced that things will be over as easily as he suggests. She heads for the shower and brushes her teeth before slipping on a fluffy white robe. She can't help thinking of Tina in her robe at The Majestic Inn. In the bedroom the curtains are drawn, and the table lamps are on. Gates is curled up on his bed fast asleep. As she covers him with a throw Hannah examines the now-familiar face. She sighs with what she suspects might be disappointment. But when her own head hits the pillow, she too is out like a light.

27

In the early hours of the morning, Hannah wakes with a start. She hears Gates getting back into bed after a bathroom visit. She rolls onto her side, but sleep eludes her. She is hyper-aware that Gates is lying three feet away from her. She has an overwhelming urge to slip into bed next to him and curl herself around his body.

What might happen if she does brings a blush to her cheeks and a tingle to her belly. She's grateful for the dark and shuts her eyes tight. It's a very long time since Hannah has thought about being physically involved with a man. In fact, there was a time when she was convinced that the chances of her ever wanting to have sex again were zero. Yet here she is, in the eye of an almighty shit storm, and all she can think about is her bare skin beneath Gates' beautiful hands.

Hannah sighs and rolls over again.

She directs her thoughts to the morning, to meeting Olly and flying to Scotland. She tries to focus on this, but her imagination escapes. It flies into the adjacent bed where it sees and hears and feels only Gates.

She has no idea what to do with these feelings.

God help her.

Hannah closes her eyes and lets her thoughts ramble over the last few days. She tries to work out what was bothering her at Glenn's but it's as if something is hovering on the edge of her vision. She begins to drift into sleep and suddenly it's there.

Hannah sits bolt upright and calls across to Gates. He is awake in an instant, both wondering what woke him and aware that Hannah is distressed.

'Hannah, what is it?'

He moves across to her bed and switches on the bedside light. He looks like a schoolboy with his sleep-ruffled hair and blinking eyes.

'At Glenn's,' says Hannah, 'when Dan came to the door. He told her he was a police officer.'

'That was probably a ruse to scare her.'

'That's what I thought at first. But what if it's true? What if he really is a police officer? What if that's how my records were tampered with, how he knows about the trackers, how he follows us so easily? You've already pointed out that the attacker must have extensive knowledge of forensics and crime scenes. And how come he was at the Majestic Inn just as Tina's body was brought out? How did he know to be there? How did he know where I lived? How did the tracker get on my keys at the station? Because that's the only time it could have happened. It all adds up, doesn't it?'

Gates sits back. Even in the yellow half-light of the bedside lamp, Hannah sees the colour drain from his face. It's a full minute before he speaks.

'Jesus Christ.'

Hannah stares at Gates, willing him to come to the same conclusion. If she's correct and Dan is a police officer, he will have untold power and authority to influence the investigation of both her own rape and Tina's rape and murder. Hannah is a call handler. She listens to gossip in the canteen. She knows how these things work.

Gates seems to gather himself together before he speaks.

'You could be right, Hannah.'

A surge of adrenaline bursts through her body.

'Do you think I am?'

Gates shrugs.

'We can't know for sure, but if you're right, if Dan *is* a police officer, it could help us.'

'How?'

'The police have something called a Contamination Elimination Database or CED. Serving police officers likely to come into contact with physical evidence must give DNA samples. It's because there's a risk they could contaminate the physical evidential chain. So, if multiple DNA is found on a murder weapon, for example, the DNA from the officers who attended the scene can be eliminated.'

'So, Dan's DNA will already be on the police system.'

'Exactly. If there is suspicion to arrest, the police database DNA can be used in connection with other crimes. If we can confirm that he's a police officer and we can name him, DI Waterhouse would have grounds to check Dan's DNA against the samples found at your crime scene. The important thing is that Dan won't know it's happening, so he won't be triggered to run. They can't use the database DNA in court though, so an evidential set of fingerprints and DNA would have to be provided separately for use in court.'

'Which wouldn't be a problem.'

'Shouldn't be.'

'And what about Tina's crime scene?'

'If any DNA is found, it can be checked against Dan's. But bear in mind that Dan's DNA will only be on the police system if he's in a role that requires him to attend crime scenes.'

'And if he isn't?'

'Then that's a problem. If an officer gets moved to an office job, say, and has no contact with the physical evidential chain, then the DNA is supposed to be destroyed within twelve months.'

'How do you know all this stuff?'

'It's my job to know it.'

'The witness has not answered the question,' jokes Hannah.

'Let's just say I have friends in the right places.'

'But if I can name Dan as my attacker, his DNA gets taken anyway.'

'Exactly.'

'And if he is in the police, we can look at police mug shots, can't we?'

'We can.'

'Can I start now?'

Gates shakes his head. 'We still need to get to Olly's for work like that. I will need to access personnel records at the local station as a starter. If he is an officer, it makes sense that he's probably based there given that your witness statement was leaked.'

'Dammit.'

Gates gets up and returns to his own bed.

'Try and get some sleep, Hannah. We have a long day tomorrow.'

Hannah settles herself into bed even though she is buzzing with excitement. There is a murmur from Gates' direction. 'Well done you.'

***

'Penny for them,' says Gates.

Hannah starts. They are waiting for the lift and Gates must have sensed that Hannah is troubled this morning. She has no intention of discussing her muddled feelings about Gates.

'I was thinking about the tracker on my keys,' she says. 'Given that it had been there since my visit to the station to work on the facial composite, Dan would already have known we were in Exmoor before I switched on my phone.'

Gates smiles but it's not a relaxed, natural smile. It's stiff and square.

'Hannah, switching on your phone saved us.'

Hannah is alert. Curious.

'How?'

'I contacted the farmer in Exmoor. Dan arrived twenty minutes after we left.'

'He was following the tracker.'

'He must have been.'

Hannah's mind is in a whirl.

'Twenty minutes. So, he was already well on his way when I switched on my phone?'

'It looks like it. I'm truly sorry, Hannah.'

'But why didn't he come after us on Saturday? Why wait till the next day?'

'Who knows,' shrugs Gates. 'While your phone was switched off, he probably assumed you were still inside your flat and may not even have looked at the tracker. Maybe he couldn't get away. He may have been waiting to see where you went before coming after you.'

The lift arrives and they wait for an elderly couple to exit.

'So, it wasn't my phone.'

'It wasn't.'

A small smile of satisfaction fights for control over Hannah's mouth, but she sets her lips into a grim line. It's enough that Gates looks awkward and uncomfortable. She will not gloat.

'Still,' she says as she steps into the lift, 'it taught me a lesson.'

***

After a quick breakfast they get ready to hit the road. Hannah stuffs her rucksack with the car blanket, torch and her few clothes liberated from the caravan by Gates. She holds up the burner phones with a flourish and Gates takes them from her with obvious pleasure.

'Ah, good girl,' he says, and changes the SIM on his current phone with one of the new ones. He grinds the old one with his boot then flushes it away.

Check-out is a key drop and Gates leads the way to the car park at the side of the hill. He has rented an SUV and Hannah enjoys the view as they roll through the Welsh countryside towards Cardiff. The journey takes less than an hour and with Olly not due until the afternoon, they park the car and take some time to sightsee around Cardiff Bay.

They enjoy a late lunch at a restaurant overlooking the water. Gates eats with his usual relish. When he has finished, he leans back in his chair and examines Hannah until she squirms.

'Have I got a boil or something?'

'I still don't know much about you.'

'I could say the same. I have no idea what you were doing with your life before you moved into your flat.'

And I don't know if you love someone, she thought.

Gates' next question suggests he's thinking along similar lines.

'Did you have a partner? Before all this?'

Hannah is thrown by the left-field interrogation.

'Husband, fiancé, boyfriend, girlfriend?' Gates adds.

'Why do you want to know?'

172

'Just curious, I guess. We're spending a lot of time together and I know so very little about you. You never mention anyone.'

'Neither do you.'

What harm is there in answering? Hasn't Gates opened up about his sister? She grimaces before speaking.

'I had a fiancé. In fact, he was four days away from being my husband when he left.'

Gates gives a long whistle. 'What a pillock. Who was he?'

'We were both teachers. We met at school. It was my first job; he was Head of Department. We'd been a couple for three years and living together for one. I had my whole future mapped out.'

'What happened?'

There's a sharp edge to Hannah's voice as she speaks. She tries to soften it. She doesn't want to sound bitter.

'He started an affair with another teacher. Right under my nose, under everyone's nose. I didn't suspect a thing.'

'What a prick. That must have been quite a shock.'

'To say the least. What got me the most was that she wasn't younger or prettier than me. She was older than him and divorced with two young kids. Everyone said it was like he fell for his mother.'

Gates raises his eyebrows. 'Maybe he did.'

Hannah grimaces as she remembers the weeks and months after the discovery of the affair. The scar in her heart has healed but remnants of the shock and humiliation remain.

'It wasn't the affair that hurt so much. It was the fact that he made a fool of me. I felt so embarrassed. Every day at work I had to see them together then face sympathetic glances and commiserations from the other staff. It was awful.'

'And you had to see them every day?'

'They both left at the end of term, thank God. Last I heard she was pregnant and a stay-at-home mum.'

'What did you do?'

'Apart from return the presents, inform the guests, and lose a lot of deposits? I left the school. Couldn't face everyone. I taught for a few more years but everything felt tainted, and my boredom grew with every year that passed. On top of that the kids seemed to get rowdier and less attentive almost every day. I ended up hating the job, so I quit.'

'No significant others since then?'

Hannah snorts.

'Let's just say that men and I don't mix.'

'I find that hard to believe.'

'Why?'

'You seem easy to get along with.'

'Maybe that's because this is a working relationship. No romance involved.'

Hannah regrets the words as soon as they are spoken. She wants to qualify them. She wants to say that she's open to romance. From Gates. He nods his head in acknowledgement. It's too late. She's angry with herself. It makes her tongue sharp.

'I don't trust men, Gates. They put on an act to ensnare you and the minute you're hooked they drop their guard, and you find out who they really are.'

'Ouch, that's a bit cynical.'

'It's a lot truthful.'

'Don't you ever get lonely?'

Hannah lifts her shoulders and drops them in an exaggerated shrug.

'I thought I did. I accepted a few dates. Mostly guys trying to get into my pants. That's how I met Dan.'

'So that was the end of that.'

Hannah shrugs.

'I try and keep myself safe.'

'Not very exciting though.'

Hannah draws a breath.

'Dan was not exciting, Gates.'

'Oh God, I'm sorry. You know I didn't mean it that way. Dan is a criminal, and most men are not like that.'

'But how do you know? How do you know who's good and who's bad? Who's genuine and who's a sham? We're supposed to trust the police, aren't we, and look at Dan. Can you ever really know another person?'

Gates holds his hands up.

'Sorry,' says Hannah. 'You touched a nerve.'

Gates looks as if he has more to say but his face has closed. Hannah wonders if she has been too forceful in her denigration of men and relationships. But then, how else can she cover up her emerging feelings for Gates? She has to keep him on her side and now is not the time to complicate matters. She is struggling with what to say next when Gates forestalls her.

'Well, we'd better get back to it. It's probably time we headed to the airport.'

28

ardiff Airport is larger and busier than Hannah expects. Gates heads to an area on the perimeter of the airfield where private planes are housed. Hannah waits in the car while he goes inside a squat rectangular building. She is watching a small, sleek jet take off when Gates bursts from the building and hurries to the car. He looks bewildered.

'What is it?'

'I've been asked to go to the main airport to speak to someone there.'

'What for?'

'They wouldn't say. But something's up.'

Gates' mouth is set in a grim line and a small rope of anxiety starts to coil inside Hannah's stomach. Gates parks opposite the terminal building and they hurry inside to search for a desk marked *Security*.

After her past quiet days, the crowded hubbub makes Hannah cringe until she feels like the only skittle left standing. The noise is layered beneath the roof of the cavernous departure hall. There is the immediacy of human presence: snatches of conversation, whining kids, trolley wheels and the clatter of cups and saucers from the coffee shops. Above this lies the sounds emanating from the airport itself: the beep of electric carts, the rumble and thump of the baggage conveyors and the clunk of lift doors closing. And each time the huge exterior doors sweep open, the sounds of traffic and aircraft rush inside and the scent of jet fuel scents the air.

Hannah shuffles after Gates as he searches for the desk. Confusion weighs her down and she finds herself incapable of helping. When he locates the correct desk, Gates suggests that Hannah sits down while he sorts things out. She accepts at once and flops onto an inflexible plastic chair. Foreboding settles on one side of her, dread on the other.

Gates is a long time. Hannah shifts from surveying her surroundings to examining Gates. He is facing off to two uniformed men. He pulls himself to his full height and his back is stiff. He seems agitated, waves his arms, and gesticulates with his hands. He looks so unlike his usual self that Hannah tenses, anticipating their discovery by the police.

Gates pulls away from the two men and wheels around towards Hannah. She gasps at the sight of copious tears rolling down his white face. She stands as he comes towards her. Her mouth struggles with a half-formed question that doesn't make it into speech. She reaches a hand towards Gates. He shrugs it aside. He slumps down into a seat and puts his face in his hands. His whole body heaves. Hannah sits back down and puts her arm around his shoulders. He slumps against her. She inhales his distress, catches it at the back of her throat.

It's like Ruth, she thinks.

What the hell has happened? Hannah's legs are jittering.

'What is it? Gates, what's wrong?'

Gates releases a long haa of air and lifts his hands from his face.

'Olly's plane crashed after take-off at Dundee. He's dead.'

Hannah sits back in her chair and absorbs Gates' words. Olly is dead. Hannah doesn't know what this means for them, but she has some idea of what it must mean for Gates. Her hands are trembling. She feels hot and sweaty. Her ears roar. Gates' body still heaves. The two uniformed men approach but keep their distance as if Gates is someone to be afraid of. They both look at Hannah.

'We have a private room,' offers one.

'Gates. Do you want to go somewhere quieter?' asks Hannah, her voice gentle.

Gates shakes his head.

'Can you give us a few minutes, please?' she asks the men. They nod with relief and step away into the clamour of the airport.

Hannah doesn't believe there is a chance in hell of Gates recovering himself in a few minutes, a few hours or even a few days. She's not sure what she should do, or what she should say. She is trained to deal with people who have witnessed sudden death, who are shocked and distressed and disoriented, but that's different. She has a screen and a headset. They provide distance, protection. She is never present to witness the still and silent corpse, to smell blood, to feel the sorrow, distress, and anger of sudden bereavement. She doesn't feel about her callers the way that she feels about Gates.

'Can I get you anything?'

Gates shakes his head.

'Can I leave you for a few minutes?'

There is no response so Hannah stands on her wobbly legs and walks across to the security desk. The din from the busy airport echoes around her. She is forced to sidestep happy holidaymakers and harassed businessmen with their shiny briefcases and shinier shoes. A crying child is slapped by his mother and then cries louder while his two siblings sob in sympathy. Hannah glances back at Gates' collapsed form and shaking shoulders. Not one person stops to ask if he's okay.

At the desk Hannah questions one of the men. He's sorry but all he knows is that Olly's plane crashed soon after take-off from Dundee Airport. It headed east in contravention of the flight path and plunged into the North Sea minutes later. There is an investigation underway. It will take some days to recover the wreckage and the pilot's body. They're very sorry but they have no further information at this stage.

'Thank you,' says Hannah.

She returns to Gates who remains crumpled but quiet. She explains what she has found out.

'What do you want to do?'

'We have to go up there.'

'Are you sure you want to do that?'

'We have no choice. Olly is a good pilot. He's a great pilot. We have to go up there and find out what happened.'

Hannah goes back to the desk and makes the arrangements.

The airport staff are kind and supportive. Hannah and Gates are led to a quiet room and plied with pots of tea until they can board a commercial flight bound for Dundee. The Loganair flight takes an hour and fifteen minutes, and Gates sits immobile with his eyes closed for the duration of the journey. On arrival they are escorted from the plane and taken to the car hire counters.

Gates produces ID and a credit card, both in a name that Hannah has never heard before. The clerk barely glances at them. Inside the car Hannah takes the driver's seat and programmes the satnav with the address that Gates provides. When that is done, he sits back and shuts his eyes.

They head west towards Perth and then northwest into the Cairngorms. Beyond Pitlochry they leave the main road and Gates opens his eyes to direct Hannah towards a low stonewalled cottage with a slate roof. Hannah is tired and stiff from the journey and looks expectantly at Gates once she has parked the car.

'Olly's place,' says Gates.

He climbs from the car and disappears around the back of the cottage. His shoulders are rounded, and his head bent. He walks like an elderly man. Hannah's heart aches for him.

Gates shuffles back with the key to the front door, and beckons Hannah inside. She heaves herself from the car and stretches her limbs, inhaling the scent of heather-clad moorland. The sun is shining but a hint of autumn swirls around on a lively breeze. She shivers after the warmth of the car.

Inside the cottage Gates slumps onto the settee while Hannah takes a quick tour. There is an open-plan kitchen/dining area with a log burner, a lounge with a second log burner plus two bedrooms and a bathroom upstairs. One bedroom has a large double bed, and the second room can only be described as a computer den. All the same paraphernalia that Gates possesses seems to be in this room but there is none of his neatness and order.

In the kitchen Hannah pauses at the sight of Olly's breakfast dishes left in the sink and in the double bedroom the bed is unmade. She has never met the man, but the remnants of his presence emphasise his absence to such an extent that Hannah finds sadness overwhelming her. She would have imagined a solitary computer nerd living in a hovel of dust and grime but although untidy, the cottage looks and feels loved and cared for. Hannah stares out of the kitchen window and sees that the trees in the garden are filled with bird feeders. Beyond the garden a hill rises steeply into a cloudless sky. Hannah returns to the lounge.

'Is it okay for us to be here?' she asks Gates.

'It is.'

Gates reaches for a photo frame on a bookshelf. It shows a man in his mid to late forties. He has a full beard and too-long hair hidden under a woolly hat with a bobble on top. He is dressed in hiking clothes and heavy boots and stands on top of a mountain with his rucksack at his feet and his arms spread wide. His grin feels large enough to fill the frame.

'Is that Olly?' asks Hannah.

'Yes. In his happy place.'

'I wish I'd met him.'

'You would have liked each other.'

'I'm so sorry.'

Gates replaces the photo frame. He turns away. 'I'm going for a walk. I need to think. I'll be back later.'

Hannah watches him leave the cottage. She goes through to the kitchen to watch from the back window. Gates passes through the garden gate and heads towards the mountain. Her instinct is to call him back, to ask him to wait for her, to at least take a warm coat or some water. She's too late. Gates is already out of ear shot and shows no signs of slowing down. Hannah sees that he needs to do this.

'Stay safe,' she whispers.

***

Evening falls and there is no sign of Gates. Hannah feels his absence as a physical pain pressing along the length of her spine. While her back aches, she rocks between reassuring herself that Gates is a grown man who can look after himself and picturing him huddled in a frozen heap on the side of the mountain. She wonders if she should phone someone to say that he is up there alone then quails at the thought of his temper if he finds out she's compromised his anonymity. She tells herself that it's still only the very beginning of September and while it's a degree or two colder than in the south, there is not yet any sign of winter frosts or stormy weather.

She considers going after Gates but dismisses the thought. There are no discernible paths on the mountain and it's getting dark. She has no idea where Gates might be or how she would find him. Within a matter of minutes, Hannah would be lost and a liability.

Her mind flits towards Dan but she shuts down those thoughts. Gates has reassured her that Olly's home is as safe as it gets. They are off the grid and untraceable. There are no more trackers and there has been no contact with anyone other than Olly. Instead of jumping at shadows and creaks she remembers Glenn's words. She can't stop fear, but she can choose how she deals with it.

She secures all the doors and windows and lights a fire, more for comfort than warmth. Although Olly's death has been a shock for them both, Hannah sees no reason why she and Gates should change their plans. Olly's house is still a safe refuge. They will use Olly's gear to identify Dan then let DI Waterhouse know. As soon as he is arrested, Hannah will go home. Satisfied with her plan she beds down on the sofa and goes to sleep, though not before checking a burner phone is underneath the pillow.

***

The next morning Gates is still absent. Hannah decides to give him a few hours to return before she contacts the DI. With nothing better to do to pass the time, she busies herself tidying the cottage. It's strange clearing up after a man she has never met, especially when she knows he will never return. Nevertheless, it satisfies an inner need to create order for the dead man. She washes his last used dishes, changes the bed linen and towels, dusts, hoovers and mops the kitchen floor. Outside she finds a wooden shed with garden implements and a sack of bird seed. She fills the bird feeders and dead-heads the summer flowers. Who will look after the birds now Olly is gone?

There is a small vegetable patch to the side of the house where pumpkins grow. Hannah cuts one to make pumpkin soup and finds yeast and flour for crusty rolls. The apple tree and rhubarb patch provide the base for a fruit crumble. It's the first time she has cooked for Gates, and she puts the food away for his return. He will be hungry.

While the kettle boils for tea, Hannah retrieves the card that DI Waterhouse gave her on the day of her interview. She reads it several times and turns it over and over between her fingers. Although she feels safe in Olly's house, she is sensible enough to realise that she shouldn't wait too long before calling.

She is standing on a rickety step ladder washing the outside of the kitchen window when a crunch of gravel alerts her to Gates' return. Her senses tell her it's him. The measured stride can only be his. She climbs down the ladder and turns towards the corner of the house to welcome him.

He is dirty and dishevelled. He needs a warm bath and a shave, but his eyes are bright, and he offers Hannah a crooked smile.

'Welcome back,' says Hannah.

She warms soup and bread and while he eats, she runs a hot bath and brings fresh towels. Gates says thank you for everything and there is a new gentleness in his tone as if he has exhausted his emotions. He has rediscovered his unhurriedness.

'Were you cold?' asks Hannah.

It's her way in. She wants to ask him where he went, why he went, what he did, did he eat, sleep, walk, rest? She can ask him none of these things. She is afraid that interrogation will upset him. She feels that to do so would be an invasion of his privacy. But Gates must recognise Hannah's need for information.

'I'm sorry, you must have been worried.'

'Yes, and no.'

'Does that mean you were worried some of the time?'

'No, it means I was worried for the emotional part of you. I knew that the physical part of you would be okay. Although, I was just about to call DI Waterhouse.'

Gates finishes his soup and puts the spoon down inside the bowl. He dodges around it with a piece of Hannah's homemade bread as he mops up the last of the soup.

'There's work to be done. We still need a name.'

He's not ready to share.

'Have your bath,' says Hannah, 'then we can work all night.'

29

Gates emerges refreshed from the bath and the slightest lift of Hannah's heart tells her that she likes to see him like this. His troubles scrubbed away with the grime. At least for a little while. Not his grief though. That remains visible in the dark shadows etched below his eyes and the grim set of his jaw.

'I'll get set up,' says Gates.

Hannah makes two steaming mugs of tea and carries them up to the bedroom that she thinks of as the computer den. Gates looks so at home she wonders out loud if he has been here before.

'Many times,' answers Gates. 'This place has been a bit of a bolt hole over the years. I love it here.'

He has already brought the computer screens to life.

'I'm going to access the personnel files at our local force, and you can scroll through those on an iPad. While you do that, I'll use facial recognition software on the mug shot from the CCTV.'

He hands Hannah the iPad, and she looks at the first face.

'How many staff are there?'

'About 1,500 but I've prioritised the police officers first followed by immediate support staff and then civilians. Take your time and take a break every 20 minutes. It's easy to lose focus.'

Hannah nods and goes next door to lie on the bed. Gates' eyes are already fixed on the screens as he clicks and scrolls for Hannah's freedom.

***

After an hour of scrolling Hannah is nowhere. Although she dismisses the females and individuals clearly outside Dan's age range, the flow of faces is endless. Her initial excitement at the thought of spotting Dan on the screen has leached away as she realises her confidence was misplaced. She tosses the iPad onto the bed and goes downstairs to make a cup of tea. She is in the process of adding milk to the two steaming mugs when a noise from upstairs startles her and milk splashes onto the worktop. Half yell, half cry, followed by the thunder of Gates' feet as he rushes down the stairs. He anchors himself against the door frame to prevent his body hurtling like a torpedo into the kitchen.

'I've got him.'

Without either of them saying another word, Hannah follows as he races back up the stairs and she is pushed into the chair which Gates rolls forwards towards the screen. On one side is the CCTV shot of Dan as he takes Tina from his car. On the other is a mug shot of DI Keith Sullivan.

Hannah's emotions leave her speechless: shock, surprise, delight, and overwhelming relief. She sits and stares for what feels like a very long time. It's only when Gates' fingers squeeze her shoulders that she finds her voice.

'He *is* a copper.'

Gates drops a light kiss on the top of Hannah's head, and she doesn't mind.

'He is indeed a copper. A detective no less.'

'Why didn't I find him?'

'Wrong station,' says Gates. 'In fact, the wrong force. Our man has moved around. Suspiciously so.'

They examine the record together. Forty-year-old DI Keith Sullivan has been in the force for twenty-two years. He has been at his current station for the last three years. He has an unremarkable record with a marked absence of commendations or disciplinary actions. The only item of significance is the number of transfers he has requested.

'He's moved a lot,' observes Gates. 'Twice as a constable and twice again as a DI.'

'Is that unusual?'

'My understanding is that police officers have to give a good reason for wanting to make a lateral transfer, but if they have a clean record there's nothing to stop it happening.'

'It sounds like there's a but coming.'

'I just wonder why an officer with a record like his would want to keep moving. He would have to re-establish himself in a new area with a new team. It can be tough. It can also mean they miss out on promotion. I would have expected him to be a DCI by now.'

'So why would he do it?'

'Your guess is as good as mine,' muses Gates. 'But my guess is that he needed to leave town for more than a change of scenery.'

'To avoid disciplinary measures, for example?'

'Could be. Who knows?'

'Shall we call DI Waterhouse?'

'Have you got the card?'

Hannah hands it over and Gates types in the number. He turns to Hannah.

'Before I call there are some rules. Please don't reveal

anything about our location. Try not to talk about me but if you do, don't mention my name. Call me a friend, a colleague, a mate, anything but a name. And of course, no mention of hacking. If there are difficult questions, I will answer them but only if there's no other choice.'

Hannah agrees. She understands Gates' need for anonymity. She hopes she can complete this call without having to ask him to speak.

'Can he trace this call?'

'It's routed through a labyrinth. We're safe.'

'Okay then. Dial it and be damned.'

Gates clicks the mouse. The DI answers on the fourth ring. Gates puts him on speaker.

'Waterhouse.' For Hannah, the voice that she heard for the first time little more than a week ago offers her a strong connection with her life before the call. Tina's call. She is sucked back to the police station, to home, to normality. She so wants this to all be over.

'Hi,' she says, 'it's Hannah Ridley.'

'Thank goodness you've called,' says the DI. 'I've been trying to find you.'

The DI has been trying to contact Hannah since she left her flat. He has been worried for her safety. So much so that he applied for an order to track her phone. It revealed a location in Exmoor, but Hannah wasn't there, and her phone has gone dead.

'I lost my phone,' improvises Hannah, a response which earns her a thumbs-up from Gates. No need to explain about Exmoor at least. 'I haven't got round to replacing it yet.'

'We tried your flat, Hannah, and you haven't been at home or at work,' says the DI.

'No, I've been away.'

'Can you tell me where?'

Hannah looks at Gates who nods.

'I've been to Wales.'

'Okay, we might come back to that. Hannah, can you come into the station?'

She doesn't have to look at Gates. She can feel his whole body shaking an adamant no.

'I'm sorry. I would prefer not to.'

'Can you tell me why?'

'I don't feel safe.'

'What do you mean by that?'

'DI Waterhouse,' she begins. He interrupts her.

'Hannah, unless we're in the company of senior officers, please call me Neil.'

'Is that meant to make a difference?'

Hannah's response is sharper than she intended, and Neil picks up on her tone.

'You need to explain what's going on, Hannah. Take your time. I've got all night.'

Gates nods an emphatic yes.

'I've been able to identify the man who attacked Tina. The same man who attacked me. He's been chasing me. He's used trackers and I think he means to harm me.'

Hannah pauses.

'Go on,' says Neil.

'I've been hiding because if I come forward, I think he will get to me.'

'Why do you think that?'

'Because the attacker is a police officer.'

Both Hannah and Gates hear the sharp intake of breath.

'Can you prove this?'

'I can identify the man as my attacker,' says Hannah. 'After my attack, the police were called to the room where it happened by hotel staff and DNA was recovered. I believe it will match the officer in question. If there is any DNA found at Tina's scene, I'm positive it will match.'

'How do you know all this?' There is an element of disbelief in the DI's voice, but Hannah knows she can't give Gates away.

'You can examine the evidence yourself. You'll see that I'm telling you the truth.'

There is a brief silence. Hannah can almost hear the DI thinking. She waits.

'Hannah,' Neil's voice is urgent. 'Can you give me a name?'

'DI Keith Sullivan,' says Hannah.

After the search for the officer's identity and the build-up to the call, the name slips from her tongue with unceremonious ease. It just slides away. No fuss, no drama.

Hannah remains calm. She is in control of this conversation and it's a good feeling.

'Will you arrest him now? And put him away.'

Neil replies without pausing.

'Are you prepared to testify in court, Hannah? About your rape. About the evidence. Your recognition of his voice.'

'There's CCTV too.'

'What CCTV?'

'From a private store. It shows the attacker parking his car and walking with Tina towards the hotel.'

'How the hell did you get that?'

Gates scribbles on a scrap of paper and holds it in front of Tina. It says PI.

'A private investigator,' she says.

'Will he come forward?'

Gates shakes his head, no.

'No, he won't. But he will provide details of the store and the owner will be happy to hand over the tape.'

Hannah crosses her fingers.

'Hannah, you must realise this makes you a key witness in the case.'

'I do.'

'I want to put you in a safe house.'

Hannah looks at Gates, but he shrugs.

'What does that mean?'

'It means that you will be assigned a Personal Protection Officer and taken to a safe location. It's usually somewhere in the country and it will be away from your home. If necessary, we'll then help you find a further safe place to move on to.'

Something in that last sentence unnerves Hannah but right now there's too much else to think about.

'How long for?'

'The average stay in a safe house is three to seven days. Quite frankly if we haven't arrested this guy in that time, it will all be over. He'll be long gone. We'll act fast. I'll have him tailed and I'll gather the evidence to have him arrested, charged and in custody in far less than three days.'

Gates is nodding in Hannah's peripheral vision.

'What do I need to do?' asks Hannah.

'Give me all the evidence you have. I promise you no-one else in the police force will hear Sullivan's name until it's written on the arrest warrant. You'll be in a safe house long before that.'

Hannah's thoughts swirl around inside her head. She's seen the TV shows, read the novels. She knows what it means to go to a safe house. It can be a comforting and protective place of safety for a few days, but it can also lead to a lifetime in witness protection. A lifetime of pretending to be someone else, learning and remembering a new name and a new history, never going back. Never seeing Gates again. Can she live with that? It's a huge decision. She needs more time.

'Can I think about it?'

Next to her Gates sucks in his breath. He doesn't like her response.

'Of course you can. But you don't have long.'

'It's the thought of the safe house. I need to think about it.'

'I understand.'

'Can I call you back? Say, in an hour?'

'I'll be waiting.'

Hannah puts down the phone and turns to Gates.

'This is it, isn't it?'

Gates nods and takes her hands. 'It is.'

'You want me to go, don't you?'

'If we keep running, I'm confident I can keep you safe for the immediate future. But eventually we'll run out of places to hide. I don't know how long I can keep you safe, especially now that Olly is gone. If you go to a safe house, you'll have a whole team of people looking out for you.'

'Will you come with me?'

'No,' says Gates. 'Much as I would like to, you know that I can't. There would be too many questions. My life and work would be over.'

'If I do this, will I see you again?'

'Of course you will.'

Hannah is not sure how Gates can know this. He can only have a vague idea of how things will work out, and he knows that if DI Keith Sullivan is not successfully prosecuted and imprisoned, Hannah will be at risk. Even if the DI goes down, Hannah could still be vulnerable. Who knows how far the crooked DI's network stretches?

'I need a bath,' says Hannah. 'It's where I think.'

She soaks in warm bubbles and considers her options. Keith Sullivan will only be prosecuted if she goes in the witness box. She has promised herself that she'll be brave. That she'll get justice for herself and for Tina. That the attacker will be taken off the streets. When she made those promises, she had no idea how much terror she would feel at the thought of fulfilling them.

Prosecuting criminals is all about getting justice for the victims but who looks out for the witnesses? What about the damage done to their lives? Hannah's fear is that Sullivan will come for her. If he evades arrest, she will be a fugitive forever.

And there is Gates. The man who has supported her and risked his way of life for her. Olly, whose life was taken. The least she can do is follow through. Walking away is not an option. It never was.

As her hour ticks away, Hannah makes her decision. After Tina's call she promised herself she wouldn't hide anymore. The last twelve days have taught her that she can cope with whatever is thrown at her. Yes, she's frightened but fear won't kill her. Leaving Sullivan free, however, could result in more rapes and murders, more ruined lives. One day, he could come back for her. He could find Gates.

Washed and scrubbed she presents herself back in the computer room. Hannah feels slightly nauseous, but she also feels positive and determined. This is her decision. In the end it was an easy one to make.

'I'm going to do it.'

Gates features soften in relief, and he offers her his gentle smile.

'Good decision.'

Gates places the call.

30

It's clear that Neil has not been twiddling his thumbs for the last hour. He is all business with his priority being to remove Hannah to a place of safety without delay.

Gates does not want his location revealed so with the help of his scribbled notes, Hannah claims that she is in Newcastle-upon-Tyne. Gates will drive through the night to cover the five-hour trip by road. Neil suggests a rendezvous at the Gateshead Metrocentre. Plenty of parking and crowds. They agree to meet at a Starbucks.

Even though she is confident that she has made the right decision, Hannah is in agony at the thought of the move to a safe house. Her insides feel hollow, and her mouth tastes like metal. Being protected but being watched, restricted, following orders; it sounds like prison. Most of all it will be tough leaving Gates. She hopes the nausea she is feeling is nervousness. Gates wants her to eat before they hit the road, but she can't muster an appetite.

While she packs her few pathetic belongings into her rucksack, Gates puts together a package of evidence and hands it to Hannah on a flash drive. Even with Olly's gear he does not trust email. Before they leave the house, he hands Hannah the flash drive and a burner phone.

'The phone is clean, Hannah. You must memorise my number in case you need to call me. If you do, I'll give you a new number before you end the call.'

'You'll trash your phone every time I call you?'

'Only the SIM card. But Hannah, you must only call me if it's something urgent. We can't chat. And you can only call me once on each number.'

'Once.'

'They'll ask you if you have a phone and you have to say no. I'm hoping you won't be searched.'

'You want me to lie to them?'

'It's the only way you'll get to keep a phone. The rules are there for your safety. You can only turn the phone on and use it once. After that you must remove the SIM and trash it. I've put a new SIM with the flash drive, so you have two calls. Don't waste them.'

Hannah's face drops. Gates touches her shoulders. 'Three to seven days, Neil said. It's not long.'

Hannah thinks of all those lonely hours without Gates.

'You still haven't told me what you were doing on the mountain.'

'Walking, thinking, sheltering in a shepherd's hut. Getting my head together. Shivering sometimes.'

He demonstrates and Hannah laughs as she's meant to. In response Gates hands her one of his jumpers. 'To keep away the shivers,' he says.

Hannah is touched. 'Thank you. What will you do?'

'I'll be watching, Hannah. But you mustn't ever look for me. And if you catch a glimpse of me, do nothing, look away.'

Hannah feels her heart shrink at the thought that this separation could be forever. If she goes into witness protection, she will never see Gates again.

'This is so hard.'

'I know, Hannah. But you know it's the only way. Now, one last thing. Look out for a bright light.'

'What?'

'I'm assuming you'll be taken somewhere in open countryside. The Protected Persons Service like to use properties that are out in the open so they can see who's approaching. If I need to contact you, I'll use a bright light. It will be my signal to you to use the phone and contact me. It will be urgent. Do you understand?'

Hannah nods and turns away. Her throat has thickened but now is not the time for tears. She must do this.

'Where will you be?'

'Once I know where you are I'm going to find out what happened to Olly. It will help me to know that you're safe.'

Hannah turns her head to look at Gates but this time it's Gates who is looking away.

***

At the Metrocentre, Gates steers the car into a space at the edge of the vast parking area. Hannah must find Starbucks in the Lower Red Mall. It's a long walk and Gates wants her to be on time for her meeting with Neil Waterhouse.

'Force yourself to forget me,' advises Gates. 'These people are trained to follow tails and are always alert to anything or anyone out of the ordinary. If you draw attention to my existence, I'll be forced to disappear.'

'I understand,' says Hannah. There's no way on earth she will ever forget Gates, but knowing he is watching over her will prevent her from taking so much as a casual glance over her shoulder. Hannah half hopes that Gates will kiss her goodbye. An affectionate peck on the cheek will do. Instead, he takes her hand and gives it that gentle squeeze of his.

'Now go. Stay safe. And don't look back.'

Hannah weaves between the vast ocean of parked cars. The lump in her throat feels bigger than her backpack. She swallows it down and walks with purpose, her head held high, and her eyes fixed ahead.

Despite the vastness of the Metrocentre and the overwhelming cacophony of chatter, music and screaming kids, Hannah finds the normality around her comforting. To see families and children enjoying their day wandering through the shops is a timely reminder that normal lives are still being led away from the stress and tension of rapes and murders and the evasion of criminals. Even though she has no interest in shopping nor any intention of buying anything other than a very large coffee, she feels her eyes drawn to the colourful window displays. The ordinary nature of everything attracts her. She feels as if she's floating along a river of innocence and ignorance.

If only these people knew what the world is really like.

She pretends she's on a day out. She's looking for something to wear for dinner with Gates. Dinner with Gates? Where did that thought come from? *Get to the caffeine queue, woman, you're losing it.*

Hannah finds Starbucks without any trouble and heads towards the counter to place her order.

'Hannah.'

She is dragged from her reverie by DI Neil Waterhouse who has materialised beside her.

'Do you mind if we get on our way?' he asks.

Hannah does mind but she pretends otherwise.

'Not at all, I was just killing time.'

Neil leads Hannah towards the nearest exit and out towards the car park. They head for a black BMW. Unmarked and unremarkable, it could belong to any successful businessman.

A middle-aged man is sitting in the front seat and a woman of similar age in the back. They are both dressed casually in jeans and shirts. Neil opens the rear door for Hannah, and she slides in next to the woman.

'Hi, I'm Jackie.'

The woman holds out a hand to Hannah who takes it. The hand is dry and worn and Jackie's eyes crinkle with a ready smile. The man in the front turns sideways and addresses Hannah. His bulk prevents him from offering his hand, but he smiles too and waves his fingers towards Hannah.

'I'm Al, Jackie's husband. Nice to meet you, Hannah.'

'You too,' she replies.

Neil settles into the driver's seat and fastens his seatbelt. Hannah feels confined and claustrophobic wedged into the car with three other humans. Neil seems to sense her discomfort and, as if anxious to be underway, he starts the engine and eases the car towards the exit.

'Jackie and Al are from the Protected Persons Service, and they are your Personal Protection Officers. Their job is to look after you and keep you safe until Sullivan is remanded in custody.'

'Where are we going?'

'The Yorkshire Dales,' says Jackie. 'It's isolated and it's safe. There will be some rules to follow, but we'll go through those when we get there.'

Hannah nods and turns to face the window. She doesn't want to be rude. She has nothing more to say.

31

*H*e is seething with anger. How dare that fucking bitch send him on a wild goose chase across Wales? Did she think it was funny? It was bloody expensive to stay the night in that posh hotel too. The key ring tracker was in the dining room, and he had to sit there all night watching the guests come and go as he lingered over five courses and umpteen drinks. Not a sign of her and no sign of the tracker either. He could hardly start tearing the room apart, could he?

If only he knew what car she was driving. Christ, she is going to pay for this. He is going to enjoy dealing with her. He will not hurry. He will take his time, watch her eyes, linger. Only when he is ready will he dispose of her. The body too this time. No chance of forensics getting anywhere near her. There are plenty of reservoirs and disused mine shafts in Wales. Any one of them will do.

First, he must find her. It will take him a while but there are only so many exits from Wales. Time to call in some favours.

32

The safe house is a detached double-fronted stone-built property with sweeping bay windows balanced either side of an imposing front door. The woodwork is tired, and the corners of the stone are crumbling, but it does nothing to detract from the warm welcome that the house offers.

'It's lovely,' says Hannah. She had pictured an enclosed abode where she would be contained and subdued and is surprised to find how wrong she was.

An armful of late summer flowers and cuttings from garden shrubs are arranged in a vase in the hallway and a cluster of coats and assorted boots jostle for space along one of the walls.

'Come through,' says Jackie.

Hannah follows her down the hallway to a large kitchen where she is almost bowled over by two excited retrievers. Al shouts at the dogs and they sit obediently although their bodies continue to quiver with joy at the appearance of humans and their tails wag like kites fighting a gale.

'This is Jemmie and Steven,' says Al, rubbing two hairy heads simultaneously. 'Two boys, too boisterous and far too friendly.'

Hannah strokes the silky hair on the dogs' backs, and they turn their heads to gaze at her adoringly.

'Room or a cuppa first?' asks Jackie as she fills the kettle.

'Cuppa, please,' says Hannah.

Before the tea is brewed, Neil settles opposite Hannah. He is bursting with questions.

Hannah sticks to her story about a private investigator and tells him all she knows. She makes it sound as simple as she can. Partly because she doesn't understand everything that Gates has done but also because she wants her story to sound as if any half-competent private investigator could have obtained the same results.

She hands over the flash drive and Neil powers up his laptop. As he watches the CCTV footage of Sullivan with Tina, Hannah can see growing horror take over his features. When Sullivan glances in the direction of the camera, Neil freezes the frame and studies the face caught there. He stares at it while Hannah starts to fidget.

Hannah caves and speaks first. 'Do you know him?'

'No, I don't,' he informs Hannah, 'he's not from our patch. Thank God.'

Neil reads the file giving details of Hannah's attack including the date, the name of the hotel and the call to the police. When he's finished, he removes the flash drive and tucks it into his inside jacket pocket.

'And you're not going to tell me how you got hold of this?'

'No,' says Hannah.

Neil shrugs.

'I need to deliver this myself, Hannah. I can't trust it to the internet, and I certainly can't risk it circulating around the station. Sullivan must have a friend there to have been able to get your statement tampered with. It's imperative that he is kept in the dark until his arrest. I've no doubt that if he gets wind of this he will run. He's a clever son of a bitch and if he gets away from us, we won't see him again.'

'So, what happens now?' asks Hannah.

'I can't use the material that you've given me without a verified source, so I'll have to access the original CCTV and the DNA from your crime scene. The next step will be to apply for access to the police DNA database so that I can confirm the DNA from your attack is Sullivan's. If it matches it will be enough to arrest Sullivan. For your attack, at least.'

'How long will it take?'

'Thirty-six hours if everything runs smoothly.'

'What about Tina's case?'

'It's the Crown Prosecution Service who decide whether to prosecute a criminal case. Their lawyers must be satisfied that there's sufficient evidence to provide a realistic prospect of conviction. They may decide we have enough, but I would feel happier if we had Sullivan's DNA at Tina's crime scene. In the light of this new evidence, I'm going to request another look at the crime scene and Tina's belongings. That bastard must have left something behind.'

'What if you don't get it?'

'This is a murder inquiry so I can hold Sullivan for ninety-six hours. In that time, I have to get this case watertight. If I can link him to Tina, we'll have him. He'll go down for life. And whatever happens with Tina's case, we'll get him for your rape.'

Neil gathers his things and stands up.

'I have no idea how you did this, Hannah. Maybe when this is all over, you'll tell me. Or at least tell me who helped you. I just want you to know how grateful I am. This is brilliant work and it's given us a real chance to get this guy. The police force is there to serve and protect the population and it's a bad day when something rotten is unearthed.'

'I'm glad I could help.'

'I'll be in touch as soon as I have some news. You'll be safe here providing you do everything that Jackie and Al tell you to. With a bit of luck, you'll only be here for a few days.'

Al follows Neil to the front door and Hannah hears a short, whispered conversation between the two men before Neil says goodbye, gets into his car and drives away. Hannah remains in the kitchen of the isolated house in North Yorkshire, alone with two strangers. *Now what?* She feels abandoned.

Al returns to the kitchen and he starts going through the rules.

'Do you have a mobile phone, Hannah?'

She is prepared for the question.

'It's long gone. It got smashed in Exmoor.'

If you're going to lie, said Gates, stick as close to the truth as you can.

'You can't contact anyone. No social media, no telephone calls, no letters, texts, messaging, nothing. Right now, no one knows you're here and we need to keep it that way.'

Don't think about Gates, she tells herself, afraid that she will smile.

'This is for your own safety as well as the safety of your friends and family.'

What friends and family?

'We've spoken to your employer, and you're on paid leave for as long as required.'

'Where do they think I am?' asks Hannah.

'They don't know where you are, but they know that you're helping the police with a case.'

Hannah wonders what Angie must be making of that. She'll be upset that Hannah hasn't been in touch. But it's not like they've been bosom buddies meeting for drinks after work or nights out. They're work colleagues who have established a rapport based on similar ways of thinking. Hannah knows she mustn't let nostalgia feed sentimentality. It won't help anyone.

Christ, it's bad enough that Gates has taken up residence in her cerebral cortex.

'Any questions for me so far?' asks Al.

'No, I can't think of anything, thanks.'

'I'll show you round,' says Jackie. 'We prefer you to stay inside at all times, but we understand that people can get cabin fever. You can go out into the garden but tell us if you're planning to leave the house and one of us will come outside with you.'

Oh great. Prison guards. A walk around the exercise yard with a warder three paces behind. What was that about welcoming?

Jackie shows Hannah the living room, dining room, study, kitchen, and a huge conservatory across the back of the house. Upstairs are five bedrooms. Hannah is shown to a spacious room with far-reaching views across the countryside. It has a comfortable-looking double bed and an ensuite bathroom. Jackie points across the corridor to a closed door off the landing.

'That's our room. If you're worried during the night, don't hesitate to knock and wake us. Feel free to explore the rest of the house at your leisure but remain indoors. I'll leave you to get settled. Lunch will be ready in half an hour.'

It doesn't take long for Hannah to unpack her rucksack. Her meagre belongings fit into one drawer. She conceals the mobile phone in the sleeve of Gates' sweater and rolls the woollen garment around it before pushing it to the back of the drawer. She isn't anxious to hurry downstairs. After the car journey, Neil's questioning, and Al's orders, it's a relief to have some time alone.

Hannah stands at the window and surveys the landscape. The safe house really is in the middle of nowhere. Hannah had imagined the area to be sparse and flat, but she's surprised and pleased to see how the ground undulates, rolling and climbing between peaks and valleys. The area around the house is devoid of human habitation but potential hiding places proliferate. There are more trees than she expected, scattered stone shepherd's huts and rocky crags. In between are sheep. Lots of sheep. She opens the bedroom window and faint baas are carried on the breeze. She thinks of Exmoor and the bundles of wool that gathered curiously around the caravan's door then skittered away if she dared to hold out as much as a hand towards them.

Almost without realising what she's doing Hannah's brain is plotting the route she will take if she needs to run. She will do the same from the other side of the house too.

There is a knock on her door.

'Lunch is ready, Hannah.'

'Thanks, Al, I'm coming,' she calls.

She picks at the lunch that Al has prepared.

'Are you okay, Hannah?'

Hannah is jolted back to the lunch table by Al's voice.

'Yes, fine, thanks.'

While Hannah destroys a slice of quiche without managing to eat very much of it, she faces another bombardment of questions. This time about her job. Jackie and Al are both trying so hard to make her feel welcome, but all the attention is starting to get on her nerves. Hannah assumes that Jackie and Al know why she is here. They must know about the call from Tina. Are they working up to asking about it?

Hannah can't go there. She longs for peace, quiet and solitude. She puts down her fork and takes her plate across to the sink. Her offer to wash up is declined.

'Would you mind if I borrow a book and go and read somewhere?' she asks.

'Of course not,' says Jackie. 'Go through to the sitting room. There's a bookshelf in the corner.'

The sitting room is at the front of the house and there's a welcoming, if subdued, log fire glowing in the grate. It scents the room with the bonfires that Hannah's dad lit on his allotment when she was six or seven years old. Hannah likes the feeling of nostalgia that the burning logs evoke but soon realises that the fire is a necessity. The old house is draughty, and she throws on another log before choosing a book from the shelf.

It's an eclectic collection no doubt designed to meet the tastes of a wide variety of witnesses. Hannah selects a book she has read before in case she is questioned on its contents. She has no intention of reading. She wants privacy so that she can think. She opens *The Man Who Mistook His Wife for a Hat* by Oliver Sacks at a random page and settles herself in a chair near the window so that she can gaze across the Yorkshire Dales.

Hannah's thoughts, as always, are occupied by people. By Tina and Dan and Gates. But for once she's not occupied with the case or the potential arrest of Dan. It's the afterwards that is concerning Hannah. If Dan is convicted of Tina's murder, he will be locked away for life. And if it can be proved that he killed the women in the other two unsolved cases, he will more than likely die in prison. Like he deserves.

So, what if that doesn't happen?

What if Dan is only charged with Hannah's rape?

What if he doesn't get the maximum sentence?

What if he's out in a few years and comes looking for her?

What if he's not convicted at all?

What if he has friends that will come for her?

Hannah remembers Googling rape conviction rates in the UK. It was less than 2% of reported attacks. Over 50,000 women put themselves through the agony of going to the police, subjecting themselves to examination and investigation, and what was the result? Certainly not justice for the women or punishment for the perpetrator. And what about all the women who choose not to report their attacks? It's no wonder Hannah didn't feel she could report hers. So how many rapists do it again knowing they can get away with it?

And when do you ever hear about men being sexually assaulted? Because Hannah knows from her job that happens too. How many men report sexual violence and how many of their attackers are convicted? Hannah doesn't know and she has no facility to Google, but anger and frustration makes her head ache.

She wants to scream. Will it be possible to ever feel safe again?

33

Hannah spends Tuesday in the sitting room with the unread Oliver Sacks book on her lap. From time to time, she gets up to stretch her legs and throw another log on the everlasting fire or wanders through to the kitchen to fill her large mug with tea or coffee. Al has left the house to run errands and Jackie is dealing with paperwork. Hannah feels that she should offer to help with something, but she is overcome with an unaccustomed listlessness. Most of all, she doesn't have the energy to answer any more questions. About anything.

With Al absent for the day Hannah escapes a formal sit-down lunch in the kitchen by making herself a sandwich and taking it to the sitting room.

'Do you mind?' she asks Jackie.

'Not at all. You go and relax. You need to rest.'

Hannah is nodding in her chair when the barks of Jemmie and Steven alert her to Al's return. Hannah forces herself to her feet to help carry bags of groceries from the car then remains in the kitchen to help prepare dinner. Jackie and Al chat about the people he met in town and share news from the locals. They demonstrate the ease of a couple that have been together a long time.

Hannah finds herself smiling and nodding throughout dinner then taking herself to bed early because she wants to be alone. When she's ready for bed, she curls under the cover with Gates' sweater wrapped around her and the curtains drawn back in case there should be a bright light on the horizon.

She is waiting. She just doesn't know what she is waiting for.

***

Now it's Wednesday and Hannah's heart sinks at the thought of another day of confinement. It's three weeks since she answered Tina's call and her world was disrupted. She still feels lost and disoriented. She's living in a strange house, in a strange place, with strange people. She has no idea when this will end or how it will end. She's lost her bearings and is bobbing about in an uncertain sea. She needs to steer herself home. Wherever and whatever that is.

'Are you okay, Hannah?'

It's another day, another meal. It's early. This must be breakfast.

'Yes, fine thanks.'

After she has eaten, Hannah asks if there's anything she can do.

'I can't think of anything at the moment,' says Jackie, 'but if I do, I'll come and find you.'

Hannah is disappointed and she feels her face fall. Al stares at her.

'Cabin fever?' he asks.

'Boredom. I'm always doing something at home.'

'Fancy some weeding?'

'Yes, I do.' Hannah jumps to her feet. 'Anything.'

'Boy, you must be bored,' says Jackie.

Hannah smiles. Weeding means going outside. A few extra yards of freedom and lungfuls of fresh air. The thought of another day of confinement feeding logs to the fire in the sitting room brings on a feeling of oppression. She dashes upstairs to put on Gates' sweater. She hides the phone in a sock.

Al directs Hannah to the front of the house where four wedge-shaped raised beds form a semi-circle of tattered summer flowers and weeds.

'Do you know much about plants?' he asks Hannah.

'I'm afraid not. I'm a flat dweller.'

'Don't worry, it's easy.'

Hannah's job is to dig up the spent annuals and weed the beds so that Al can plant spring bulbs, heathers and winter pansies.

'Just leave the big shrubs. Everything else can go,' says Al.

Hannah sets to work. The soil is loose and easy to turn over and Hannah is soon absorbed. Her mind flashes back to the day she met Gates in the garden of her flat, but the memories make her chest ache, and she shuts them down. Sometimes the plants still have flowers blooming and Hannah is reluctant to pull them up, but when she questions Al, he reminds her that the first frosts will be arriving in a matter of weeks and the plants will be killed by the cold. Satisfied with Hannah's progress, Al disappears around the back of the house. Within a few minutes Hannah hears the buzz of a hedge trimmer. Without Al as a supervisor, she sits back on her heels to admire the scenery.

The sun is low in the sky but still has enough warmth to tempt Hannah to turn her face towards it. This is a spectacular part of the country and Hannah wishes that she could take a packed lunch and explore the area while she's here. Hmph. She knows what Jackie and Al would say about that. She is about to return to her digging when a silver flash catches her eye.

Hannah stands up and stares in the direction of the light. It flashes again. It's coming from a small copse of trees directly ahead of the house but some distance away. Hannah turns her head back towards the house. There is no sign of Jackie, and the whine of the hedge trimmer tells her that Al remains hard at work. When she looks back towards the light it flashes directly into her eyes. Once, twice, and then there is a flurry of short, repetitive flashes.

The light is purposeful, and Hannah has no doubt that it's targeted at her. It has to be Gates. He promised he would locate her but only if it was for something important. It must be urgent.

But what if it isn't Gates? What if it's a trap? How can it be? Who else could know about their arrangement? Who else has given her a phone?

Hannah makes an immediate decision. She slips into the house by the front door, tiptoes up to her room and retrieves the phone from the sock. She locks herself in her bathroom, switches it on and dials Gates' number without any hesitation.

'Thank goodness you saw me.'

She doesn't need to pick up Gates' anxious tone to know that something has happened. The fact that he would risk signalling in daylight is enough of an indication.

'I need you to leave the house tonight and come across the dale to meet me. Pinpoint my next signal, while it's daylight. Head towards me. I'll find you. Come as soon as you can.'

'What's wrong?'

'Turn off your phone, Hannah. I'll tell you tonight.'

Hannah switches off her phone without saying goodbye. Her hands are sweating and her heart thudding. She removes the SIM and flushes it down the toilet. She washes her hands and face. Her stomach is roiling with nerves. In the bedroom she replaces the SIM with the spare and conceals the phone in her sock then goes back outside. There is one more flash of light. If there is a moon tonight Hannah will be able to orient herself towards the copse. She still has Gates' torch, but she won't be able to flash it around the Yorkshire Dales in the middle of the night without being spotted. She will take it anyway. She will fill her water bottle and dress in warm clothes. She returns to her weeding.

'Good work, Hannah.'

The voice behind her causes Hannah to start.

'Sorry,' says Al. 'Thought you might like to come in for some lunch.'

'Yes, of course.'

Hannah hurries inside to eat her sandwiches, anxious to get back to the garden.

'It's nice to see you with an appetite,' observes Jackie.

'It's all the fresh air,' says Al.

Hannah finishes her sandwich and takes her plate to the sink. She is about to head out to the front garden when Al's telephone rings. He goes out into the hall to answer.

'DI Waterhouse, how are you?'

Hannah meets Al's gaze, and he indicates with his hand that she should wait. She goes back to the kitchen and sits down. When Al enters the room both Hannah and Jackie are sitting, waiting.

'It's good news,' Al says straight away.

Hannah feels herself relax.

'The police have picked up some DNA.'

'Where from? Is it Dan's? I mean, Keith's?'

Hannah has half lifted herself from her seat. She feels Jackie's hand on her arm, steadying her.

'The DI is waiting for the results but it's being fast-tracked at the lab. What he does know is that it doesn't belong to Tina and it's male.'

'Where's it from?' asks Hannah.

'From a hair slide that Tina was wearing.'

'How could they have missed that?' asks Jackie.

'They weren't looking there. Apparently, the slide is sparkly and scratchy. It's possible Tina's attacker caught her by the hair and scratched himself without noticing.'

'When will we know?' asks Hannah.

'It will take a bit of time. The DI will drive here once he has the results. He wants to discuss next steps.'

Hannah's feelings are in disarray. She nods to Jackie and Al and stumbles outside. Her hand trowel tears through the plants and soil like a whirling dervish. Her mind is a tumult of emotions. They have DNA. It must be Dan's. Please let it be Dan's. Is this why Gates has contacted her? Does he know? Why else would he want to see her?

After dinner she watches an action movie with her hosts, then claims exhaustion and the need for an early night. Upstairs she packs her bag and uses her pillows to make a human shape in the bed. It's a childish trick but it always works in the movies. Besides, Hannah is not aware that anyone checks up on her at night.

She does know that Al bolts the doors and sets an alarm each evening. She must leave the house before he does so tonight. She switches off the lights in her room and creeps down the stairs. Jackie and Al are watching the news and discussing a political scandal involving an MP and two young girls. Hannah creeps to the back door. The dogs greet Hannah and wag their tails. They know her now. She gives them a quick pat on the head and lets herself out. She clambers over the post and rail fence that borders the west side of the garden and says thank you to the half-moon that throws a veil of light over the dale.

Aware that she can't afford to twist an ankle on the uneven ground Hannah resists the urge to run and half walks, half trots towards Gates, her feet propelled by her surging, hopeful heart.

34

Hannah's thoughts whip between Gates and Keith Sullivan. Thinking about the two men is like hanging from either end of a balanced plank. Gates represents safety, guidance, and comfort. Keith Sullivan represents fear, danger, and even death. They are like two opposing forces. One she can lean on, the other she wants to destroy.

The irony is that she believes both are fighting for their freedom, albeit in different ways. Sullivan does not want to be caught for the crimes he's committed and is fighting for his physical freedom. Gates is fighting for oppressed victims of the justice system and to avenge his sister's death. And Hannah in the middle? Hannah wants to free herself from her self-imposed shackles of isolation. From her fear of being harmed and her fear that Keith Sullivan is waiting for her around every corner.

She wants to live her life in the open, at Gates' end of the plank.

She wants justice and retribution. Most of all, she wants vengeance.

What makes her smile at this moment, in the dark, in the middle of a vast, empty Yorkshire moor, is the knowledge that the police are closing in on Sullivan by the hour. Meanwhile, Hannah is learning to handle her fear. She is growing stronger.

She is halfway between the safe house and the copse when a dark shadow materialises in front of her.

'Hannah,' whispers Gates.

Her heart lurches with relief and her whole being is suffused with joy. Her primary concern had been that she might miss Gates in the dark. Just the sight of him is enough to centre her and she stands still so that she can drink in his presence. He takes her hand and leads her forward. Hannah moves faster with Gates' support, and they soon reach the shelter of the small copse of trees. They pause to catch their breath.

'What's happened?' asks Hannah.

'I'll fill you in when we get to the car,' says Gates. 'Right now, we need to keep moving. Once they discover you've gone, they'll probably have the dogs out.'

Hannah shudders and readjusts the straps of her backpack.

She follows Gates in the semi-darkness. There are few clouds in the sky but when one does slip across the moon they have to slow down and move with care.

It's still dark when they reach the car Gates has hidden behind a roofless stone barn. Hannah drops her backpack onto the rear seat and throws herself into the passenger seat. Gates is driving onto the narrow road before Hannah has fastened her seatbelt.

In the moonlight Gates' features look like a rockfall.

'Gates, what is it?'

'Olly's alive.'

Shock and relief grip Hannah's limbs.

'What? How?'

Why doesn't Gates look happy?

'How can you know that?'

'I followed you here on Monday but left as soon as I knew where you were. I drove back to Olly's place. I planned to hang out there and make use of his kit until Sullivan is arrested.

When I arrived at Olly's, he was there in the house. Living and breathing and eating the last of your soup and bread.'

'You must be so relieved,' says Hannah. Gates has his friend back. The man he described as his family.

'Relieved is the last emotion I feel.'

Hannah is confused.

'But why? I don't understand.'

'To say it's complicated is an understatement. The short story is that Olly tried to fake his own death. He wanted to disappear. The problem is that like me, he's a ghost. He swaps identities the way some people change their underwear. He needed to die in front of someone that knows his real name so that he would be officially recorded as deceased.'

Hannah's jaw drops open.

'It was all planned?'

'Arranging to come and pick us up from Cardiff provided him with the opportunity to do something he'd been planning for a while. He assumed I'd hear the news, confirm his identity, and he would cease to exist. He was hiding when we arrived at his place, half-expecting us to appear. When we left, he assumed he was safe and went back to the house. He was gob-smacked when I turned up again. There he was, living and breathing.'

'So, who died?'

'No one. Accident investigators are diving for the wreckage, but they won't find a body. Olly landed in the sea and swam away before anyone got to the wreck. The plane sank like a stone. With Olly's help, of course. I gave the guys at Cardiff Airport Olly's real name and told them he was the pilot. I suppose he will eventually be declared dead.'

'So, he used you?'

'He shafted me, Hannah.'

Gates slows the car to turn onto a main road then speeds up.

'How?'

'I've always shared my work with him. I trusted him. I thought we were a team. He's been selling my programs and algorithms to anyone that will pay him.'

'Anyone? You mean crooks?'

'Some of my work involves testing systems for organisations who want to keep their data secure. If I can find a way in, I can also show them how to close and bolt the door. Olly has been helping himself and making a shedload of money.'

Gates' hands are gripping the steering wheel so tightly, Hannah can see the outline of his bones. She is trying to understand what Gates is saying but it's impossible to make sense of his words. Her head begins to thump.

'But he's your friend.'

Gates scoffs.

'Not anymore, he's not.'

'Why though? Why would he do this?'

'Freedom, money, escape?'

'What do you mean? Help me out here, Gates. I don't understand what you're saying.'

'It seems my best friend is a gambler who has got himself into serious debt with the wrong sort of moneylender.'

'So he's stolen from you?'

'That's exactly what he's done. But worse than that. He's given away my secrets. If I want to carry on doing what I'm doing I will have to start from scratch. Nothing will be secure. And worse than that, he knows the location of the safe house. I'm afraid he has given you away to get at me.'

'Do you know that for sure?'

'Not for sure, but I can't take the risk of leaving you there.'

Hannah rests her hand on Gates' forearm. His muscles are rigid with tension.

'I can't believe this.'

'I feel such a fool for trusting him. In fact, Olly was the one and only person I did trust. I thought we were close. I thought we were the same. I'm an idiot.'

'But why would he turn against you? I still don't get it.'

Gates shrugs and lets out a long sigh.

'I'm the cash cow. I suppose he doesn't have anyone else.'

Hannah wonders if she should ask him to stop at the next service station and take a break while he tells his story. She says nothing. He is already talking again.

'He used me. Olly is a good hacker but he's also a games addict who plays for money. He's lost everything and borrowed more. He's been selling my work to clear his debt and then he was going to disappear. Even from me. Especially from me. If I thought he was dead, I wouldn't come looking, would I?'

'Except you did come.'

'His only way out of the mess was to play dead.'

Hannah rubs her face with her hands.

'What will happen to Olly now?'

Gates shrugs as much as he can without letting go of the steering wheel.

'He's dead. That's what he wanted. He's free. I suppose he'll start a new life.'

'Can't you report him?'

'Not without exposing myself. He knows that. And anyway, what's the point? He's too clever. He'll have a new identity. No one will ever find him, even if the police believe me. Remember we are both ghosts.'

'This is so unfair.'

'I know it is. I can't get my head around his betrayal and what he's done. There are things I could try but Olly would hit back without a second's thought. Tit for tat. It's how wars start, and we could both end up in prison. We could get ten years. It's best left. As far as I'm concerned, he really is dead.'

'Jesus. I could kill him in real life.'

'Join the queue.'

'How can you be so calm?'

'I wasn't calm when I found out.'

There is an edge to Gates' voice that alerts Hannah to the 'but' that is surely coming. She remembers his temper in Exmoor.

'What did you do?'

'I disabled his equipment.'

Gates' smile is so wide Hannah can see his teeth shining in the moonlight.

'You smashed his gear?'

'To smithereens.'

The sheepish grin on his face gives Hannah a glimpse of the schoolboy he once was. Hannah pictures the computer room in Scotland, Gates standing knee-deep in debris.

'Olly thought I was leaving but I went round the back to the woodshed and helped myself to his axe. There is nothing functional left.'

'Well, I wouldn't have been shouting Exmoor.'

'I was hoping you'd feel that way.'

Hannah has one final question. For now, at least.

'Is Olly still a threat to us?'

Gates shrugs.

'I doubt it. He's got what he wanted. He'll disappear.'

'Are you a threat to him?'

Gates hisses with frustration. 'I wish. Olly has all my codes, routes, and gateways. He can monitor anything I do and share it or wreck it. He's closed me down.'

'Can't you do the same to him?'

'Yes, but I won't.'

'Why not?'

'I told you. Tit for tat. That's when the war starts. I don't want that.'

'What will you do?'

Hannah can see the approach to the M6 motorway and Gates indicates to take the ramp heading south.

'That is something I will sort out when this is over. It can wait. But honestly? Probably nothing.'

'So where to now?' asks Hannah.

'We're going to Runcorn.'

'Runcorn, what on earth's there?'

'Nothing, but that's the whole point.'

'Another caravan?'

'Airbnb.'

'Luxury. And who will I be staying with?'

'Mike.'

'Hi, Mike. Pleased to meet you.'

Hannah's thoughts drift to Jackie and Al.

'I hope my hosts will be okay.'

'I'm sure they will be,' reassures Gates. 'At least Sullivan has a penchant for keeping things tidy. I don't think he'll pick a fight with trained Personal Protection Officers.'

'Good,' says Hannah. 'They're nice people. Did you hear about the DNA?'

'From Tina's hair slide? It's great news. The results should be back by now.'

'Can we check?' asks Hannah.

'As soon as we get to the Airbnb, yes. I need to be extra careful now.'

'Of course. Neil said if they get a positive DNA result, they can arrest Sullivan. Do you think we can go home then?'

Gates hesitates before he speaks. 'I've never been in a situation like this. I don't fully understand what has gone on with Olly. I don't know how a police officer can get away with committing these horrendous crimes, and I still don't understand why he's not in prison right now. It's all to fight for and I can't predict anything.'

35

o these guys have no sense? Are they really all blithering fucking idiots? If a pack animal is being hunted by a predator, they all run and hide. If a meerkat senses danger, they all pop down into the safety of their burrows and stay there till it's safe to come out. It's a basic animal instinct to run and hide. They all do it.

Not the UK police though. Not at all. God, they make his life so easy. They just stroll around in full view without a care in the world. Do they have to be so obvious? It's so disappointing. He likes the chase, loves the challenge of escape and evasion. For fuck's sake, it's half the fun. The DI didn't even try and keep out of sight. It was like following a schoolboy on a bicycle.

She is the only clever one. He admits that. Sending him off on a wild goose chase in Wales. He respects her initiative even if he is still riled at the fucking waste of time and money. He was apoplectic when he realised the trackers were useless. She was probably feeling very pleased with herself. Except you don't become as successful as he has been without a plan B, even a C and D if needed. Always have a backup.

Follow the leader. In this case DI Neil Waterhouse. It was no effort to call his office and sweet-talk the floozie on the phone, he is a DI himself after all. Ask her to take a peep into the incident room and survey the board. Easy to locate the hotel always used by the police. Took a bit longer to get up north, of course. Foot down all the way. Pity he didn't have the location of the safe house, but he couldn't go there in daylight anyway. The DI's hotel was good enough. Especially when Waterhouse turned up in the car park begging to have a tracker attached to his car. Stupid man.

He was braced for another uncomfortable night in his own car, but the DI came racing out in the middle of the night and screamed off across the moors. At first, Sullivan kept his distance and used the tracker to follow. But he was already bored senseless. He was entitled to have some fun. Headlights on main beam and scream up to the DI's bumper. Let the chase begin.

No such luck.

He wasn't even close when the DI appeared to lose control, shot off the road and his car disappeared into the darkness. As the DI's car plowed into a jumble of rocks the explosion of sound resonated through Sullivan's steering wheel. He felt disappointed that his potential fun had been curtailed. The DI's headlights were still shining but there was no sign of any movement.

He drove slowly by with a shrug. Not his problem. Stupid, stupid man.

He would find him at the hospital.

If he was alive.

36

Hannah wakes to a fresh morning and a view of the River Mersey. She's not surprised to find Gates is already up and has managed to procure good coffee and croissants from somewhere.

'Yum,' says Hannah as she helps herself. 'The benefits of civilisation.'

Although Olly's betrayal still weighs heavily, this is about as relaxed as she's been for a very long time. It's as if this is her new normal. It's a normal she likes. Since the first day she asked for his help Gates has made her feel safe. Yet that hasn't made her feel helpless and dependent, it's made her feel stronger and more determined. Maybe because she wants to prove something to him. Maybe because she knows he has her back. Maybe it's enough to have someone on her side. Whatever the reason, Hannah feels good.

'So, what's the plan?'

Gates has his computer equipment set up and flexes his long fingers, ready to start work.

'My priority is to check the DNA results and talk to Neil. We need to let him know that you're safe and find out when they plan to arrest Sullivan. Until he's behind bars, we continue to lie low.'

'Anything I can do?'

Gates looks doubtful.

'Go on, what do you need?'

'I don't want to be sexist, but we do need groceries.'

Hannah laughs. 'If I could do what you can I might fight you, but under the circumstances, let's say I spotted a Co-op on the way in. How long do you think we'll be here?'

'I've booked two more nights.'

'I'm going to need to get some clothes too.'

'Take your phone,' says Gates, 'but only switch it on if you need to. And here.' He hands Hannah a bank card. 'Use this. Double six, three, eight. It can't be traced. Don't worry about the spending limit, get what you need.'

Hannah is happy to leave the house and drive off to do the grocery shopping. It feels normal, as if the last two weeks haven't happened. She even feels brave enough to enter local supermarkets into the car's satnav and manages to find an Asda, where she purchases food and clothes for herself plus socks, underwear, and a rugby shirt for Gates. His rucksack is a bit of a TARDIS but he's going to run out of clean things sooner or later. She also buys herself a small selection of toiletries, a wash bag to hold them in, and a small towel. The delight she feels at owning something as simple as a nice toothbrush again is enough to plaster a toothpaste ad smile onto her face.

Until she gets back to the house. His voice calls from the lounge. Sharp, urgent.

'Hannah, get in here.'

Gates is sitting in front of his computer screen. The rockfall has happened to his face again. He motions Hannah to join him. She doesn't ask questions. She still clutches the shopping bags.

The screen shows a local news channel. An ambulance, fire engine and police cars surround the wreckage of a car, blue flashing lights and hi-vis jackets providing a kaleidoscope of colour. Hannah can see the Yorkshire moors rolling away from the scene. They look familiar. As the camera zooms in she sees that the roof of the car has been cut away and the air bag billows in the wind. Skid marks on the road lead to deep ruts and gouges in the surface of the moor. The car has rolled away from the road and become wedged against a rock. Headlines run across the bottom of the scene.

Police detective's car forced off the road.

'Turn it up,' Hannah says.

The newsreader's voice is bland and impersonal.

'In the early hours of this morning a car driven by a police detective was chased and forced off the road on the Yorkshire Moors. The car rolled several times before being stopped by rocks. The victim has been identified as DI Neil Waterhouse who was on duty at the time of the accident. He has been transferred to hospital by helicopter where he remains in a critical condition.'

Hannah shivers.

'He was on his way to me.' She is so sure of this her words are a statement, not a question. Gates nods.

All Hannah's feelings of safety and security are whipped away by the tornado whirling and screaming around her. She can see from his face that Gates is as shattered as she is. She is forced to search for her voice before she can speak.

'Sullivan?'

'Who else?'

'Jesus Christ.'

Hannah is holding it together but only just. She likes Neil. He's a good man. And he was on their side. Hannah trusted him and she knows Gates did too.

'What do we do without him?'

'Nothing for now,' says Gates. 'We lie low and let the authorities do their jobs. The more Sullivan gets involved, the stronger the trail he'll leave behind. No-one knows we're here. Not Sullivan, not Olly, not Neil. There are no trackers and no listed mobile phones. I think we should let events run their course and wait to see what happens with Neil. Meanwhile I'll track the police and NHS systems and keep an eye on what's happening.'

'And what about Sullivan?'

'Running the DI off the road was a stupid move. It's a sign he's getting desperate. It's only a matter of time before he messes up big time.'

'You think he will?'

'Almost certainly.'

'What does that mean for us?'

'It's time for us to be ready. For anything.'

***

Although she is not a fan of morning TV, Hannah is awake early the following day to scroll through the TV channels. She finds a short report about Neil's accident that says he is in ICU in a critical condition. The car that forced DI Waterhouse off the road was found abandoned and burnt out at a derelict and remote hill farm. Forensics officers are examining both scenes.

Gates sits next to Hannah. He stares at the screen.

'What do you think?' asks Hannah. She turns to Gates and is shocked to see how tired he looks. There are purple stains beneath his eyes and his skin is grey. He doesn't answer.

Hannah feels as if her insides are rusting. Her body feels unyielding and heavy. Even lifting her hand to zap the remote control at the TV is an effort. Something is wrong. She wants to question Gates, but his body is stiff besides her, his eyes fixed on the TV screen.

'This changes things, doesn't it?'

Gates starts as if his thoughts are a million miles away.

'It does. The minute Neil wakes up we must find a way to get into the hospital to see him. We have to find out what's going on with the case.'

Hannah asks the question that has kept her tossing and turning all night.

'What happens if we don't get anywhere with all of this?'

Gates pauses as if he's thinking but Hannah suspects he's already worked out the answer.

'You run.'

'How?'

'You go into witness protection, or you disappear.'

Sweat breaks out between Hannah's shoulder blades. Running means giving up, returning to her life in the shadows. She can't. She's over that. She wants to keep fighting.

'I can't...' she begins.

Gates interrupts. It's unlike him to be so abrupt.

'You may not have a choice. Sullivan has upped the stakes. He tried to take out the senior officer in charge of this investigation. He won't hesitate to take you out too.'

Hannah shakes her head. 'I'm sick of hiding. What good has that done?'

'You have to stay safe, Hannah.'

'I've been staying safe and where has that got me? It's time to do something real, to take some action. The minute Neil is awake I'm phoning the hospital.'

'Think about this.'

'I have thought about it, and I've decided. I would love your support, Gates, but I'm going to do this with or without you.'

Gates shakes his head and Hannah detects a ghost of a smile.

'So that's who you are,' he says.

227

37

ates has set up a call to the hospital. Despite some nerves Hannah finds it easy. The female voice that answers the telephone sounds harassed and when Hannah introduces herself as Neil's niece, she's not questioned. However, says the voice, we can't give out patient information over the phone.

'Can I visit?' asks Hannah.

'Not until he wakes up, I'm afraid.'

'Can I call again tomorrow?'

'Yes, of course.'

She gets a thumbs-up from Gates but there is no further conversation.

Apart from soup and bread in Scotland, Hannah has yet to cook for Gates, who has been feeding her for the last two weeks, albeit mostly on pastries and coffee. She takes pleasure in spending the morning making a cottage pie from scratch before rummaging around the Airbnb for a book. It's a fruitless search. She's aware of Gates muttering into his headphones from time to time, but she leaves him to work and spends the afternoon watching TV shows. She takes nothing in.

Gates washes up after dinner before joining Hannah on the settee. She is watching re-runs of *Friends*.

'I needed something light and fluffy,' she explains.

'Fair enough.'

Gates' response is curt, unfriendly; his body language is closed and cold. *Have I done something to upset him?* A feeling of dread is blooming inside Hannah, even though she knows that right now, in this house, she is safe. Perhaps it's nerves for tomorrow. Her decision to act feels good and right but it doesn't stop a few butterflies from flexing their wings. She wants to thank Gates again for all his help but remembers that he doesn't like constant thanks. They sit side by side. Gates' long legs stretch out in front of him, and his body has slid down the cushions. His hands rest palm down on his thighs and as Hannah examines his slender fingers, Gates places his hand on hers.

The sudden movement takes Hannah by surprise, and she takes a sharp intake of breath. A thrill flutters around her belly, beating the butterflies into submission. She waits for the gentle squeeze and release, but Gates holds on to her hand.

'There's something I have to tell you.'

What now? she thinks.

His voice has changed. It's quiet and croaky. Whatever he's about to say is going to be unpleasant. Hannah's tummy flutters turn to ice. She leans forward to look Gates in the face, but he won't meet her eyes. She pulls her hand away from his to rub her forearm. Gates picks up the remote and turns off the television.

'What is it?'

Gates grimaces. 'My wife is sick.'

Hannah is still silent, her brain trying to compute what she has just heard. His *wife* is sick? Every hair on her body stands up. Her ribs have turned into iron claws around her lungs squeezing out the air even as she is trying to suck it in.

What did he say?

He has a wife?
A sick wife?

What does she say to that? I didn't know you were married. Where is this wife? Why is this news such an enormous blow to my guts? Hannah turns her head away from Gates so that he can't see any of this confusion in her features. He's waiting for her to speak. Hannah forces her strangled voice down to its normal register. How do you hide devastation?

'I had no idea you were married. Where is she?'

'We've been separated for four years,' explains Gates. 'We've been leading our own lives and only communicate occasionally. She left me a message that I picked up this afternoon.'

So, they only communicate occasionally but the wife has communicated today.

'What does she want?' Hannah knows her voice sounds harsh, but she's hurt. No, she's devastated. Her voice is all she has.

'She has ovarian cancer,' explains Gates. 'By the time she was diagnosed it had already spread to stage four. She's riddled with it. Liver, lungs, brain. She's terminally ill.'

Hannah wants to say, what's that got to do with you? She can't. She can't be that unkind. Gates is a kind man, a good man. He wouldn't turn his back on someone who needs him.

'I don't know what to say.'

'There's nothing you can say. It is what it is.'

'Where is she?' Hannah repeats.

'She's in Birmingham. Still at home but needing more and more support all the time.'

Hannah knows what's coming.

'So, you need to go to her.'

Her words are a statement. She knows this man. He sighs with relief.

'Yes, I do. I don't know why. She left me for another man. We were together for five years, but she had been shagging other men the entire time. She fell in love with one of them and left. A bit like you and your guy. I felt like such a fucking fool. All people could do was ask me how she got away with it for so long.'

'And you never suspected?'

'Never. I loved her. I thought she loved me, and I trusted her.'

He loved her. Past tense but even so. The cancer card is a tough one to be up against. How can Gates *not* go to a dying wife?

Gates shakes his head and scoffs. 'She said I was boring. I always had my head stuck in my computers. She didn't know why I bothered marrying her. It was the truth, I suppose.'

'Is she still with the man that she left you for?'

'No, he scarpered. I guess I feel sorry for her. I did neglect her, and she was a high-maintenance wife. Our marriage didn't stand a chance.'

Hannah feels her insides beginning to uncurl. Just a little.

'Did you not divorce?'

'We never got around to it. I suppose if one of us had wanted to remarry, we would have. I guess I didn't want to be the one to suggest it. I was always waiting for her to make a move. Maybe a small part of me hoped she might come back.'

Hannah's stomach drops.

'Do you still feel like that?'

He reaches for her hand and delivers the gentle squeeze she didn't know she was longing for.

'Not for a long time.'

Hannah doesn't know what this means. She feels deeply sorry for the man beside her who is turning out to be far more complicated than she could ever have imagined. She also feels a sense of relief that the marriage he bowled at her a few minutes earlier is a far softer and slower ball than she at first thought.

But even so. He has a sick wife, a dying wife. Hannah knows him. She knows he will go to his wife.

***

Their time at the Airbnb is up. It takes Hannah less than a minute to pack. She thinks of the bathroom in her flat with eye cream, deodorant, body lotion and hair products, all replaced with basic soap, shampoo, and toothpaste. She now has a few changes of underwear, three tops, one pair of jeans and Gates' sweater. She considers returning the sweater to Gates but even as she folds it, she knows she'll keep it. A little bit of Gates will be better than nothing at all.

Their breakfast is sombre and awkward, both trying to avoid catching the eye of the other. How quickly things can change. Hannah wonders if this is why Gates didn't tell her about his wife before last night. Why not tell her when they were discussing their families? Because she isn't family anymore, is she? They're separated. Why should he tell her?

Let's face it, the best way Hannah can describe the two of them is as friends and colleagues. Gates has never said or done anything that suggests he sees Hannah as anything more than a victim who requires his help. It's Hannah herself who is getting doe-eyed over a man she barely knew until three weeks ago. Three weeks. A lifetime. Life-changing.

'Hannah, are you listening?'

'Sorry, miles away.'

Gates studies her for a few seconds longer than he needs to and Hannah wonders what he sees. She meets his eyes squarely as she gazes back, challenging him to something. Hannah wishes she knew what the challenge means. She isn't sure what she's wishing for, and it's this uncertainty that is clawing at the edges of her concentration.

'I've been monitoring the hospital systems during the night. Neil is off the ventilator.'

'That's good news,' says Hannah. It means she can go and see him.

'It is, but he's still in intensive care. He has multiple fractures and has had surgery to repair a tear in his liver. He's conscious and responsive but I don't really know what that means. If he can talk and you can get in to see him, that's great. Otherwise, we're no further forward. We're going to have to busk it.'

'What does that mean?'

'Fly by the seat of our pants. We'll head to the hospital and see if you can blag your way in.'

'I think Neil will want to talk to me,' says Hannah.

'I agree with you, but I wonder if the medical staff will feel the same way.'

'I'm willing to try.'

'Well, I'll be there to back you up.'

'I thought you were going to Birmingham?' asks Hannah. Her words are sharp, and she sees Gates flinch as she delivers them.

'Yes, I am. After you've seen Neil. I need to know where Sullivan is and if he's being arrested. That's my priority. Your safety is my priority.'

Hannah is mollified but only a little. She is annoyed that Gates has been keeping his wife a secret from her. Especially after she shared the story of her almost wedding. He says her safety is his priority, yet it can't be if he's rushing off to his wife. Hannah feels as if they are at some sort of crossroads and Gates is turning left or right instead of moving forwards with her.

Things are changing. That's okay. One of the things she has learned over the last couple of weeks is that she can do this. On her own if necessary.

38

They are both subdued in the car and Hannah is relieved when they turn into the hospital entrance. It's a large hospital with a selection of car parks for visitors. Gates chooses a dark corner in the basement of a multi-storey. He pulls a baseball cap low over his face before he leaves the car.

It's a brisk ten-minute walk to the main hospital entrance. They pass a Costa coffee shop crammed with visitors and uniformed hospital staff and turn right towards a bank of lifts. The foyer of the hospital is vast and airy. The echoes of voices and footsteps merge with Hannah's breathing as she walks with faux confidence. She belongs here, she is not an imposter.

There are four lifts in a row and a huddle of people in front of each one. There's no point trying to find the smallest huddle because even as they pause to look more people cram in behind them. When the lift doors open, Gates and Hannah are pushed forwards. Hannah smells dirt and human sweat.

This is a hospital, for God's sake. Why are people acting as if they're in a football scrum? Fortunately, the opened doors of the lift have revealed its voluminous capacity and Hannah and Gates make it inside. Gates steers Hannah to one side where he stands in front of her to protect her from the shoving and squashing of the few individuals who refuse to accept that they can't fit in. Hannah is reminded of the London Underground in the rush hour and wonders how people can bear this every day.

'Let's take the stairs on the way down,' she whispers to Gates.

They escape the claustrophobic lift on the third floor and turn left along a wide corridor. Hannah can see the sign for the intensive care unit on their right, but Gates walks past without so much as a glance. When they are a good distance away, he stops at a window and pulls out his phone. Hannah watches without speaking as he dials and then hands her the phone.

'ICU, how can I help?'

Hannah explains that she is Neil's niece. She understands that he's awake and wonders if she could visit. She freezes when the female voice says that she will just check with the patient's wife. Hannah puts the phone on speaker. The voice when it returns is brusque and to the point.

'DI Waterhouse does not have a niece and reporters are not permitted on the unit.'

'I'm not…' begins Hannah, but the line disconnects.

'Dammit.'

Hannah is annoyed with herself. She should have thought things through, had a more convincing story. She hands the phone back to Gates.

'Don't worry,' he says. 'I can try.'

He dials another number. A woman answers on the second ring.

'Mrs. Waterhouse? My name is Rick Henderson. I've been working with your husband.'

Hannah listens in awe as 'Rick' explains that Neil has uncovered evidence relating to a corrupt police officer. Neil's car crash was not an accident. Rick wants the police officer responsible brought to justice. He needs a few minutes with her husband if he is well enough to talk. He's here in the hospital. Outside the ICU.

Gates ends the call with a smile. With skilful fingers he removes and replaces the SIM card in his phone and hands the old one to Hannah.

'Take this and destroy it. I'll meet you back at the car.'

'Let me come in with you.'

'They'll be looking out for a female reporter. It's better if we don't arouse suspicion.'

Gates walks back to the door to the ICU. When it opens, she sees him shake hands with a woman who must be the DI's wife. Hannah is too far away to see her expression or hear her words, but she gestures to Gates who steps inside. Can it really be that easy?

Hannah is annoyed with Gates for taking charge. She accepts that he is only trying to help but she feels thwarted, diminished even. It hasn't occurred to him that she needs to feel in control of her own destiny. It's that crossroads again. He's turned the wrong way.

Unable to face the lifts, Hannah chooses to walk down three flights of stairs to the ground floor. She takes her time, not knowing how long Gates will be with Neil. She's relieved that the DI has started to recover from his accident and that his wife is beside him. The stairs are quiet and peaceful, and at the bottom Hannah pauses before she pushes the door open with both hands. A small beat as she takes a breath and prepares for the noise of the foyer to engulf her. Time to glance through the window embedded in the top half of the door.

Time to freeze.

She's hidden by the door for the few seconds it takes Sullivan to enter the lift. There's no doubt it's him. Her first instinct is to draw back and cower behind the door. Her pulse races and her heart throbs in her chest. Her scalp prickles. She gathers herself and peers through the window. When the woman behind is shoved into him by the surging crowd he kicks back. His shoe scrapes her shin. The box of chocolates in her hands slips from her grasp and her mouth forms a small 'o' of surprise. She falls away from the scrum, the lift doors closing in her face.

Hannah pushes through the door and rushes forward. She already hates and despises Sullivan, so his treatment of the woman makes little difference to her feelings about him. But anger erupts, and the anger crushes her fear along with her instinct to run. It occurs to her that Sullivan is now the fugitive. He's the one that needs to hide.

She picks up the fallen chocolates and asks the woman if she needs help. There's a hole in her tights and beads of blood decorate her leg. A gentle smile brightens the careworn face.

'I'm fine, thank you, love. It's always the same here at visiting time. I think I'll use the stairs.'

'What about your leg?'

The woman looks at her leg and seems surprised to see the drops of blood already clotting on her bare skin.

'Well, look at that. I'll need a new pair of tights before I go. Never mind. I'll ask the nurses for a plaster when I get to the ward.'

'Are you sure you are okay?'

'I am, love, but you're a sweetheart to ask. Thank you.'

The woman pats Hannah's arm and heads for the stairs. From the rear, Hannah notes her worn shoes and old coat. She clutches her box of chocolates under her arm. Hannah is engulfed by an over-powering memory of her mum. It comes from nowhere. Hannah falling from a swing in the back garden. Her mum had been out shopping and was still in her coat when she ran out to comfort Hannah and mop up her tears and bloody knees. The coat. It's identical to the one her mum used to wear. The same bottle green as Hannah's school uniform but faded with age and wear. The exact colour of Gates' jumper. The colour of safety and comfort.

There is a huge lump in Hannah's throat as she heads outside. She tries not to think about her mum these days. It's something that's always been too painful, so she's pushed the memories away. Why are they coming back now?

Hannah is almost at the car park before she pulls herself together and realises that Sullivan was heading up to the intensive care unit. What if he finds Gates? What should she do?

She remembers the SIM card. She rushes back into the hospital and follows the signs to the toilets. Remarkably there is no queue. Inside the cubicle she grinds the SIM card underneath her heel, wraps it in a wad of toilet paper and flushes. The wet bundle disappears but she flushes again just to make sure. Gates has changed his SIM card and Hannah doesn't have his new number.

How can she warn him? She can't. Sullivan will already be upstairs. But there are gatekeepers: the medical staff, Neil's wife, Gates himself. Sullivan can't get in. And even if he does, will he know who Gates is? And what can Sullivan do in the hospital? He's a man on the run. It's Hannah he's after and the last thing she needs is to be seen by him. So, while her heart tells her to run to Gates, her head directs her to the car park where she can wait out of sight.

She hurries back to the underground car park and waits a few rows away from the car. It doesn't take long for Gates to appear. He may be tall and lanky, but he moves like a panther. She crosses the rows of parked cars to intercept him.

'Thank God,' says Gates when he sees her.

'I saw Sullivan getting in the lift. He hurt a woman.'

Gates has unlocked the car and they both get in and fasten their seat belts.

'He's out of control, Hannah.'

'Don't we already know that?'

'This is different. He must know he's been identified yet he's just marched up to ICU without a care in the world. He's aggressive, drawing attention to himself. He's even more dangerous than I thought.'

39

As they head towards the motorway Gates fills Hannah in on his visit to the ICU. Neil was still very sick but awake. As soon as Rose was satisfied that Neil was happy to see his visitor, she left them together.

'Five minutes,' she had said.

Neil was attached to a myriad of tubes and monitors and lay immobile in the high bed, but he was eager to talk.

'Neil told me his crash was an accident. He was informed that you were missing, and he was driving to the safe house. A car came up fast behind him and he assumed it was Sullivan. Then Neil lost control on a sharp bend. I told him I just needed to know where the case was at so I could keep you safe.'

'What did he say?'

Gates' mouth twitches.

'That the case is with the CPS.'

'Thank God.'

'It's the CPS who take the decision to prosecute though, so Sullivan's arrest can't happen until they give the okay.'

'What? How long is Sullivan going to be allowed to walk the streets? How can that be right?'

'The case must be watertight, but Neil thinks it's a matter of hours. Once Sullivan is arrested and charged, he'll be remanded in custody, and he'll be off the streets. Except.'

'Except what?'

'Sullivan is AWOL.'

'Jesus Christ. I know that. I've just seen him at the hospital.'

Hannah covers her face with her hands.

'The police let him get away, didn't they?'

Gates nods. 'He hasn't been seen since before Neil's accident.'

'Can't we call them and tell them he's here?'

'Mrs. Waterhouse has seen to that.'

Hannah's brow is furrowed.

'What is it?' asks Gates.

'How was he at the hospital?'

'The accident was on the news. And I told you he's getting desperate. My guess is that he's trying to find out how much Neil knows and where you are. And if he has the chance, he'll go after the evidence. He still has his warrant card, remember. Nobody bothers to check them.'

'But even if he gets his hands on the evidence we gave to Neil, it won't do him any good. We have copies of everything.'

'That's true, but Sullivan doesn't know that. He certainly doesn't know about the DNA.'

'Did he see you at the hospital?'

Gates shakes his head.

'Thanks to Rose. She's like a rottweiler. Guards Neil with her life. I told her who he was, so she asked the nurse not to let him in, informed the police then steered me out through the fire exit.'

'But Sullivan will keep trying, won't he? Is Neil safe?'

Gates smiles.

'Rose was on the phone demanding security for her husband while I was walking down the stairs.'

Now Hannah is shaking her head.

'This sounds like a right mess.'

'In a way,' responds Gates, 'but there is a light at the end of the tunnel.'

'Shining on what?'

'The fact that Sullivan is on the run and a warrant is about to be issued for his arrest. Up until now, he's been hiding in plain sight. Now he's a suspect, he won't find it quite so easy to move around. He will have to remain hidden and that will clip his wings.'

'Are you certain the CPS will decide to prosecute?'

'Neil believes so.'

Gates has taken a breath as if he has more to say but then he stops.

'What?'

'He attacked you. You know him. You heard him attack Tina. Your evidence is crucial to Sullivan's prosecution. Without you, a good barrister can argue that the DNA and CCTV is circumstantial.'

Hannah scoffs with frustration.

'Circumstantial. Come on.'

Gates shrugs.

'The CCTV? He was helping a drunk girl back to her hotel. He left her in reception. Blood on her hair slide? It happened when she fell against him. DNA at the scene of your attack? You consented.'

Hannah is aghast.

'This is not justice.'

'It's the system, Hannah. It's all we've got to work with.'

'Sod the system.'

Gates laughs. 'Succinct and to the point. Ah, damn.'

The sky has darkened, and a deluge of rain sweeps across the sky. After weeks of dry weather, the surface of the motorway is slick where water meets accumulated oil. Forty miles per hour restriction signs flash but Gates crawls at less than thirty. Six lanes of near stationary traffic face them.

'It's like looking at Christmas lights,' observes Hannah. 'Red on our side, white on the other.'

Gates delivers one of his snorts.

'You're the only person I know who is capable of comparing a traffic jam to Christmas.'

'Ah, but you love me for it,' retorts Hannah with a chuckle. Her response is delivered as a joking rejoinder but there is the tiniest awkward pause from Gates. Just a fraction of a second, but a pause, nevertheless. Hannah feels the tinge of a blush develop at the base of her neck.

She fiddles with the radio in an attempt at distraction. 'I'll try and get the traffic report.'

They both stare ahead as if news of traffic jams and flash floods is of paramount importance. The moment passes.

By the time they reach Keele, they have slowed to a walking pace. Stop-start driving at its most frustrating. Gates turns off the radio. Hannah gazes out of the window at the oily road verges. Even the weeds have given up on existence, their sunbaked roots unable to stand up to the battering rain. If there is an elephant in the car neither of them is going to acknowledge it.

It takes them so long to reach Birmingham that by the time they approach the city centre the car is filled with a fuggy warmth. Hannah opens her window a fraction to let in as much air as she can get without the rain squeezing in behind. She turns her face to the narrow gap and is surprised at how fresh the polluted city air feels against her face.

'Almost there,' says Gates.

They are travelling along a dual carriageway as clogged with traffic as the motorway and just as slow. The road is bordered on both sides by an endless jumble of small hotels and bed and breakfasts interspersed with fast-food joints and takeaways. The gap in Hannah's window allows the scent of hot oil and vinegar to pervade the car's interior. Her stomach grumbles.

'Where all the best travellers come,' she remarks.

'That's us,' replies Gates.

After several miles and many, many sets of traffic lights, Gates steers the car into the car park of a mid-sized hotel with a purple neon vacancies sign outside. The rain still lashes down, so he parks as close to the front door as possible. They grab their backpacks and make a run for it.

Inside they find a modest, slightly run-down establishment but one that's clean and the landlady is friendly. She shows them to a twin-bedded room at the front of the hotel. To Hannah's relief, there's an ensuite bathroom. There's nothing worse than tiptoeing down a cold corridor in the middle of the night and finding the engaged sign on the toilet door.

They're too late for dinner, they are told. The chef has switched the ovens off. Gates raises an eyebrow at Hannah, and she suppresses a giggle. For an excuse, at least it's on topic. However, cheese toasties are available if they wish. They do wish. They wish for two toasties and a tray of tea. For good measure, Gates also orders two muffins for dessert. The muffins arrive packaged in cellophane.

'Not the Ritz,' he says, flicking his thumb and forefinger at the muffin which rolls to the floor and bounces. 'Now that's scary.'

Hannah picks up the muffin and squishes it with interest. She pretends to read. 'Not for eating unless you want your tongue glued to your palate.'

'Or you are starving.'

'Hey,' she says, 'we're warm and we're safe. I'll take that.'

'Me too,' replies Gates. 'I'm going to take that muffin too.'

Hannah picks up the second muffin and tosses it to Gates. 'Have mine too. It's a gift.'

Gates catches the muffin in one hand. 'I just love buying my own gifts.'

They finish their supper and empty the teapot. There seems to be a new ease between them, and Hannah likes it. She wonders if Gates feels the same way and if it has anything to do with him unburdening himself about his wife. She's trying to pluck up the courage to ask him without embarrassing herself when he stands up.

'I need to go.'

Hannah frowns but doesn't speak. She won't ask. He has to say it. She waits.

'I have to go and see my wife.'

Hannah feels the sharp retorts jostling for space amongst her vocal cords.

So that's why we came here.

You'd better go then.

Why am I not surprised?

I can see where your priorities lie.

But then she looks at Gates' face and she sees her unhurried friend gazing back. He's unashamed and unrepentant because he has nothing to be ashamed of, nothing to repent for. He's a kind man about to visit the dying woman that he once loved. Hannah meets his gaze and her heart swells at the sadness she sees there. She gives a self-conscious little wave of her hand. She is not that person. She cares about him too much to be unkind.

'Of course, you must go.'

As soon as the words leave her lips, she sees Gates' face relax. He had been afraid to tell her, worried about how she would react. God, what a bitch he must think she is.

'It's okay. I'll be fine here.'

'Are you sure?'

'Sure.'

Before he leaves, Gates hands Hannah another burner.

'It's okay to contact me but only if you really need to. A text is best, but a brief call is okay in an emergency. Keep the phone switched on and always keep it with you. Mine is a new burner too so we can't be traced.'

'I know the drill,' Hannah reassures him.

'And one more thing.'

'I know,' says Hannah, 'don't go out.'

Gates grins. 'Unless the building is on fire.'

'Or falling down.'

'Or flooded.'

'Or bleeding to death.'

'People bleed, Hannah, not buildings.'

'You win that one then.'

He leaves with their banter still dangling in the air. Hannah feels bereft. It's something that she feels deserves an explanation yet there isn't one to be found. There's just a huge part of her that's filled with the knowledge that Gates exists and is part of her life. Even in the moments when her thoughts are consumed by Sullivan and the threat he poses, Hannah is calmed by a different thought. The one that tells her Gates is on her side.

40

Gates doesn't return. At half past midnight he sends a text to say that he's going to stay the night at his wife's place. There are things to sort out. She needs him. *Stay safe*, he ends.

You too, sleep well.

Should she add a kiss? Hannah adds two kisses. No, too much. She deletes one of them.

You too, sleep well x

It looks like she's sending love. Still too much. She deletes the kiss and presses send before she can change her mind. Hannah is in bed, but she gets out to check that the door is locked. Before she climbs back under the duvet, she pulls Gates' jumper from her rucksack and falls asleep with it cuddled against her.

The following morning the rain has eased but it's still drizzling. Despite the close, grey sky, the city street beneath Hannah's window looks freshly rinsed after a long summer of heat and dust. There's a bus stop outside the hotel and Hannah examines the commuters waiting to travel into the city centre.

Office workers and shop girls perhaps? A teenage girl with heavy make-up looks like she works at a beauty counter.

A young guy with glasses and a backpack straining at his shoulders. Must be books, perhaps a librarian or student. What about the older guy? Smartly suited and yes, he has a black umbrella. Going to the bank.

Hannah amuses herself for some time watching the changing lines of individuals setting off for a day's work in Britain's second biggest city. She wishes she could catch a bus into the heart of the shopping district and wander through the Bull Ring without a care in the world. Will she ever be that free again? The ping of her phone disturbs her reverie.

So sorry. Need to stay another day. Back tomorrow. Really sorry. Let me know you're okay.

Hannah's spirits sink down through her torso, but she replies straight away.

All well. No need to worry.

Hannah takes her coat and bag down to breakfast, and as soon as she's finished, she steps outside, intending to find a newspaper, a magazine or even a book. She has a whole day to kill and right now her horizon stretches only as far as the end of the street.

A newsagents is wedged between a bookies and a charity shop. The door is propped open, and Hannah slips inside to examine the racked newspapers and journals. The first thing she sees is her own face. Right next to Sullivan's. The warrant for his arrest has been issued. At last. Relief washes over her. That will clip his wings.

Hannah can't afford to hang around in the shop reading the article, so she grabs *The Times* and the *Telegraph*, two random women's magazines and a book of Sudoku. As she passes the cold cabinet she adds a meal deal to her pile, sandwich, fruit juice and crisps. Hannah is anticipating a day indoors.

She pulls up her hood before she pays for her goods. The photograph used by the press is a poor one purloined from work. She remembers the day it was taken for her security pass renewal. Her shoulder-length hair is scraped back, her face make-up-free and her features trace the road map of a long and busy night shift. It looks nothing like her.

The young guy behind the till barely acknowledges Hannah. He rings up her goods and shoves them into a blue and white striped carrier bag. His eyes search for her hand so she can take the bag and simultaneously hand over a twenty-pound note. Her change comes back to her in the same way. No eye contact, no smile of acknowledgement. When did people stop looking at each other? She might as well not exist. Hannah takes the proffered receipt from him, says thank you and leaves the shop. Amazing. A transaction between two humans without any real human interaction. So, this is big city living. *Suits me*, she thinks.

Back at the hotel Hannah goes straight up to her room and puts the *Do Not Disturb* sign on the door. She throws her coat onto a chair and spreads out the newspapers on the bed. Both stories are succinct. Sullivan is the man wanted in connection with the rape and murder of three young women.

Three, thinks Hannah. *They've connected the cases, good.*

Plus, the rape of a fourth woman. Police also want to question him in connection with a road accident in the Yorkshire Dales in which a detective inspector was seriously injured. The officer is recovering in hospital under police protection. Sullivan is considered dangerous and should not be approached under any circumstances.

Hannah's story is brief by comparison. She is a key witness for the case and police are concerned for her safety. If anyone thinks they have seen her or know anything of her whereabouts, please contact the number below. Hannah snorts at the photo which truly is a dreadful likeness. She wouldn't expect her own mother to recognise her from that.

It's a long day. For a large part of it, Hannah is glued to the television news features. For the first time she sees close-up photographs of the three women that Sullivan is alleged to have killed. They are all young, blonde, and pretty but Tina is especially attractive with her elfin face and white-blonde hair. Her voice still echoes in Hannah's head, and she discovers that she can concentrate better if she folds the newspaper over so that she can't see Tina's blue eyes staring at her.

Hannah's own face on the news makes her uncomfortable. She feels embarrassed knowing that resources are being expended searching for her when she's safe and well. Perhaps she should call the helpline, explain who she is, say she'll come forward once Sullivan is arrested. But they might track her, take her to another unsafe safe house while Gates is away tending his wife. Hannah looks down at the phone in her hand and sighs before she puts it back in her pocket.

She will wait for Gates.

Her fingers itch to text him.

When will you be back?

Will you be back?

Missing you.

No. No texts. He's with his sick wife. She can't be a nag. Her stomach gurgles. Her meal deal is long gone. Dare she go for another? Not with Sullivan on the loose.

She tries a few press-ups, managing six before collapsing on the scruffy carpet. She starts numerous games of Sudoku, finishes none of them. She stands at the window and watches the morning's commuters returning from work. The buses travelling away from the city centre stop on the opposite side of the road. Hannah is thrilled when she spots the young girl, her make-up still immaculate. No sign of the banker or the librarian/student.

She makes up lives for those people that have caught her

attention. Ordinary lives. Going home to loved ones for dinner and an evening curled up in front of the television. Maybe a bowl of popcorn and a movie or a favourite box set and a bag of Maltesers to share. A goodnight kiss and cuddle.

Hannah thinks of her tidy, lonely flat. Will she go back there? Will it be safe? Does she even want to return after all that's happened? She feels different, changed somehow, stronger, more confident. Maybe this shake-up could be the start of something new.

There's a scratching at the door and before Hannah can react, it swings open. Gates is preceded by the aroma of an Indian takeaway and it's possible that the carrier bag of food in his arms is the only thing that prevents Hannah from throwing herself at him. He looks tired but manages his unhurried smile.

'You're back,' she says.

Gates upturns a hand in reply. It's all he has available until he's deposited the food on a small table.

'Thought you might be hungry.'

'Ravenous. Have you seen the news?'

'I have. No idea who that woman is they're looking for though.'

Hannah giggles. 'It's a terrible photo, isn't it? It was taken for my security pass at work.'

'I'm surprised you ever reach your desk.'

'It's touch and go sometimes. Oh my God.' Hannah has bitten into an onion bhaji, and the spices are melting on her tongue. 'You'd better sit down and get stuck in if you want to eat.'

They eat in their usual companionable silence while their facial expressions indicate the levels of ecstasy that the delicious food induces. Gates has also brought a selection of ice-cold drinks. He sips a beer. Hannah has a Diet Coke. Between them they manage to devour all the food.

'What a feast,' says Hannah.

'Fit for a cover girl.'

'Ha ha. Very funny. I haven't been outside since I saw that.'

'Wise decision, mug shot or not.'

'How's your wife?' Hannah asks.

Gates shrugs. 'She's struggling.'

'I'm sorry.' Hannah's words are sincere. She's sorry for anyone dying before their time, but she's also sorry for Gates. He blows out a long stream of air and leans back to regard Hannah. Somehow, she has the feeling that he's not seeing her.

'I spoke to her doctor today. It's the main reason I stayed over. I wanted to catch him and get an accurate view of things.'

'And what did he say?'

'That she's terminally ill. She doesn't have long. He couldn't be precise. It might only be two weeks, but it could be two months. No longer.'

'Is she being well looked after?'

Gates nods. 'Nurses are going in every day, and she has a neighbour who's helping. She's been referred for a hospice bed. She should get a place within the next week or two. I've been sorting out the practical stuff for her.'

Hannah imagines what it must be like to know that you're dying, to leave your home aware it's for the last time. How do you cope with the realisation that your life is over? You won't go anywhere else; you won't do anything else. You will never make the dream trip, learn a new skill, live your best life. It's done, finished.

'I don't know her name,' says Hannah.

'Alison.'

Hannah wants to reply, to say something, anything in response to the name, to the sadness of the moment but nothing comes. Gates starts clearing away the debris left from their meal, pushing the empty containers and plastic cutlery

252

into the carrier bag.

'I'll take this lot downstairs, so the room doesn't smell in the morning.'

'Thanks.'

Hannah gives herself a shake and busies herself boiling the kettle for tea.

When Gates returns, he asks Hannah to be ready to leave after breakfast the following morning.

'Where to?'

'To the seaside. South Devon.'

'Another Gates residence?' asks Hannah.

'Indeed,' replies Gates, pausing to take a sip of his tea. 'Wow, that's disgusting.'

'UHT milk from a plastic pot.'

'Well, my residence will have fresh milk from a carton.'

'A carton. Not a farmyard caravan then?'

'Sort of a caravan, but more upmarket. It has a bathroom.'

'I'm in,' laughs Hannah. 'You had me at bathroom.'

41

The journey down the M5 is uneventful but long. Traffic is heavy, and they have two service stops for coffee, sandwiches, and bathroom breaks. Each time she leaves the car Hannah pulls her hair loose around her shoulders and wears Gates' baseball cap and sunglasses. She looks nothing like her press picture and does her best to walk with confidence. Even so, she's relieved each time she's back in the passenger seat buckling her seatbelt.

They stop for the third time at a Morrison's supermarket. Stepping from the car Hannah pauses to assimilate the scent of the sea and the squawks of the seagulls. The sun warms the top of her head and there is a brightness to the sky that you only find near the sea. She's dragged back to Weymouth almost three decades ago where, as an almost five-year-old, she stood with her dad admiring a sand sculpture.

The sculpture was a depiction of George slaying the dragon, every scale of the dragon carved in meticulous detail. A wire fence protected the sculpture from damage by members of the public and those wanting to get as close as possible, wanting to touch. Hannah remembers pressing her face so hard against the wire mesh that the pattern became embedded on her face.

When her dad tried to leave Hannah pulled back, begging her dad to let her stay. Only when he started to become impatient did she drag her reluctant feet after him.

She wanted to stay because she was worried that if she left, it might rain, and the beautiful dragon would be washed away. It would be gone forever, wouldn't it? Her dad had said yes, nothing lasts forever. Hannah had cried at this, and her dad had lifted her up and carried her to the ice-cream van. When he handed Hannah a cornet of whipped ice-cream he said, 'Eat it quickly, Hannah, it won't last forever but you can really enjoy it before it goes.'

It was a clever and appropriate lesson.

Today, the scent of the sea and the cry of the seagulls bring it back vividly. The sculpture, the ice-cream, and her dad's words that nothing lasts forever.

How apt this is, thinks Hannah, as she looks across the roof of the car at Gates. This moment, this precise moment is over even as it starts. She turns towards the supermarket entrance. When will this whole situation be over and more importantly, what will be left?

Gates grabs a small trolley and Hannah can't resist raising an eyebrow.

'Hopeful, aren't we?'

'This is a good place, Hannah, and every police officer in the country is on the lookout for Sullivan. We deserve a few days at least.'

'Describe the kitchen facilities to me?'

'Er, sink, hob, cooker.'

'So somewhere we can cook and get the dishes washed?'

'If you want. We can heat up pizza or something.'

'No to the pizza. I've only cooked you one proper meal since we've been on the road. I'm making a lasagna. Don't try and stop me.'

Gates laughs and raises his palms. 'Perish the thought. Any chance of garlic bread?'

Hannah grabs a bulb of garlic and tosses it to Gates who makes a show of sniffing the bulb with exaggerated extravagance before he drops it into the trolley. Hannah is energised at the thought of having a real kitchen after all these weeks and shops for a prawn stir fry and a chicken and leek pie. Gates follows behind with a bemused expression on his face.

'I can cook, you know.'

Hannah lowers her voice. 'You can hack too but I can't. So, you do what you do, and I'll feed us for the next few days at least. Much as I love coffee and croissants, they do not feed my soul. Besides, I like to cook. You can provide breakfast and do the washing up.'

'There's a dishwasher.'

'You'll have time to clean the bathroom then. I'll buy some bathroom cleaner for you.'

As she and Gates unload the contents of the trolley onto the conveyor belt Hannah is aware of a rare feeling in the pit of her stomach. It bothers her for a matter of seconds before she recognises it as the first tendrils of happiness. She's at the seaside with Gates and is shopping for the meals she will share with him.

Oh my God. Her face drops.

'What is it?' asks Gates, looking over his shoulder, half expecting to see Sullivan in the queue.

'You're not vegetarian, are you?'

'I'm working on it but no, not this week.'

'Don't worry,' says Hannah with a sigh of relief. 'I have a good repertoire of plant-based meals if I say so myself.'

Why did she say that? Like she's going to carry on cooking for him in the future. This is so close to being over. She can't make assumptions about life after this. Who knows what it will look like?

They unload the groceries into the boot and as they descend the hill from the supermarket Hannah can see the silvery waves of the sea dancing and glinting below them.

'Oh, it's beautiful,' she sighs, as she feels her heart physically lift within her rib cage.

'I know,' replies Gates. 'I love it here.'

They turn onto a road bridge that spans the water. Gates slows down so that Hannah can absorb the view. She feels his glance on her as she gazes towards the mouth of the estuary where a collection of small boats negotiates a channel marked by bobbing buoys.

Back on dry land the road passes through a village of stone cottages before climbing up and around the side of a hill. Once they're above the village Hannah sees a vista of coastline sweeping in an eastwards curve towards Dorset. Her breath catches in her throat. She has no idea why this landscape is affecting her so much. Except that she feels safe and happy. She feels empowered. That will do.

'We're here,' says Gates.

***

The view falls away as Gates turns off the main road. They follow a driveway into a holiday park where Gates pulls into a small car park surrounded by a high privet hedge.

'We walk from here. Just carry what you can.'

Hannah pulls her rucksack onto her back and grabs two bags of perishables. Gates manages his rucksack, his laptop bag, and the rest of the shopping. He locks the car. The walk is short but steep. They follow a tarmac driveway which forks after a few hundred yards. The left-hand turn leads further up the hill where Hannah can see neat rows of identical caravans lined up in front of the breathtaking view of the bay below them.

Gates follows the right-hand turn which takes them to a line of impressive lodges.

'This is it.'

The lodge is beautiful. It's set into the side of the hill anchored by wooden decking on three sides. The surrounding lawns are trimmed to perfection.

'It's immaculate,' observes Hannah.

'There's a twenty-four-hour maintenance and security service. They keep things tidy, and the guys keep an eye on the lodges when the owners aren't here.'

'Wow, good service.'

'And they charge us for the privilege.'

'Fair enough,' says Hannah.

'But I pay extra,' adds Gates.

'For?'

'They call it special services. If you're ever here alone and you're worried about anything, night or day, they are the guys you call. Their number is on the fridge. You can trust them with anything.'

Gates has the door open, and he steps inside. Hannah follows through a small utility area with a washing machine and tumble dryer into an open-plan lounge, dining area, and kitchen. The air smells fresh and clean and the well-designed kitchen has a full-sized oven, fridge-freezer, and the promised dishwasher. In the comfortable lounge a large plasma screen hangs from the wall. The place is spotlessly clean. Hannah is impressed.

But it's the view that draws her forward. She's still clutching a bag of shopping in each hand as Gates pulls back the bi-fold doors to reveal a one-hundred-and-eighty-degree view of the sea. She steps out onto the wooden deck and leans against the clear balcony. She feels like Rose in *Titanic*. She has no words.

Gates comes up behind her and takes the shopping from her hands. Hannah doesn't notice. She stands motionless and overcome. She inhales the view. This is paradise. Gates is back.

'Nothing to say. That's not like you.'

Hannah shakes herself before she can respond.

'There's something about being near to the sea. It's the space, I think. The sky is endless, and it makes the light different. This is magic.'

Gates smiles. 'I like it.'

'I'd spend all day transfixed by this view. I love the water.'

'We can walk to the beach later,' promises Gates.

He goes back inside the lodge and starts putting the groceries away. Hannah leaves the deck with some reluctance and goes to help but her eyes stray at intervals to the spectacular view of the sea. Something is stirring inside Hannah and for the first time in a long time, she finds herself thinking about the future, forming plans, imagining a life. A stable life. A shared life.

42

Gates sets up his computer gear on the dining table while Hannah explores the rest of the lodge. Two bedrooms, one with an ensuite, a bathroom and a boiler cupboard. Everything is compact, clean, and perfect.

She returns to the main area and starts to prepare the lasagna for supper. The only thing Hannah likes better than cooking is having someone to cook for. As she stands in the kitchen layering pasta, meat, and sauce she finds herself smiling.

'You look happy,' says Gates.

'Do you know something? I am.'

Gates gives Hannah a long look which she is unable to interpret. Except to say that he too looks content. Maybe that's the best she'll get from him.

'Are you free for a minute?'

She is. Hannah gives the lasagna a last sprinkle of black pepper and joins Gates at the table. As she sits next to him on an upright dining chair, she almost feels nostalgic for his flat and the sound of Deborah dropping her books or bumping up the stairs. Despite all the worry and fear, how much better this world has turned out to be.

'I've checked everything I can and so far, the situation

is unchanged. Everyone is looking for Sullivan. No-one has found him yet. We're as safe here as anywhere so we might as well settle in and enjoy it. My concern now is the search for you. It's too much attention. I don't like it.'

'But we decided I'm better staying away from the authorities.'

'We did. The problem is that you are their prize witness, and they obviously want to have contact with you. I think we should offer them that. It should take the heat out of their search if they know you're safe and you'll come forward when Sullivan is in custody.'

Hannah tips her head to one side. 'Sounds fair.'

'Okay, good. I'm going to make a call to Mrs. Waterhouse. See if she can suggest the best person to contact and we'll take it from there. I don't want to call a Helpline and end up with some Jobsworth. I want to speak directly to someone in authority. Neil's wife will have a pretty good idea of who he trusts and who he doesn't.'

Hannah goes back to the kitchen to tidy up while Gates makes the call. She only half listens to the conversation. *This place is like a cocoon*, she thinks. Her concerns have scattered on the wind and been whipped away across the sea. Only when the call ends does she give Gates her full attention.

'Neil is doing well. He's out of ICU and recovering on a normal ward. He's decided to retire.'

'I'm glad to hear that.'

'Me too. And I have a name and a private phone number.'

'Who?'

'An assistant chief constable no less.'

'Straight to the top.'

'I know. There are plenty of good coppers apparently, but she doesn't know any of them well enough to trust them. This assistant chief constable she does know.'

'Is there a story there?'

'Nothing salacious. Somebody married somebody else, and it made them relatives of a sort.'

'That'll do. Let's dial.'

Gates dials the number through his computer. The call is answered after three rings. Gates introduces himself as a friend of Neil Waterhouse. He explains that he is with Hannah, and she is safe but in hiding. She'll come forward when Sullivan is arrested.

The questions come thick and fast, and Gates answers them without hesitation. The assistant chief constable asks to speak to Hannah. She joins the conversation after identifying herself. As expected, the assistant chief constable wants Hannah to come into a safe house, but she resists. Her experience, she explains, has not been a good one. She feels safe where she is. She declines to give a contact number but promises to call if anything changes. Gates ends the call.

'That was easy,' Hannah says.

'Let's hope it's enough for him to call off the dogs. We could really do without the attention.'

Gates closes his computer and packs it away in his backpack.

'Going somewhere?' asks Hannah.

'Do you fancy a walk on the beach?'

'I thought you'd never ask.'

***

At the entrance to the holiday park, they cross the main road and climb a stile into a steep field that falls away, offering breathtaking views of the sea. Sheep graze although this late in the year the grass has been nibbled almost to its roots and pickings are sparse. Hannah and Gates amble to the edge of the field where they stop at a sturdy fence. A large wind-battered sign attached to the wooden crossbars reads *Danger unsafe cliffs, do not cross*. The sign is repeated at intervals. Gates beckons Hannah towards the fence, and they lean over.

The bay sweeps away either side of them. Hannah admires the dark red cliffs of the Jurassic Coast in the distance. Wind stirs their hair.

'It looks so wild from up here,' she says.

'Wild and dangerous. Rain erodes the rock and sections of the cliff tumble down onto the beach. People have been killed.'

Hannah peers over the fence. From where she's standing it looks like a near vertical drop to the sand below.

'Do you have a problem with heights?' asks Gates.

'I don't love them, but I don't get vertigo.'

Gates points to Hannah's left where she sees a small outcrop of grass just wide enough for one of her feet. 'See that step?'

'I don't see a step. I see a death wish.'

Gates pulls a heavy piece of metal and a length of blue string from his pocket. It looks like a number eight with one half bigger than the other.

'This,' says Gates, 'is a standard figure eight descender.' He doubles over the string and pushes it through the larger metal circle before hooking the loop over the smaller circle. He demonstrates how releasing the rope allows it to pass through the descender in a controlled manner.

Hannah starts to feel queasy.

'Why are you showing me this?'

'In case you need to run, for any reason, this is the place to come. If you drop over the lip of the cliff you can hide.'

The queasiness blooms into nausea.

'Drop over the lip of the cliff? You are joking, aren't you?'

'I'm serious, Hannah. With a piece of rope around the fence post for safety, you can descend the cliff a few feet. Only in this one spot. There are eight grassy steps at the top of the cliff. Just enough to give you some support and keep you out of sight.

'Keep the descender in your pocket. This bit of metal and a piece of rope will hold you. In an emergency it will get you safely down the cliff. Just don't let go of the rope or there's nothing to stop your descent. Do you understand?'

Hannah wonders if Gates is being serious.

'You want me to throw myself over a vertical cliff? Are you mad?'

'That's not what I said.'

'Well, that's how it sounded.'

'It's the perfect hiding place and it's safe.'

'I beg to differ.'

Hannah peers at the grassy step but can see nothing step-like about it.

'Just tell me you could find it. Even in the dark.'

Hannah assesses the distance between the danger sign and the lump of grass that Gates seems to think will hold the weight of a human body.

'I see it.'

'Good enough.'

He holds out the string and descender for Hannah.

'Show me.'

Hannah takes the descender and the string, pushes the doubled string through the big hole and hooks it over the smaller one. She holds it up for scrutiny, more uncertain than triumphant. Gates gives it a tug.

'This bit of metal could save your life, Hannah. If you run, you take it with you.'

'What about rope?'

Gates leans over the fence and points. Attached to the fence post Hannah can see a black cord.

'There's a waterproof bag there with a length of climbing rope inside. I'll check it every day.'

'You've really thought about this,' says Hannah.

'It's my back door. The truth is you won't be able to outrun Sullivan for any distance. If it comes to it, this is the optimal escape route. No-one will expect you to disappear over a sheer cliff. If you need to, descend all the way down to the beach. Once you're on the beach you can use the tunnel, or you can clamber over the rocks in either direction to get to the next bay. Just watch the tides. You might get a soaking.'

Hannah peers over the cliff to the sand below.

'Have you been down there?'

'Of course.'

Of course he has. Gates is a risk-averse person. He assesses risk and produces his contingency plans. He won't take a chance unless he's forced into it. And likewise, Hannah has no intention of descending a sheer cliff face unless she's forced into it.

'And what tunnel?' Hannah asks.

'I'll show you that next.'

Gates moves off and they walk along the fence line in silence. Gates appears calm and reassured but Hannah is appalled that he could even consider asking her to climb over the fence and sneaks frequent, anxious glances at the cliff. Just the thought of stepping off the cliff edge makes her heart beat faster. She feels a physical sense of relief when they leave the field and cross a narrow road leading to a municipal car park, but her pulse continues to race.

It feels like a premonition.

43

They walk along the narrow road until they reach the municipal car park. Skirting the car park, they head into a dark tunnel carved through the cliff face. It's lined with crumbling bricks which, according to Gates, were laid by smugglers wanting a speedy exit from the beach. There are intermittent, cobweb-draped ceiling lights which penetrate the gloom, but do nothing to disperse the sense of twilight that envelops them. The walls are wet, and the cloying scent of damp earth irritates Hannah's nostrils. The sound of waves echoes around them. The air is moist and stale. They descend three long sets of concrete steps to a puddle-covered landing where they turn sharp left. A fourth set of steps carries them through an opening to emerge into bright sunlight. They blink and squint and Hannah hears, before she sees, the thundering surf pounding the beach.

They're standing on a small, square, concrete landing with a metal rail. Hannah leans against it to marvel at the stretch of gritty red sand below her. Belligerent waves are rolling into the bay and the wind whips Hannah's hair across her face. The beach is almost deserted bar a pair of dog walkers and an elderly lady searching for something in the wet sand. Her feet are bare, and she is close enough to the bottom of the steps for Hannah to see wet sand squelching between the woman's toes.

'It's stunning, Gates.'

Gates leads the way down the final flight of steps, which end in the deep, red sand. Hannah flings off her socks and boots, rolls up the legs of her jeans and runs to the water's edge. She squeals as the freezing sea engulfs her feet. A laughing Gates joins her and takes her hand as they splash and paddle along the edge of the waves.

They are having far too much fun to notice the roller until it hits them with so much force, they both topple into the surf. Hannah screams then howls with laughter while Gates clambers to his feet shouting, 'Fuck, fuck, fuck.' For a moment they stand in the water, fully clothed, soaked to the skin and laughing like drains. Then Gates has his arms around Hannah, and he is kissing her with such passion she is devoid of the oxygen required to speak, to breathe, even to think.

She kisses him back.

She has no thoughts of Sullivan, of rapes or attacks, of being betrayed or chased or shut in an unsafe safe house. There is nothing but this moment with Gates' arms around her, his lean torso pressed against hers and the salty taste of him on her lips. Their bodies mould together, and the fit is perfect. Then Hannah is stumbling backwards as Gates pushes her away. Her lips feel scratched from the salt and her heart races. Gates clutches his head with both hands and turns in circles.

'I'm sorry, I'm so sorry.'

Hannah is confused. Why isn't he smiling? Why is he turning away? What is he sorry for?

'I shouldn't have done that.'

'Why not? I wanted you to. I think I've wanted you to kiss me for a long time.'

'Fuck it.' Hannah hears anguish in his voice.

'Gates, what's wrong?'

He runs his fingers through his hair and the salt from his hands makes it stand up in every direction. He looks at Hannah as if beseeching her to understand. She doesn't. Her body is on fire from this man's kiss and her lips vibrate with her need for him. She reaches out a hand to touch his arm, but he steps away from her.

'Come on, we should go back and get out of these wet clothes.'

'No, Gates. Don't do that.'

'Do what?'

'Avoid the question, change the subject, go quiet on me, anything other than answer my question. Didn't you castigate me not so long ago for doing the very same thing? You promised we would always be honest and open with each other. Speak to me and tell me what's going on.'

There is an edge of anger to Hannah's voice. She has just experienced a moment that she believes is life-changing and Gates is backing away as if it were nothing. His sigh is almost enough to split Hannah's heart in two. He was the one who kissed her, for God's sake. What is wrong with him?

'Walk back to the lodge with me and we can talk on the way.'

Hannah wades out of the knee-deep water. Her clothes are soaked and her jeans squeak and rub against her thighs as she walks. She decides to carry her socks and boots. Gates does the same and they pick their way slowly back up the steps into the tunnel.

They hadn't spoken on the way down and when Gates starts to talk Hannah is surprised at the resonance of the echo. Although they're alone, Gates lowers his voice.

'When I met you for the first time,' says Gates, 'I felt like you were someone who was hiding from people. You barely left your flat except to go to work, you didn't have a partner, you never had friends come to visit. From what I could see, you were a hermit.'

'So?'

'When we chatted in the garden, and more recently when you came to me for help, I realised that you *were* hiding. You were afraid. And you were afraid because you had reason to be. I wanted to help you so much, Hannah. Not just because you made me think of my sister but because you *deserved* my help. I wanted to make your world less frightening, I wanted to protect you.'

'And you've done that.'

'Hannah, you were like a deer in headlights. I couldn't risk startling you. I thought you'd run away.'

'Gates, this is all very well but you're talking in the past tense. I know I've changed. I can feel it. That Hannah has gone. For God's sake. I've slept alone in the forest. I've escaped from a safe house. I've just fallen into the sea fully clothed.'

Her last statement lightens the atmosphere but only a little.

'And now look at you.'

He gestures to Hannah who is walking up the steps beside him, slightly out of breath now from the steep climb.

'Yes. Look at me, please. Can you really see me? Or do you only see the old Hannah? The dependent Hannah. Do you see that I'm happy? For the first time since my attack, and despite everything that's happened with Sullivan, I am truly happy. So, please, tell me what's so bad about a kiss. We're both grown-ups.'

Gates starts to count on his fingers.

'Don't do that, I find it annoying.'

He shoves his hands into the pockets of his jeans.

'I can't be in a relationship, Hannah. With anyone.'

So now we're getting to the truth, she thinks.

'Why not?'

'How about the way I make my living?'

'That doesn't bother me. I'm in the process of exploiting the way you make your living for my own benefit.'

'Living permanently off grid wouldn't bother you?'

'You've got to do better than that.'

'We're hiding from a killer and the police.'

'Irrelevant. That's temporary and in any case, that's down to me.'

'I have a wife.'

'Separated wife.'

'Who is dying and who needs me.'

Hannah looks up at this. She almost says, 'who will be gone soon' but manages to catch the words before they escape.

'Because you're a good man, Gates. I admire you for supporting her.'

'Things are complicated, Hannah. The kiss was a mistake.'

His words are a blow to Hannah. What was he playing at if this is how he really feels?

'So why do it?' demands Hannah. 'Why make me feel like I did just now and then shove me away, claiming it's a mistake?'

'Hannah, I didn't shove you.'

'You may as well have. Why did you do it?'

Gates raises his hands then lets them fall to his sides.

'You looked so happy and so beautiful. I couldn't help myself. I want…'

'No!' Hannah shouts the word which echoes and reverberates around the tunnel. Anger is rising through her body. 'You don't get to say what you want. I have feelings too. Feelings that you have just exploited and hurt.'

Hannah doesn't want to hear any more of what he has to say. How dare he take a giant wooden spoon to her feelings, stir them up and then back off. What sort of man does that? She looks Gates in the eyes.

'I want to say that this is over but there's nothing to be over, is there? Still, you don't get to mess me around. You don't get to play with my feelings, raise my hopes then dash them to the ground within the same frigging minute. I can't deal with that. So, let's agree, right now, that you never, ever touch me again.'

Gates opens his mouth as if to speak then closes it again. He nods once then turns to walk gingerly across the car park in his bare feet. Hannah follows two paces behind so that he can't see her tears.

44

*W*ow, what a high.

Walking into Waterhouse's station was a bold and audacious move, even for him, but Jesus, what morons. A flash of his warrant card, an authoritative demeanour, and a firm voice. That's all it took. Not one of them bothered to check. They all took his warrant card at face value. Then again, why wouldn't they? It's authentic, after all.

Within minutes he was in the incident room, surveying the boards. That gave him an even bigger kick because they haven't got a fucking thing. Nothing except the woman, Hannah. And they only have her as a witness to a rape that took place over a year ago. Her word against his. And what use is she without DNA? The CPS will never agree to prosecute anything on that basis, call handler or not.

He was about to sidle away before anyone asked him what he was doing when he saw it. The reg number of a car that followed the DI when Hannah was delivered to the safe house. The car turned away and although it was followed up, the owner could not be traced. But Sullivan knew who it was. The guy who is helping Hannah. Has to be. He was following to get her location. That's how he got her away by the skin of his teeth.

And that's how he is going to get caught.

He calls an ex-girlfriend at his own station and gets her to run the number through the ANPR system. If questioned, he will claim the car almost ran him off the road. Of course, it's marked. That's what comes of following a car on its way to a safe house. He writes the car's latest location on a scrap of paper and saunters away. South Devon is a long drive, and he has a job to do. It's time to end this.

Once and for all.

45

The seagulls screech like a pack of injured monkeys and the silvery waves have turned a miserable grey. Hannah's brain is heavy and dull. Her limbs stiff and unresponsive. Gates is subdued and sits staring at his computer until it's time for Hannah to serve her homemade lasagna and garlic bread. To Hannah, the food is tasteless, and she regrets the love and anticipation that she put into its preparation. Apart from soup and bread in Scotland, this is the first proper meal she has cooked for Gates in all the time they've been together. Will it be the last? One way or another, she can feel the end of their odyssey drawing near. Hope and anticipation are turning into regrets. How different this evening is to the one she had envisaged.

Gates clears his plate and helps himself to seconds. He makes no attempt to initiate conversation with Hannah, nor does he meet her gaze. The only satisfaction she gets is the slight shake of his hand as he manoeuvres the serving spoon. He scrapes his plate clean and takes it to the sink.

'Thank you.'

'You're welcome,' replies Hannah, wondering if all future conversation will be reduced to polite exchanges such as these. But no. Gates is disappearing again.

'I need to go and see Alison.'

Hannah starts. *When was this planned?*

'That's a long drive.'

Gates shrugs. 'She's worse. They're going to transfer her to the hospice tomorrow. I'm going to help with the transfer.'

Now you're telling me, thinks Hannah. She nods. 'Okay.'

What can she say? She can hardly ask him to stay and neglect his sick wife. Nor does she want him to. He's no use to her if a simple kiss sends him psycho. *Stop it*, she tells herself. *You're turning into a bitch.* Besides, she knows the final reckoning with Sullivan is close. She is ready and she is prepared to face it alone. She doesn't need Gates here for that. She doesn't want him to deal with Sullivan on her behalf. Sullivan is her nemesis, and she will be the one to defeat him. She wants him to see her face.

'Hannah?'

'What?'

'Same deal as usual with the phones. I should be back tomorrow evening. If not tomorrow, then the night after that.'

'Yes, of course. I'll be fine here. Don't worry about me.'

'I'll tell security you're home alone, so they'll increase their patrols after dark. They try not to spook the residents, but they may knock to check you're okay. If they do, they'll call out, so you don't get scared.'

'Knocking would scare me. Quite a lot. I'd prefer them not to knock.'

'I'll tell them. I'll give them your number and ask them to text.'

And he's gone. Again. He doesn't look back, he doesn't wave. He leaves with his head down and his shoulders collapsed towards his chest. Hannah's ribs ache. She regrets her failure to offer him any comfort before he left.

Who can compete with a dying wife? thinks Hannah.

Who can deal with a man whose kiss turns her insides to jelly but tells her he doesn't want a relationship?

Could she live off grid? Honestly? Hannah doesn't know. She doesn't fully understand what it would mean for her. The bigger question in Hannah's eyes is whether she wants to live without Gates. She knows the answer to that question.

It's a no.

***

She goes to bed with the phone under her pillow. When it rings half an hour after midnight she wakes with a start. She checks the time before she answers. She's been asleep for two hours.

'Hannah?'

It's Gates. There's something wrong with his voice. As if he's trying to speak without enough air or attempting to form words without using his teeth and tongue. His breathing is harsh and ragged. Fear tugs at Hannah's senses. She knows these sounds. Her previous sour mood is forgotten. This is the voice of someone injured, someone hurting. She presses the phone to her ear to still her shaking hand. Dread seeps into the room.

'Gates, what is it?'

Hannah's listening skills are on high alert. Something has happened. Gates is not himself. She hears a muffled voice and then brusque words thump into her ear. They are delivered by the one voice she hoped never to hear again.

'Gates is with me, Hannah.'

She stops breathing.

The way he says her name slithers around inside her brain. He is deep within her head. He sounds smug. Any nervousness Hannah may have been anticipating at the thought of speaking to this man slides away. He thinks he's going to mess with her thoughts, with her emotions. *Not this time*, she thinks, *not again*.

This time she's not going to be afraid. She's not going to run. She can deal with this. She can deal with him. She breathes.

Go ahead, caller, you are through to the police, thinks Hannah. Her voice is calm, professional.

'And you are?'

His voice is arrogant, mocking.

'Oh, I think you know who I am.'

Hannah has been bracing herself for this moment for the last thirteen months. In a strange way it's almost a relief that it has finally arrived. She recalls Glenn's words at the farmhouse in Wales. You can't stop yourself feeling scared, but you can change the way you react to it. This time she is ready.

'And what do you want, Mr. Sullivan?'

He sniggers. His voice is high and singsong. 'Oh, please call me Dan. You know it turns me on.'

Hannah almost chokes on the bile that surges into her throat. She swallows and speaks in her calm, professional voice.

'Do you want something, Mr. Sullivan?'

'I want you to come and collect your boyfriend.'

'I don't have a boyfriend.'

'Call him what you like, Hannah. I don't want him. So, you come and get him, or I'll leave him somewhere the coroner can scrape him up.'

This is a call. Just another emergency call.

'Don't you think that would leave rather a lot of DNA?'

'It would leave plenty of his, none of mine. I always make sure of that, as you know. So, are you coming or not? I must tell you he's not much company. Not very chatty. I think his jaw might be broken. I'll be quite happy to finish him off now if you're not interested in him.'

Hannah's belly contracts but she stays icy calm. She's trained to deal with difficult phone calls. Hell, this is how she makes a living.

'What do you want?'

'I want you, Hannah.'

'Where are you?'

'That's better. I'm in the Quantock Hills. Nice and quiet. Head to Taunton. Stop there and call me on this number. I'll ping you a location. And I don't need to tell you to come alone, do I?'

Hannah doesn't answer. The less she engages with this man, the better. She wonders how Sullivan has found her. Then realisation dawns. He hasn't found her. It's Gates that he has caught. And now Sullivan is using Gates to lure Hannah to an isolated place so that he can do whatever he has been planning over the last weeks.

Sullivan laughs. He actually laughs. He's enjoying Hannah's silence. He thinks he's in control. But he's not. He's desperate. Hannah believes he will kill Gates. She's not going to let that happen. He thinks Hannah is afraid. He thinks she will be compliant, a victim. Oh no. She's played that role once already. This time she's prepared to fight. Hannah's initial fear has metamorphosed into a vibrant surge of anger that makes her eye sockets ache.

'I'll be there,' says Hannah.

'I knew you were a clever one.'

She ends the call.

Hannah takes some time to think. Gates is hurt and Hannah's only option is to go to him. She is not afraid to face Sullivan and it's with a slight sense of detachment that she goes to the kitchen drawer and removes the sharpest knife she can find. At the same time, she acknowledges how physically slight she is. She has never been aggressive: no playground brawls, no pushing, shoving, or slapping. Mercifully, she has few memories of her rape but before her eyes closed, she felt Sullivan's hands on her, pushing her face into the bed. He's tall and strong and he will use that to his advantage. It's what he does. All his victims have been small and slight.

She has no idea what condition Gates is in, but he sounded hurt. He might need support to move. A plan is already forming in her head, but it will require two people. The second to help Gates get away while Hannah deals with Sullivan. And how she longs to do that.

She finds the number for site security on the fridge and dials. Within minutes there's a voice at the door. Hannah is impressed by the size of the man who stands there. He's six feet of solid muscle and steps sideways as he passes through the small utility room into the lodge's main living area. He's Craig and he's here to help. What does she need?

It doesn't take Hannah long to fill Craig in on what's happened. She understands that Gates has somehow fallen into the hands of Sullivan and that he is being used as bait. Hannah is the one he wants and he sure as hell is not planning on taking her to dinner. Hannah does not want to enlist the help of the police. They are slow and who knows how trustworthy. She needs to get in quickly and take Sullivan by surprise. If Gates is badly hurt, she will need help to move Gates.

Craig listens carefully as Hannah outlines the details of her plan. He's ready when she is.

'I'm really anxious to hit the road.'

'Get yourself sorted,' says Craig. 'Meet me at the gates in five minutes.'

Hannah dresses in warm clothing, including Gates' jumper and her faithful boots. She hurries out to the gate and climbs into the passenger seat of a Range Rover. As the car pulls away a further set of headlights swings in behind them.

Craig catches Hannah looking. 'Back up,' he says.

'I'm so sorry to put you to all this trouble,' says Hannah as they turn onto the main road and head for the estuary bridge.

'Trouble?' grins Craig. 'We'd pay for nights like these.'

Hannah has no answer. She focuses on the road ahead and stills her shaking hands by wrapping them around her phone.

46

Traffic is light in the early hours of the new day and Craig takes no prisoners as he breaks the speed limit of every road in Devon and Somerset his tyres touch. Even so, it takes forty minutes to reach Taunton. Hannah dials the number of the last call on her phone.

'Speedy,' mocks Sullivan. 'You must have put your foot down.'

Hannah uses her professional call handler voice.

'There's not exactly a lot of traffic at this time of the morning.'

'I'll see you soon then.'

The call ends.

Hannah's phone pings. She looks at the map. Sullivan has given her the location of an isolated car park. It's going to take a further twenty minutes to get there. *Hang on, Gates,* she thinks. Craig pulls to the side of the road and parks on the verge.

'Okay, Hannah,' he says, studying the phone. 'I'll just have a word with my mate.'

The backup car is parked behind them. Craig takes Hannah's phone and walks back to brief the driver on their final location. Hannah can't see if anyone else is in the car, but it doesn't matter. She's ready. It's great to have Craig beside her but Hannah is prepared to get Gates back, whatever it might cost her. And that includes going it alone if necessary. When Craig reappears, he opens the passenger door. As he lifts his hand to help Hannah from the car his jacket gapes and she catches a glimpse of a gun holster. It contains an ugly and lethal-looking weapon. Hannah finds the sight of the gun both scary and reassuring.

'Your turn.'

As planned, Hannah walks around to the driver's seat to drive the final few miles. It's imperative that Sullivan thinks she has come alone. Although she should be frightened and feeling shaky, it seems that her body has slammed the door shut on any potential fears. At least for now. Her hands are steady as she takes the wheel, and her breathing is even. Craig notices her calm.

'You're one tough cookie, Hannah. Gates will be proud of you.'

Hannah couldn't wish for a better affirmation than that.

'So, let's go get him,' she says.

Craig gives Hannah clear and concise directions, so she doesn't have to squint at the phone to stay on the correct route. Once out of Taunton she drives on full beam first along a main road then on a minor road heading into the countryside. She can see the dark shadow of a large wood on the horizon. *What a great place to hide*, she thinks.

She glances in the rear-view mirror, but the backup car appears to have fallen away.

'He's there,' reassures Craig, 'he's driving dark.'

'How?'

'Night vision goggles.'

'Oh,' is the only response that Hannah has. These men are more than just security guards. They're something else entirely. Thank God Gates has paid for their special services. The parking spot is approaching, and Craig releases his seat belt. He secures the phone in a holder on the dashboard for Hannah and climbs into the back seat.

'I don't expect him to be in the car park,' says Hannah. 'I believe he'll be watching from somewhere nearby. So, you can't show yourself until I'm out of the way. He'll want to get me out of the car and on foot. He likes to use his height and physical presence to intimidate. I know Gates is hurt but I don't know how badly. As soon as I move on Sullivan, I need you and your mate to grab Gates and get away him away. You get Gates out of here in one of the cars. The other car and driver can wait for me.'

'Understood,' says Craig. Hannah loves that he doesn't disagree or question her.

She drives the last minutes in a state of surreal calm. For the first time since her attack, she feels ready to meet Sullivan head on. She can't explain when or how she began to feel stronger and braver. She just knows that it's happened.

It doesn't make any difference to Hannah that Gates has backed away from any potential relationship with her. That he has chosen his precarious and illegal lifestyle over her. How Gates feels about her isn't important. What's important is how Hannah feels about Gates. She wants him to be safe and free to do whatever he wants, with or without her. And if she can get Sullivan at the same time, it will be the ultimate serendipity.

'We're here, Craig.'

'Okay.'

His voice is muffled, and Hannah realises he's buried beneath a layer of car rugs.

She gives a small gasp as she catches sight of Gates' car.

'Tell me what you see.'

'Gates' car. It's smashed into a tree. The front end is crumpled, and the side is dented.'

'Sullivan's doing, no doubt. Can you see the roof?'

'It's okay.'

'That's a good sign, he hasn't rolled. What about the air bag?'

'It's been released.'

'Good.'

As Craig speaks Hannah's phone rings. She grabs it and puts it on speaker.

'Yes?'

'I see you made it.'

Sullivan's voice is all but crowing. If he were to walk towards Hannah right now there would be a swagger in his gait and a smirk on his face. She can hear it in his voice. He thinks he's won. *Not yet you haven't.* When she speaks Hannah's voice is composed.

'Of course I did.'

'Leave your car where it is and head to the end of the parking area. You'll see a path leading into the woods. Follow the path.'

'For how long?'

'You'll know how long. Just keep walking.'

Hannah ends the call. An arm appears between the seats and offers her a torch.

'Don't turn around, Hannah. Leave the car unlocked. Do exactly as he says. He'll probably jump you but stay as calm as you can. There are three of us. We'll be right behind you.'

'Thank you,' whispers Hannah. She steps from the car.

Before she goes towards the path Hannah looks at Gates' car. She shines the torch around the interior and is relieved there is no sign of any blood. On an impulse she crouches down and shines the torch around the wheel arches. Near the off-side rear wheel she finds a small rectangular box. She gives it a sharp tug and the magnetised tracker comes away in her hand.

'Oh, Gates,' she sighs. 'You didn't check.'

The bright torch illuminates the path ahead. It's a well-trodden route, and Hannah sets off at a steady pace. She's anxious to get to Gates but suspects Sullivan is watching. He can't be allowed to see her concern. That will give him power over her and she will not let him play his psychological head games with her. Not again.

She walks with studied ease, thinking back to her meeting with Sullivan in the bar. She remembers the way he charmed and flattered her. Right up to the point where she refused her drink. That's when he demonstrated his disappointment. A sharp flicker of anger. Enough to discourage and unnerve her. Enough to make Hannah realise she wanted to get away from him and return home.

Of course, that's his weak spot, thinks Hannah. Sullivan thinks he's in charge, he must be in control. If he controls the woman; he controls the scene. He's like a movie director. The action and the dialogue must all be within his power. Each of his victims has been a rehearsal for the next. That's why his crimes have escalated.

This revelation almost causes Hannah to stop walking. Almost. If Sullivan is watching, he'll have seen nothing more than a slight hesitation in Hannah's step. Hannah can use this knowledge against him. She feels as if she's acquired some ammunition. If she fights back Sullivan will feel he has lost control. That will make him weak.

The path through the forest is easy to follow, but the ground is rising, and Hannah becomes breathless. She stops for a few moments and listens. There is no indication that there's any other living creature amongst the trees and undergrowth. She assumes her footsteps have frightened away the night creatures, but neither is there any suggestion of a human breath other than her own. She glances at her watch. She's been walking for eleven minutes. She's concerned at the ever-increasing distance between her current position and the safety of Craig's car.

The ring of her phone breaks the silence. Hannah starts and drops it. She keeps her swear words to herself and sweeps the torchlight around her feet. The phone is close. She picks it up and answers.

'You're taking your time.'

Hannah's retort is quick and instinctive. 'You didn't say I had to hurry.'

'Well, I'm saying now. It's getting boring out here.'

Hannah ends the call. He won't like that. He won't like it at all. She's fired the first salvo.

Her phone rings again. Hannah ignores it. The thought of Sullivan's anger makes her want to smile but this is not the time or the place. This is a game that she's playing with a deranged killer. She must brace herself for his next move.

It's not long in coming. As the path becomes steeper and uneven a dark shadow steps in front of her. Hannah has been expecting this but still her limbs freeze. She sweeps her torch over Sullivan. She is grateful that the darkness conceals the tremors that shake her legs.

He shields his eyes from her torch. 'Drop that fucking light.'

Hannah returns the beam to the ground and Sullivan turns away.

'Follow me,' he says.

She shines her torch at his feet and follows as he leads her away from the path. Her fingers itch to reach for the kitchen knife in her pocket and thrust it into his unprotected back. Right kidney or left? Instead, she grits her teeth and tightens her grip on the torch. She must allow Sullivan to lead her to Gates. She does her best to keep track of their route and direction but Sullivan twists and turns between the trees and the darkness disorientates her. She feels a grain of panic embed itself inside her as she realises that finding her way back to the car is going to be near impossible. Then she remembers that she has her phone and that she's not alone. There are other pairs of eyes watching her.

Control. It's all about control. Deep breaths, Hannah. Take some big, deep breaths.

Sullivan stops. A natural rock cave is almost buried amongst a dense cluster of trees. In the darkness Hannah sees little more than an impenetrable, black shadow. She shines her torch into the cavity and the beam highlights a bundle of rags tossed on the ground. The bundle shudders and groans. Hannah gasps as she realises it's Gates and he's hurt. Every instinct in her body screams at her to run to him, to check his injuries, to whisper that he will be okay, that they'll get through this.

Stay in control.

Hannah turns to Sullivan, glad that in the darkness he doesn't have a clear view of her face. She keeps her voice steady.

'So. What now?'

Hannah hears rather than sees the smirk.

'Now you get in there next to him and don't move. Say goodbye while you're at it because he won't be coming with us.'

That's what you think.

'Coming where?'

Sullivan snorts. 'You're coming with me to retract your police statement. You're going to tell them about the lovely date that we had. Except for the part where you drank too much and jumped into bed with me. But then you cried rape and got me in this mess. You are going to come with me and tell the truth.'

'Why would I do that?'

'Because if you do, I might let this snivelling heap of humanity go.'

He is stark, raving mad, thinks Hannah. *On another planet.*

'I have told the truth.'

Sullivan bends down towards her, pushing his face almost into hers. She forces herself to stand firm and not back away from his rank breath.

'If you believe that then you both die here, tonight. If you come with me to the police and tell them the truth, tell them that you consented to sex with me after a very pleasant date, then you at least will live. Fuck it up and neither of you will live to see another day. Your choice.'

'And what's to stop me shopping you when I get there?'

Sullivan shrugs and gestures towards Gates.

'You do that, he dies.'

Hannah's mind is whirling. So, he wants his life back as it was. He wants all the charges dropped. He thinks she's the one person that can set him free. He can't know that the police have the CCTV of him with Tina and his DNA from at least two of the crime scenes. Neil did keep his word. News of the evidence didn't leak. Should she play along and go with Sullivan? That way Craig could rescue Gates. *I can look after myself,* she tells herself.

But then she thinks about Sullivan. About his cleverness and duplicity. About his physical strength. About the way he fools everyone around him. Not just women but his colleagues, his bosses, probably his family if he has any. No, this man can't be trusted, and Hannah must not be diverted from her plan to rescue Gates. Left to his own devices Sullivan could still kill. And not just her and Gates; any number of women in the future. She has no choice but to take him down. She realises that he will never let her go. He wants her dead.

Not tonight. Not ever.

She shrugs and bends down to shuffle beneath the rocks. She sits close to Gates on hard, stony ground. It's cooler beneath the rocks and the scent of rotting vegetation and leaf mould is strong. Gates' breathing is laboured, and as she leans towards him, Hannah can smell the metallic tang of fresh blood. She feels the hurt emanating from his body. Gates reaches out a hand towards her but even that small movement results in a moan of pain. Hannah switches off her torch so she is less visible to Sullivan.

Her breathing is even, her hands steady. Sullivan walks a few steps away from the cave. She feels for Gates' hand in the dark and gently squeezes his fingers. She is rewarded with a slight squeeze in return.

Sullivan is now pacing backwards and forwards in front of the cave, tapping at his phone. His appearance is a stark contrast to the slick, professional man she met for a date not so very long ago. He looks unkempt, anxious, unstable.

After her attack she labelled Sullivan a dangerous man. During the last few weeks of flight, she has observed a man becoming increasingly erratic and desperate. That makes him unpredictable.

To most people.

Hannah is different. Hannah has taken calls from people who are suffering every level of distress. She knows how to handle them. She is under no illusion that Sullivan will let her and Gates walk into the sunset. This is a man who leaves his crime scenes spotless. She has no doubt that he will do the same now. Rather than terrify Hannah, the knowledge calms her. She knows what she has to do.

She leans down and whispers in Gates' ear.

'Craig's here.'

Another squeeze of her fingers.

Hannah won't let fear overcome her. Not now. She knows better. *So, follow through with your plans*, she thinks. *Sullivan will not write the ending to this story.*

Hannah leans in towards Gates again.

'Can you walk?'

There is a pause before Gates gathers himself to speak.

'Slowly. I'm hurt.'

Slowly might be enough, thinks Hannah. *If I knew which way to go.* She turns her back to shield the light from her phone and finds the direction of the car park. It's all she needs.

'I need you to try and get up. As quietly as you can. Be ready to move.'

Sullivan continues tapping at his phone, agitation coursing through his body. He is distracted. She must act now. She must destroy his sense of control.

Gates moves. He's in obvious pain and Hannah bites her lip to keep her concern under control. With her help he pulls himself into a sitting position. His breath is heavy, but Hannah has no time to be kind and caring. She must get Gates onto his feet. If only she had more physical strength. But she has her voice. A voice that sometimes must be firm and commanding so that she can take control of someone who is hurt, terrified, in pain, bathed in panic. She uses it now. Even a whisper can be commanding.

'Listen to me. You need to get to your feet. The minute I move you stand up and start to move. However much it hurts. Do you understand?'

'Yes.'

Hannah shields her torch with her hand and shines the muted beam behind her. The cave floor is covered with assorted debris. She snatches up a piece of rock. It's larger than her hand but mishapen enough for her to get a tight grip around it. The knife will be a last resort as a single thrust might not be enough to incapacitate a man as strong as Sullivan. But she checks that it's accessible anyway.

She switches off the torch and moves into a crouch. She

pats the pocket containing the kitchen knife. Just in case. She waits for Sullivan to finish tapping and walk towards her. She crab walks from the cave so that she is to the side of him.

When he is almost upon her, she launches herself.

She gathers every ounce of fear and hurt and disgust that Sullivan has nurtured in her and throws it back at him with all her strength. Sullivan is tall and strong, but Hannah has speed and agility. She springs from her toes as if she is about to score a goal in netball and brings the rock crashing down into the side of his head.

Sullivan drops to the ground with a thud.

47

He is motionless for a few seconds then starts to move. Hannah delivers a second blow and has raised her arm for a third when her wrist is caught, and the rock removed.

'Enough,' says Craig.

Hannah stares at Sullivan's still form and wants to kick him but Craig pulls her away.

'Come on. Let's go.'

They return to Gates, who is on his feet and has managed to shuffle a few feet from the cave. For the first time Hannah can see him clearly. His head and half his face are dark with dried blood. She sees as well as hears his teeth chattering. His eyes are half-closed. A dark bruise is forming along one side of his swollen jaw.

Craig places one of Gates' arms around his shoulder. Hannah takes the other and the two of them drag a groaning Gates between the trees. His eyes squint against the pain. Even so he does his best to keep his legs moving. Gates is tall but he's skinny, and Hannah sends up a quick prayer of thanks as she shoulders part of his weight. When they are some distance from the cave Craig halts.

'Rest here,' says Craig. 'I'll check on Sullivan and call the police.'

Hannah has no time to answer before she's alone with Gates. He sprawls against a tree, violent shivers shaking his body. Hannah removes her coat and places it around his shoulders before huddling up next to him, gently wrapping her arms around him. She rests her head against his, not minding that she might get his blood on her skin. All she can think about is keeping him warm until Craig gets back.

This wasn't meant to happen. It was bad enough that Neil ended up in hospital with career-ending injuries. None of this hurt should have happened. Not to anyone. But especially not to Hannah's unhurried Gates, who spends his days tapping away at a keyboard because he wants to help people like his sister. Like Tina. Like Hannah.

Hannah strokes Gates' hair and murmurs, 'It's going to be okay, Gates. Everything is going to be okay.'

Please, she asks, wishing for once in her life that she had faith. What a comfort it must be to be able to pray at times like this.

Craig's voice startles her.

'Hannah, we need to move.'

They help Gates to his feet but the long wait on the ground has stiffened his limbs and the best he can manage is a painful shuffle.

'What's happened?' asks Hannah.

Craig makes a noise that is halfway between a snort and a growl.

'Sullivan is gone.'

Hannah stumbles but regains her balance before Gates can fall.

'That's not possible.' Hannah's voice is flat. It's as if her shock is a balloon that's grown then burst so she has no emotion left to share.

'That man must be as strong as an ox.'

'I thought I'd knocked him out.'

'As did I. He was probably playing dead. On the other hand, I'm glad for your sake that you haven't finished him off. You don't need a manslaughter charge.'

'I feel the same. I just don't like the idea of him running around these woods. What about your guys?'

'They're searching as we speak but these woods are extensive and dark. Sullivan is probably hiding. He could be anywhere.'

They shuffle on but it's slow going. Hannah is worried about the extent of Gates' injuries. She wonders if he's bleeding internally, going into shock, nurturing an infection.

'We need to get Gates to a hospital,' she says.

Gates croaks again. 'No.'

'Sorry, Gates,' says Hannah. 'I'm in charge now and you're going to lose this one. Craig, where's the nearest hospital?'

'Taunton.'

'So, that's where we're heading,' says Hannah.

***

By the time the ragged threesome emerges from the trees at the car park, the sky is lightening. Craig has carried most of Gates' weight, but Hannah's shoulders scream with pain and her knees and hips ache. Gates' stumbles did little more than keep him upright as Hannah and Craig hauled him through the trees. Hannah feels tearful with relief as she catches sight of Gates' battered car. Between them, Hannah and Craig lower Gates to the ground and prop his back against the car.

'Wait here,' orders Craig as he sets off at a trot to fetch the Range Rover closer. He shows no sign of fatigue. *Is he even human?* thinks Hannah.

They settle Gates on the back seat of the Range Rover with his head supported by a rolled-up car blanket and another tucked around him. He is icy cold. Hannah retrieves a set of car keys from his jacket pocket, and rummages in Gates' car. As expected, she finds his laptop bag in the boot. Hannah knows it can't be left behind.

Craig starts the car and heads for the hospital. Hannah crosses her fingers. Apart from the sound of his laboured breathing, there is no sign that Gates is alive.

***

Twenty minutes later they pull into the hospital car park. Craig hurries inside to fetch a wheelchair. When he returns, they lift Gates from the back of the car, install him in the chair and Craig pushes him through the doors of the Accident and Emergency Department. Hannah carries Gates' laptop bag.

Seeing Gates injured has hurt Hannah deeply. Her organs ache and nausea has taken up residence at the base of her throat. Handing Gates over to the care of the doctors and nurses is a relief so enormous that her legs crumple and she half sits, half falls onto a plastic chair with an audible bump. Craig places a hand on her shoulder.

'Coffee?'

Hannah conjures a weak smile.

'Oh, you mind-read too.'

While Craig is gone a nurse approaches Hannah with a clipboard and a form for her to complete. She does her best and congratulates herself on remembering to use one of Gates' many aliases. For his address she gives the Exmoor Farm, reasoning that as the location of the caravan is already blown it's probably the least important. She enters her own name as next of kin and designates herself his 'partner', thinking this might be the only way she will be given information about him.

Craig returns with coffee and a dodgy-looking pastry claiming to be a sausage roll. Hannah is game enough to take a bite but that's about as much as she can manage. The pastry is too dry to swallow and the filling indeterminate. Even after several mouthfuls of hot brown water masquerading as coffee, she still has pastry flakes stuck to the roof of her mouth.

'Not eating that?' asks Craig.

Hannah hands it over with relief.

'Do you think he followed us?' she asks. She doesn't need to say his name.

Craig shakes his head. 'If he did, he won't come in. This is far too public. He'll be hiding somewhere and plotting his next move. And I bet he's got the mother of all headaches. Don't worry. We'll be ready.'

'Oh, I'm ready.'

Hannah recalls the dull thud as the rock in her hand bashed into Sullivan's skull. She is ashamed of just how good it felt.

It's an hour and a half later when a nurse comes to collect Hannah. She is led through to a curtained cubicle where Gates lies on a high trolley. He is dressed in a hospital gown and an intravenous infusion drips clear liquid into his right arm. A monitor next to the trolley shows his heart rhythm, pulse, and oxygen levels. A neat row of stitches decorates the right side of his forehead. His left arm is strapped. The patch of bruising along his jawline has spread to cover one side of his face and closed his eye.

Hannah's instinct is to rush forward but the presence of the nurse keeps her in check.

'He's been given some pain relief so it's best to leave him to rest for now. We're just waiting for a bed and then we'll move him up to the ward.'

'He has to stay in?' asks Hannah.

'At least for tonight. He's taken quite a beating and needs observation because of his head injury. If he remains stable, he'll probably be allowed home tomorrow.'

'Are his injuries from the car accident?'

'He got off lightly from the car accident. Probably due to the deployment of the air bag. But the beating he's taken has done the most damage. He has extensive bruising, fractured ribs, a severely sprained wrist and numerous cuts and abrasions. He's going to be very sore for a while but fortunately there's no sign of brain injury and none of his injuries are life-threatening. He's going to be okay.'

The nurse smiles at Hannah and gives a small nod as if to say, 'There you are.'

A shower of relief drenches Hannah.

'Thank you.'

'I hope they catch the guy who did this.'

'So do I,' says Hannah with a vehemence she didn't know she possessed. Now she has even more reason to deal with Sullivan.

'Would you like to sit with him?'

'Please.'

Hannah takes the proffered chair and pulls it as close to Gates as she can get. The nurse lowers the trolley so Hannah can hold Gates' good hand and she leans forward to rest her head beside their entwined hands. This is so not fair. Even though Gates makes his living on the wrong side of Britain's privacy laws, he is a good man. He's spent most of his adult life trying to make the world a better place. Despite his one and only show of temper, Hannah believes that Gates would never intentionally harm another human being. He does not deserve this.

She remembers that Gates was on his way to see his wife. Hannah wonders if she should call her? What would she say?

Your ex is in hospital because he was helping me catch a killer. How would that help? *I could make an excuse*, thinks Hannah. Say that Gates has been delayed. Say that his car has broken down. That he's been held up at work. No, she can't. It would be too easy to do or say the wrong thing.

Gates has another life and Hannah is not part of it. In fact, when she thinks about it, Gates has always had another life. This time with him was always going to come to an end.

Hannah stands up and kisses him lightly on the forehead. He does not move.

'Thank you, Gates,' she says. 'For everything.'

48

Hannah makes her way back to the hospital entrance and sees Craig sitting with two police officers. She hangs back and waits until they end their conversation. She knows she will have to be interviewed herself but is not ready. She needs more time to gather her thoughts. Only when the police officers depart does Hannah approach.

'How did the police get here so soon?' she asks.

'The hospital called them. Gates' beating has been reported.'

'Of course.'

'How does he look?'

'Battered, but peaceful. He's had pain killers, so I think he's floating.'

'The best thing.'

'They're going to take him up to a ward when they have a bed. They said he might be able to go home tomorrow, which is today. Why don't you go and get some rest, Craig?'

'I was just about to say the same thing to you.'

'I'll stay.'

Craig nods. 'You've got my number. Call me when you want collecting.'

'Thanks, Craig. And thanks for tonight. I feel like this whole thing was way beyond the call of duty.'

'It wasn't. But I'm seriously pissed that we didn't get that fucker.'

'Me too.'

But I'll get him, she thinks. *One way or another. He won't give up. But neither will I.*

After Craig has left, Hannah returns to Gates' cubicle to find him awake. His attempt at a smile is more of a grimace but it's enough to make Hannah feel that all is well in the world. She reaches for his hand.

'How are you feeling?'

Gates' face twitches.

'Like I'm eighty years old.'

'I've been told it won't last. If all is well, you can go home later today, Rick of Exmoor.'

'Ah, I was going to ask.'

'Was that the right choice? It makes you sound like a medieval knight.'

'You did good, Hannah. You always do.'

'How much do you remember from last night?'

'More than I care to. I stopped for fuel and when I got back to the car Sullivan was there, leaning on the driver's door. I was flabbergasted.'

'There was a tracker on your car.'

'Christ! I didn't check.'

Hannah touches his hand. 'Don't worry.'

'Sullivan told me he had you, Hannah. Part of me wondered how that was possible but he seemed so sure of himself. He convinced me. He handed me a phone with a location in the woods but when I arrived, he ran my car into a tree with his Land Rover. I got out of the car, but I was dazed. I couldn't fight back. He was too strong. He took me to the cave and battered me. Then you came.'

'Christ.'

Hannah doesn't know what else to say. She rubs her forearm. Gates notices.

'He got away, didn't he?'

Hannah nods.

Gates starts to release a sigh, but pain stops him, and the rest of the air is subject to a slow and controlled release. A minute passes before he can speak again.

'So, we're no further forward.'

'He's still out there if that's what you mean.'

Gates tries to shrug but clenches his teeth and whistles as pain takes hold of him. Hannah reaches for his hand. They are interrupted by the swish of the curtain which is pulled back by a nurse. Two porters are with her.

'You're going up to the ward now,' she says with a cheery smile.

She tucks a thin folder of patient notes down at the end of the trolley while the two men release the brakes and manoeuvre the trolley out of the bay.

'Can I go with him?' asks Hannah.

'Yes, go up and see him settled,' says the nurse. 'They may ask you to leave though. It's a busy time on the wards.'

Hannah grabs the laptop bag and follows the two men into the lift and up to the next floor. The porters' dexterity with the trolley is impressive and Gates is whisked smoothly down the corridor and onto a ward. He is positioned in a side room with an ensuite bathroom.

'Private room,' whispers Hannah.

'Wish you could stay,' says Gates.

Hannah can't. Because a different nurse bustles in and sends her home with a list of items that Gates will require including clean clothes and toiletries. She is reluctant to go but Gates assures her that he is in good hands.

'Call Craig,' he says.

Craig arrives back at the hospital in an impossibly short time.

'You didn't go back to the lodge,' Hannah observes.

'Nah,' says Craig. 'I caught up on some kip in the car. The NHS never keeps anyone in unless they have to.'

'Gates for one will be pleased about that. I'm supposed to get him clothes and toiletries.'

'Not from the lodge you won't. It's too far. We'll head into Taunton.'

Hannah is happy to be guided by Craig. She is short of sleep and the trauma of the night is catching up with her. Her feet drag. Once in the centre of town Craig steers Hannah towards Marks and Spencer. Hannah pauses in the doorway.

'Do you think Gates is an M&S kind of guy?'

'He is today,' smiles Craig. 'Follow me.'

In the men's department, Craig selects a pair of track pants, T-shirt, hoodie, socks, and underpants.

'You look like you've done this before,' observes Hannah.

'A few times. Though not for Gates. This is a first.'

Hannah examines the bundle of clothing as they wait at the checkout.

'Trackpants though? Gates is more of a jeans man.'

'Not with those bruises. Trust me.'

They're called forward to pay which Craig does without fuss.

'Do you want me to pay?' offers Hannah.

'No sweat, the boss will sort me out.'

Without asking, Craig heads towards the café and takes Hannah to a corner table. He deposits the shopping on one chair and indicates that Hannah should take the one next to it.

'Croissants, bacon, eggs, porridge? Or are you a toast and muesli girl?'

Hannah had no idea she was hungry until Craig mentioned food. Her empty stomach lets out a squall of protest. It has been a long night and the lasagna is a distant memory.

'Porridge and coffee, please.'

Craig returns with coffee and cutlery, and Hannah drains her cup without pausing. Craig leaves his own drink to fetch Hannah a refill. She feels a touch of embarrassment at her greed.

'Sorry,' she says when Craig returns.

'Go for it, Hannah. You deserve it after the night you've had. You did well out there.'

Their food arrives. A fry-up and a plate of toast for Craig and a bowl of thick porridge for Hannah. They eat in silence. Both hungry and both wrapped up in their own thoughts. When they've finished, Hannah leans back in her chair and wonders if it would be rude to close her eyes.

'More coffee?' asks Craig.

Three coffees with breakfast. *That's outrageous*, she thinks. But before she has a chance to reply, Craig has left his seat.

'Thank you, Craig,' says Hannah on his return. 'This is beyond the call of duty again.'

Craig's response is almost a snap. 'It's not duty.'

'What do you mean?'

Craig pauses. He studies Hannah's face but she can't decide what he's looking for. Evidently satisfied he starts to speak.

'You're fond of Gates, aren't you?'

'Yes, I am.'

'He's fond of you too, I can see that.'

'Really?' Hannah can feel a faint blush warm her cheeks and her full tummy contracts.

'He's never brought a woman to the lodge before.'

'How long has he had it?'

'Three or four years. Given last night...' Craig pauses again. He seems to be struggling to select the right words.

'Given last night, I'm assuming you know what Gates does, you know what he is?'

Hannah nods. 'I do. He's been helping me. That's why he's lying in a hospital bed right now. This is all my fault.'

Craig holds up a hand to stop her.

'Gates doesn't do anything he doesn't want to. And he's not a risk-taker. He'll have weighed up the pros and cons, considered his options, decided to act. One word you can't use to describe Gates is impulsive.'

'You seem to know him well.'

'Well enough. We met at school.'

'Wow. What was he like?'

'A right little nerd. Or should I say big nerd. He was the tallest, skinniest lad in the year.'

Hannah smiles at the thought of the lanky Gates hunched over a computer screen. She can imagine him dressed in his schoolboy uniform with the tail of his shirt hanging out and his tie adrift.

'You know, kids don't like anyone who's different. He got bullied.'

'Were you friends?'

'Honestly? No. I knew him, but we didn't run in the same crowd. Gates didn't run with any crowd. He spent all his spare time in the computer lab. The only link we had was that we lived in the same street. We somehow ended up walking home together. No-one bothered him when I was there with him, and he appreciated that. In return he helped me out of a few sticky messes. Mostly to do with schoolwork. At first our meetings were accidental and then we began hanging around waiting for each other at the end of the day. I was into sport and mucking about, a right wanker. Gates was some sort of calm in a storm. I think he stopped me from wrecking my prospects without me even realising he was doing it. He's a good guy, Hannah.'

'So, you're close?'

'You'd have to ask him that question, but I'd say so. It's all about trust with Gates.'

'He's quite wary, isn't he?'

Craig nods. 'Needs must. If he lets his guard down with the wrong people, it's all over for him. Do you know about Olly?'

Hannah scoffs. 'I know he's let him down big time.'

'He has.'

'I've never met him,' said Hannah, 'but how can someone betray a friend and colleague like that?'

Craig shakes his head. 'I don't know, Hannah. But I do know that Gates has been badly hurt by this. And I don't mean his physical bruises. This is a betrayal that's gone to the very bones of him. I don't know if he can recover from this.'

'I'm glad he's got you,' says Hannah.

'Likewise,' replies Craig. 'So, shall we go and break him out?'

'Let's.'

49

Back on the ward Gates manages a wry smile when Hannah holds up her shopping for inspection.

'Please tell me this is Craig's doing,' he says.

'Absolutely,' replies Hannah. 'Something about being kind to bruises.'

'Ha, he's got that right.'

The intravenous infusion and monitors have been removed and Gates is ready for discharge. The hospital gown, while unbecoming, makes dressing reasonably straightforward. Underwear and trackpants pulled on underneath and then the gown removed for the T-shirt and hoodie. Gates huffs and puffs and takes things slowly, and when the gown is removed, Hannah can't help her reflex intake of breath. Gates' torso is black and blue, and when she unties the gown at the back, she swears she can see a boot print.

'Christ, Sullivan did a job on you.'

'I got the feeling it was personal. He was not happy with me.'

'Well, let's keep him away from you in future.'

'The police were here this morning.'

Hannah pauses. 'What did you say?'

'Not much to be honest. I used the Rick alias but otherwise I told the truth. I gave them your home address. I said I thought you'd head back there.'

'They'll be knocking on that door for a while.'

'Exactly.'

'I assume they're searching for Sullivan?'

'As best they can,' says Gates. 'But he's a clever and elusive bastard.'

'At least everyone's looking for him now. It's a national manhunt.'

'About time.'

Gates reaches for her hand and squeezes. She helps him to stand up as straight as his bruises allow.

'You look like a teenage hunchback of Notre Dame,' says Hannah.

'All the better to shuffle off out of here,' he says.

***

Craig drives the three of them back to the lodge without incident. Gates refuses to go to bed but agrees to lie on a bed of pillows that Hannah arranges on the sofa. Craig joins them for a debrief and to discuss their next steps. Not surprisingly, Gates is concerned about his ex-wife.

'I need to talk to her and apologise for not turning up yesterday.'

'What will you tell her?' asks Hannah.

'It'll have to be a version of the truth. When she sees me, she'll know that I've been in an accident. I'll say it was a shunt on the motorway.' Gates turns to Craig. 'Can one of your boys drive me up there?'

'Gates, you need some time to recover,' says Hannah.

'Alison doesn't have time, Hannah. I need to get to her now.'

Hannah dips her head. Of course, Gates will do the right

thing. That's who he is.

'I'll take you,' offers Craig but Gates shakes his head.

'No. I want you to stay here with Hannah. That bastard is still on the loose so watch her.'

'Of course,' says Craig. 'When do you want to go?'

'I'd like to travel tonight when the roads are quiet. Before I go can you take my computer kit to a secure location?'

'No problem,' says Craig.

'Won't you need it?' asks Hannah.

'Not for the next day or two. I think my work is almost done. It needs to be somewhere safe.'

'I'll see to that now,' says Craig.

Hannah hands over the laptop bag that has become something of an appendage for her. It's odd to see it hanging from Craig's shoulder, but he shakes Gates' hand and leaves the lodge. Hannah hands Gates a phone and he manages to support it in his damaged hand while he dials with the other. Once the call has connected Hannah slips outside and sits on the lodge steps until she can no longer hear Gates' voice.

When she goes back inside the phone is on the floor by the settee and Gates is snoring gently. Hannah lies down on the second sofa so she will be nearby if Gates wakes. She falls into a troubled sleep.

She is woken by Craig.

'What time is it?' she asks. Her head feels heavy and it's an effort to open her eyes. The lack of sleep is taking its toll. She can see that Gates is still asleep. Craig leads her outside.

'The laptop is safe,' he whispers, 'and I've arranged for Gates to be driven to Birmingham. The car's ready when he is.'

Inside the lodge Gates has started to stir. Hannah hears him call her name and she returns inside.

'Go and be with Alison and don't worry about us. You know we'll contact you if we need to.'

'There's nothing more you can do, buddy,' chips in Craig. 'Let the police do their job and I'll do mine.' He tips his head towards Hannah as he says this. She pretends not to notice.

At the last minute, Gates is reluctant to leave but he's exhausted, hurt and under the influence of strong analgesics. When the car arrives to take him to Birmingham, Craig and Hannah make him comfortable with barely a word of protest. Hannah checks their phones, hands Gates his drugs and a bottle of water, and squeezes his hand. He turns to meet her gaze.

'Hannah, I need to do this one last thing for Alison. I can't let her die alone.'

'I know.'

'Everything is ending.'

Not us, thinks Hannah.

'I hope...'

Gates stops her. 'Don't, Hannah. Don't say anything. It is what it is. Everything ends. Eventually.'

She stares into his eyes hoping to find some hidden message there. All she sees is Gates. And it's enough.

'Stay safe,' she says.

Gates meets her gaze.

'You too.'

Craig and Hannah stand watching the taillights disappear down the hill and away towards the estuary bridge. Hannah has a lump in her throat.

'Jesus, what else can go wrong for that guy?' she says, shaking her head.

'There's a lot going right for him too, Hannah. You just can't see it yet.'

Craig heads back into the lodge and for a moment Hannah stands outside wondering what the hell he means by that.

Inside the lodge Craig tidies away Gates' makeshift bed

while Hannah clears up the dishes.

'I'm staying here with you while Gates is gone.'

'Good. Thank you.' There will be no arguments from Hannah. 'You can use the second bedroom if you like.'

Craig smiles. 'I won't be sleeping. But you need to. Go and get some rest but stay dressed and keep your boots, phone, and torch near to your bed. I'm expecting company.'

Hannah goes into the bedroom and takes the descender from the drawer where Gates stowed it. She pushes it into the pocket of her fleece and zips it firmly shut. *Just to be on the safe side,* she tells herself. She knows that Sullivan is coming. She can practically *smell* him. She hopes he doesn't keep her waiting too long.

When she lies down the descender rests against her heart.

50

Craig shakes her awake from a deep, dreamless sleep. She's wide awake and alert in seconds.

'Is he here?' she whispers.

Craig nods. Hannah is ready. She slips her feet into her boots, pulls on her jacket, and grabs her phone and the torch. Craig has the bedroom window open. Hannah can feel the cold edge of the night air infiltrate the room.

'Phone?' asks Craig.

Hannah pats her pocket.

'On silent?'

'Yes.'

'Descender?'

'Yes.'

'Okay, go. Up the bank at the back then head for the cliff.'

Hannah slips out of the window and climbs the bank at the back of the lodge. There is a good covering of trees and shrubs, and she reaches the top without incident. When she looks back down, she can see a dark figure trying to open the lounge window of Gates' lodge. Keith Sullivan. She climbs the fence at the top of the bank in silence and hurries down the hill, across the road, and climbs over the stile into the field.

She feels a frisson of excitement as she heads across the grass. She is strong and she knows what she needs to do. She has waited so long for this.

This will end tonight.

Nevertheless, her heart is beating a little faster than normal and from time to time Hannah's feet catch in the weeds and long grass. The night is clear, and she can see well enough to walk without her torch.

This is it.

The danger signs on the fence have an eerie glow in the dark and they guide Hannah to the boundary of the field. Leaning on one of the signs gives her a strong sense of Gates standing at one shoulder, Glenn at the other. The breeze coming off the sea is cold. She can smell seaweed and hear the powerful waves breaking on the beach below. She licks her lips and tastes salt. She moves past the danger sign to the post next to the grassy step and peers over. The grassy step is nothing more than a dark shadow. It's enough.

Hannah finds the black cord and pulls it towards her. A black bag appears as promised, the coil of climbing rope curled inside. She unwinds the rope and ties it firmly to the rough wood of the gate post. At the other end Gates has already created a loop for her to put around her body. She attaches the figure eight descender and gives it a sharp tug. It appears to be a very small piece of metal to hold her weight and the butterflies inside her begin to stretch and flutter their wings. Pity there was no opportunity to practice.

There's no sign of any activity coming from the direction of the lodges and the sheep seem calm. Hannah takes some time to pull handfuls of long grass and weeds from the cliff side of the fence to cover the rope. Just in case. She huddles down beside the fence.

And waits.

Hannah has no idea what time she left the lodge, so she has no idea how long she's been crouching in the cold. Her legs are becoming stiff, and she stands up to stamp her feet, wishing she had been organised enough to find a woolly hat or some gloves. Autumn took a firm hold on the countryside when she wasn't looking.

The wail of a siren pierces the night.

What the…?

She stands still and listens. As the sound becomes louder, a jumble of flashing blue lights races across the estuary bridge below her. They disappear as they reach the road and then reappear on the bend leading up to the lodges.

Hannah is half hoping they will go past the holiday park. She is ready to confront Sullivan and has no desire to be delayed by anything.

They don't go past. They slow and turn into the driveway. Lights start to come on in the lodges and Hannah can hear fragments of speech carried on the clear night air.

What the hell is going on? Hannah is bewildered. Should she return to the lodge and find out what's happening, or should she stay put where she is hidden away and safe? *Relatively safe*, she corrects herself. She's still standing on the edge of a crumbling cliff in the middle of the night.

Hannah feels for the phone in her pocket. Should she call Gates? No, how can she? He is with his dying wife in Birmingham. And what could he do even if he was here with his bruises and stitches and cracked ribs? What about Craig? No, Craig knows she's here. He'll come and get her when it's safe. Hannah is still pondering when a second police car screeches into the holiday park.

Hannah waits. The temperature drops further, and she begins to shiver. After an eternity the second police car leaves. Her teeth chatter, and she can't feel her feet. Her emotions have shrunk into a ball of boredom and annoyance. The disturbed occupants of the lodges begin to drift back to bed. Their dark, distorted figures remind her of the stick people in a Lowry painting. She can't distinguish between men and women and sees only height and outline. The agony of not knowing what's happening is almost too much to bear and Hannah takes a few steps away from the fence. Her pocket vibrates.

Her frozen fingers fumble to retrieve the phone.

'Yes,' she whispers.

'Are you okay, Hannah?'

Craig's voice.

'Yes, just cold. What's going on?'

'Neighbourhood Watch.'

'What?'

'One of the neighbours saw Sullivan trying to break in and called the police. Of course, he ran. Then I had to explain what I was doing here in Gates' lodge with no Gates. It's been chaos.'

'Can I come back now?'

'Yes. The police have cleared the area but be careful. I have no idea where Sullivan is, but he won't have gone far.'

Hannah releases herself from the rope but leaves it secured to the fencepost. She tries to conceal it with grass and weeds but it's too dark to see much anyway. She'll return when it's light to put the rope back in its bag.

The first police car is still parked outside the site office so Hannah retraces her steps to the back of Gates' lodge. She keeps to the shadows and stays alert, aware that Sullivan might still be hanging around. At the door of the lodge, she taps twice and puts her hand on the door handle. Craig's shadow approaches through the glass to let her in. Simultaneously, a hand is smacked across her mouth, and she feels something cold and hard pressed into her temple. Hannah's mind is blank. Shock crumples her legs.

'Stand up, you fucking bitch,' growls Sullivan.

Panic engulfs her. For a few seconds. Then it's gone and she is thinking, using logic, calm logic. It's too late to run, she's too weak to fight. The reality of her position hits her with such force that it crushes her fear and takes away any uncertainty. She can crumble right here and give in, or she can stand up and fight. This man is not going to win. Hannah can feel his body shaking against hers, the hand across her mouth is trembling, the gun slips against her temple. He is wound so tight he is barely in control of himself. All Hannah needs to do is wait. He has to be in control, she remembers.

Craig throws open the lodge door and pales when he catches sight of Hannah in the grip of Sullivan, a gun pressed against her temple. Despite his obvious shock he too remains calm.

'Come in,' he says, stepping aside.

'After you,' Sullivan replies.

Sullivan removes the gun from Hannah's temple but keeps his hand over her mouth until they are inside. His skin smells stale and Hannah holds her lips closed. Breathing in his smell is preferable to tasting his stinking flesh. Craig sits down on the sofa and Sullivan pushes Hannah forwards to sit next to him.

Hannah examines Sullivan. He still has his sharp bones, his ice-cold eyes, and his grim, downturned mouth. He also has a large bruise on the side of his head, the swelling disfiguring his eye. He looks down at Hannah and Craig with an arrogance that makes Hannah shiver. How desperate must she have been to agree to a second date with this man? He isn't even attractive. What in God's name was she thinking?

She wasn't. That much is clear.

The three of them stare at each other in silence. Craig looks relaxed but Hannah senses the tension in his muscles. He reminds her of a coiled tiger ready to pounce. And Hannah?

Hannah forces herself to present a calm front. She must not lose control. She must not let Sullivan sense any fear. That's what he wants. To be in control of her emotions. She will not give him the satisfaction. She imagines him as an obnoxious caller.

You are through to the police. What is the address or location of your emergency?

Hannah feels her limbs relax.

'So here we are again,' says Sullivan.

'It's becoming a bit of a habit,' replies Hannah.

She's aware of a miniscule intake of breath from Craig. He won't want Hannah to provoke Sullivan, but that's exactly what she plans to do. Sullivan must be in control. If he thinks he's losing control, he'll get angry and make mistakes. Right now, he's slow to respond. Beneath all that bravado he must be tired and anxious. He must know that his time is running out, that he has nowhere left to hide.

'So, what do you want?' asks Craig.

'Nothing that I haven't already got,' replies Sullivan.

'Which is?' asks Craig.

'You two, of course.'

Sullivan puts his free hand into his coat pocket and pulls out a set of cable ties. He throws them at Hannah.

'Tie his wrists.'

Hannah looks at Craig, who nods and holds out his hands with his wrists crossed in front of him. Hannah fumbles at first but uses one of the ties to secure Craig's wrists.

'Tighter,' orders Sullivan.

Hannah does as she's told but tries to leave some room for movement.

'Now put one on yourself.'

Hannah does the best she can and when the cable tie is in place Sullivan puts his gun down on the dining table and tightens

Hannah's cable tie himself. His skin is sweaty against her hands. He picks up the gun and indicates that Craig and Hannah should go to the door. Hannah is still wearing her outdoor gear, but Craig leaves the lodge in his jeans, boots, and a rugby shirt. He is shivering within seconds. Sullivan, she notices, has a full-length warm coat, hat, and gloves. He came prepared.

Hannah and Craig walk ahead of Sullivan down towards the road. The police car has gone. All is quiet. They cross the road, struggle over the stile with their bound wrists and enter the field. Hannah's stomach feels heavy as they trip and stumble towards the fence. Perhaps Sullivan is going to deal with them both. It won't take much effort. Hannah wonders if Sullivan still wants her to retract her statement or if he's decided she's better off out of the way.

Without warning Craig turns and barges headfirst into Sullivan's stomach, knocking him from his feet. Hannah doesn't need to be told to run. Sullivan lands on his back. Craig is already on his feet and running.

'This way, Hannah,' he shouts. He heads back towards the road and the holiday park.

Hannah ignores him.

She's had enough of Sullivan ruling her life, threatening her, and threatening Gates. She knows only too well that Sullivan will kill without compunction, that he wants her and Gates out of the way. This is her opportunity to protect herself and Gates. To get rid of Sullivan once and for all. To save Gates. To save herself.

She has her own plan.

She knows she can't outrun Sullivan; she can't fight him either. But she sure as hell can outwit him.

With her bound hands held close to her chest Hannah races towards the pale rectangles that mark the boundary fence. Sheep scatter before her but Hannah doesn't falter. She forgets about potholes and potential twisted ankles and runs for her life, knees pumping, gulping lungfuls of air. She knows that Sullivan will follow. She knows that she can lure him to the cliff edge. What happens when he reaches it is down to him. Hannah almost smiles because she knows this man. She can predict his behaviour.

Follow me, caller, she thinks. *Choose your destiny.*

Sullivan is winded but staggers to his feet. Hannah glances back and sees him searching the ground, presumably for his gun. She can see him. The sky is lightening. Is that good or bad?

Crack!

It's bad. That was a gunshot.

Craig has reached the fence at the side of the field. Hannah hears him call Sullivan's name. Sullivan hesitates just long enough for Hannah to put a decent distance between them. He can see that Hannah is heading towards the cliff edge where she will be trapped. Unless she goes over. Her brain has already computed her options. There is only one choice and Hannah must follow it through. She's the one Sullivan wants. He thinks he has her cornered. He isn't even bothering to run. He's strolling towards her. He's smiling.

Come on, Sullivan.

51

Hannah stumbles to the fence and climbs over without hesitation. The first few inches of grass are short where the sheep have managed to push their snouts through the wires to snatch at the tasty morsels. Beyond this the longer stalks wrap around her ankles, and she holds onto the fence as best she can with her bound wrists. A quick glance reveals Sullivan ambling towards her. He makes no attempt to hide his confident swagger. Hate gives Hannah fresh energy. She sidles sideways.

The grassy step. There it is. She steps onto it gingerly, testing its strength. Gates was right. It's solid. Thank God Hannah left the rope in place. She could never have managed to secure it with her wrists bound together. She throws the loop of the rope over her shoulders and pulls it tight under her armpits. The cable tie makes everything more difficult, and her movements cause the harsh plastic to dig in and mark her flesh. Hannah feels nothing but the urgent need to descend the cliff. She fumbles with the figure eight descender, afraid that she's going to drop it. She wishes she had practised with one hand, is thankful that she attached it earlier.

She takes a deep breath and thinks of Gates. It's all about trust, he'd said. We need to trust each other. How long ago was that? The cable ties on her wrists are awkward and painful. She will trust this rope because Gates told her it was safe, and she trusts Gates. She begins to lower herself down the cliff face one inch at a time.

To descend at a decent pace Hannah needs to use her hands separately but the ties make that impossible. She remembers her days as a schoolgirl messing about on ropes in the gym and uses her feet and ankles to anchor her weight. Still, she's forced to run the rope through her bound hands using one as a brake on the rope and the other for descent. It's an excruciatingly slow process, and with every few inches strips of skin are scraped away from her hands until warm blood is oozing down her wrists, staining the cuffs of her jacket.

Despite the pain Hannah keeps moving. She is descending inch by painful inch below the edge of the cliff.

Gates was wrong about the number of steps though. There are only five and, in any case, she is not trying to hide. Sullivan knows exactly where she is. She wants him to know. She wants him to follow her. She continues to lower herself one step at a time. She braces herself against the cliff with her feet and dislodges a handful of shale which bounces down to the beach below. She's aware that she has already descended too far to get back up. Her arms are simply not strong enough. That's okay. She must make the descent look easy so that Sullivan follows. Without a descender.

Without much conscious thought Hannah continues her descent, praying that the rope will be long enough to reach the bottom and repeating over and over, 'Come on, you bastard, come on.'

The rope isn't anywhere near long enough. *Oh, Gates, you forgot how tall you are*. When Hannah comes to an abrupt halt her heart is hammering so fast and loud Sullivan must be able to hear it from the cliff top. Scattered falls of stone and debris clatter down the rock face. Sullivan is up there searching for her. But he's too far to her left. What now?

Hannah risks a peek down to the beach. It's still too far to jump but there are several rock falls that have built up mounds of debris piled against the cliff. They don't look stable, far from it, but they are high enough to break her fall.

Hannah must remove her arms from the loop of rope beneath her armpits. The loop has tightened with her descent and the struggle to release herself with her shredded hands produces more blood and makes her arms ache. She takes her weight on the rope above so she can wriggle free from the loop. By the time she's dangling from the loop, her muscles scream in agony and her palms are on fire. She lowers herself so that her toes touch the top of the tallest rockfall. Sweat drips into her eyes and her hands are clammy. With no time to think her arms and hands give way. She falls onto the rock pile.

She bends her knees as she drops, and lands crouched on top of the rocks. Her bound wrists prevent her from grabbing a handhold. She slumps forward so that her chest is flat against the rocks and stones. There is some movement amongst the rocks beneath her feet, but the pile holds. Hannah pushes herself up into a crouch. She pauses to steady her breathing before she begins to climb down towards the ground. The flurries of shale and small rocks from above are creeping inexorably closer as Sullivan moves towards her.

'Hann-ah, where are you?' His voice is high-pitched, wheedling. It echoes around the bay.

Hannah tries to control her breathing, which is harsh and loud in her ears.

'Hannah, I know you're there. You're going to have to come back sooner or later.'

She continues her descent, placing each foot on the rocks and testing her weight before committing to the next step. She's within feet of the beach when the rock beneath her left foot shoots out from beneath her and a small avalanche of rock and shale tumbles to the beach. Hannah is thrown onto the sand, where she rolls to the side as fast as possible. The rocks above shift and settle, and several boulders crash down to embed themselves in the sand. Hannah feels rocks hit her back and arms but is too relieved to be in one piece to cry out. The minute the rocks and stones settle, she is on her feet running to the shelter of the cliff face so Sullivan can't see her. But she hears him.

'Oh, Hannah, you silly girl, what have you done? You fucking stupid bitch.'

Hannah's instinct is to hide but that would be the action of the old Hannah. The new Hannah will not be a victim. She doesn't cower or whimper. She doesn't cry or shout or scream. She wants Sullivan to come over the cliff. She stands up straight, pulls back her shoulders so that she can fill her lungs with air, and she *roars*.

'Come and get me, fucker!' she screams.

She wants to make him mad. She wants him to climb down. He's agitated and out of control. Hannah puts her hand in her pocket and feels the cold metal of the descender. Sullivan has nothing but the rope and his hatred for women. If he comes for her, he will surely fall.

'What are you waiting for, Sullivan?'

Hannah presses herself up against the cliff face. Trickles of warm blood creep down her back and the skin across her shoulders stings but she remains immobile while she waits for Sullivan's next move. The showers of stone suggest he's still searching for her. Then the rope jerks and it's hauled up into the air. He's found it.

'Stupid fucking bitch,' he shouts. 'Stupid fucking *bitch.*'

Stones and dust are falling around her. Sullivan is using the rope to climb down. While he's occupied negotiating the cliff

Hannah takes a few steps across the beach to select a rock. She has her back to the cliff as she squats to pick up her weapon. She turns at the sound of a scream followed by a crashing, cracking, crump. Hannah thinks of World War Two movies when mortar shells land on the beach. Not because of the noise from the shells. Because of the images of the battered bodies landing in the sand. She turns around. The sun is coming up and she can see all she needs to. She sees relief. And freedom. She releases a huge sigh of satisfaction.

Sullivan lies crumpled on the heap of rocks at the base of the cliff. Hannah stands and stares. He lifts an arm; the rocks shift and his body tumbles down to the sand, landing in a heap like a broken doll. He is immobile. Hannah hesitates. Half of her thinks she should go to him, but the other half remembers he has a gun. She runs. Along the beach, into the tunnel and up the steps. She is barrelling up the second flight when she's caught by Craig coming down towards her. He has a noticeable limp. He catches her and holds her tight to prevent her from falling. She drops the rock from her hand. It is red from her blood. She looks at Craig's hands on her arms and wonders how he managed to remove his cable tie. He answers by pulling a knife from his pocket and cuts Hannah's tie. She wants to massage her wrists with relief but the skin on the palms of her hands is shredded and bloody. They are beginning to throb with pain.

'Hannah. Thank God you're okay. I can't believe you went down that cliff. What happened to Sullivan?'

'He followed.'

Craig tips his head to one side. It's a question.

'He fell. He fell a long way onto a pile of rocks.'

'Where is he?'

'On the beach. I think he's hurt but I didn't check. He might still have the gun.'

Together they climb the rest of the steps.

'Have you hurt your leg?' Hannah asks.

'I think something tore when I knocked Sullivan down.' He smiles at Hannah. 'It was worth it though.'

Craig has already dialled triple nine. Hannah wishes she had been the one to take the call. The one that will see Sullivan arrested at last. He leads Hannah across the car park, and they wait behind the tourist information shack. They're out of the wind but also out of sight if Sullivan should appear. Hannah thinks that's unlikely. Despite her wounds, adrenaline is still surging through her body, and she feels triumphant.

When blue lights and sirens flash up the hill for the second time that very early morning, Hannah and Craig emerge from the shadows. Firearms officers are the first to be dispatched. A paramedic cleans the wounds on Hannah's hands and wrists and applies dressings that remind her of a pair of white mittens she wore as a child. Before too long the firearms officers give the 'all clear' and the paramedics head into the tunnel. Craig and Hannah sit in the back of a squad car with the engine running and the heater on, so they have a chance to thaw out. They're wrapped in warm blankets and hot coffee is magically produced from the hotel next to the car park. Craig holds Hannah's cup for her.

Hannah waits for a stretcher to be brought through the tunnel but when the paramedics emerge into the growing daylight, they're carrying a chair with what appears to be a body bag strapped to it.

'Oh my God,' whispers Hannah.

Craig lifts his head and stares out of the car window. He is silent.

'I have to be sure,' says Hannah.

'No, wait,' Craig calls. Too late. Hannah is out of the car and hurrying towards the ambulance.

'I need to see him,' she shouts back to Craig.

The paramedic starts to refuse but, unable to use her hands, Hannah leans her body against the chair.

'This man has been chasing me for weeks. I have to be sure it's him so that I can sleep at night.'

'Let her,' says one of the police officers.

A paramedic unzips the black bag and Hannah stares at Sullivan's face. His features have been smashed by the rocks but there is no doubt that it's him. Lifeless.

'Thank you,' she says, and turns away. Craig is behind her.

'It's over,' she says.

52

Despite their vocal protests, Craig and Hannah are taken to hospital, where they are poked, prodded, and examined before Hannah has her remaining cuts and bruises cleaned and dressed. She's given a tetanus shot. Her shoulders look as if she's been dragged across a bed of gravel by her arms but other than that and her very sore hands, she's given a clean bill of health.

Craig has a torn ligament, and his foot, ankle, and lower leg are firmly strapped, so much so that he can't get back into his jeans and is forced to wear a set of hospital scrubs on his lower half.

'How do I look?' he asks Hannah when they are reunited in the relatives' room.

'Have you got a wife?'

'I have,' he smiles.

'Well, nick a matching top and a stethoscope and you can play *Grey's Anatomy* when you get home.'

'Grey's what?'

'The TV show.'

Craig shakes his head.

'Doctors and nurses?'

A slow grin spreads across Craig's face as realisation dawns and Hannah feels a surge of genuine fondness for this tough guy.

They're hoping to be returned to the lodge but first they are transferred by squad car to the police station, where they are taken to separate rooms to give their statements. The coffee is foul. So bad that Hannah finds it impossible to drink enough of it to overcome her exhaustion. She's thankful Gates is not around. The endless questions would have been his worst nightmare and Hannah is relieved she doesn't have to lie to protect him.

When the police decide they have enough, for now, Hannah is released. Craig is already waiting for her, and they are driven back to the lodge in silence. It's past midday. Hannah had been planning to freshen up and drink coffee but all she can do is remove her coat and boots and collapse on the bed.

Craig offers the phone to Hannah, suggesting she telephones Gates, but she shakes her head.

'Too tired,' she mutters, but the truth is that for the first time ever, she doesn't know what to say to him.

'I think I need to sleep first. Sort my head out.'

'Do you mind if I call?' asks Craig.

'No, go ahead. Thank you. For everything.'

Hannah closes her eyes but listens while Craig makes the call. Gates has had enough trauma to last him a lifetime and she wants to know that he's okay. It's time he had some good news. And the news from Craig that Sullivan is dead leaves a long silence over the phone before Gates utters one word. It's loud enough for Hannah to hear.

'Good.'

'Hear, hear,' says Craig.

Gates must have asked how Hannah is.

'Fast asleep,' says Craig. 'She's a little battered but the doc says she'll heal. Christ, she's fucking plucky.'

Hannah can't hear Gates' reply.

'You know she went down the cliff?'

Hannah thinks she hears a bark of proud laughter but can't be sure.

'How are things at your end?' asks Craig.

There is a pause while Craig listens. His voice has softened when he replies.

'Sorry to hear that.'

Another pause.

'I will mate, I will. I'll tell her.'

Hannah sleeps.

The following morning they're woken by a banging on the door. The police are back with more questions. Hannah rubs the sleep from her eyes and answers as best she can. When the questions end, Hannah asks if she can go home. To her surprise, the police agree that yes, she can return to her home address. Does she need transport?

'I'll take her,' interrupts Craig.

'But your foot?'

'I don't need my left leg to drive. That's what automatics are for.'

'Are you sure?'

'Gates would have my guts for fucking garters if I didn't.'

Hannah giggles at the juxtaposition of the expletive in the middle of a phrase her granny used to use. Without the swear word, of course. *You can tell a lot about a man by the company he keeps*, she thinks. When the police have left Hannah telephones Gates but there is no reply. She leaves a short voicemail saying that she's fine, she hopes all is as well as can be expected with him and she is heading home with Craig. He doesn't call back.

Hannah sighs. She wants to share her news with Gates. He is the only person who will truly understand how she feels now that Sullivan is dead.

'Are you sure you don't want to stay down for a bit?' asks Craig as Hannah gathers her few belongings together with her awkward bandaged hands.

She shakes her head and pauses to stare out of the window at the sparkling sea.

'I love it here, but this is my fourth week away from home and from my job. I feel like I need to get back to some sort of normality.'

'I get it,' says Craig. 'But you might find it hard at first.'

'What do you mean?'

'You've been through a lot of shit, Hannah. Gates has too. Stuff like that is traumatic and it changes you. You might not realise at first. It's often when you get home that you notice you've changed. It might be hard to settle.'

Hannah regards Craig's serious face.

'Are you talking from personal experience?'

Craig lifts his shoulders a fraction. 'Afghanistan, Iraq. You live through it, hope your mates will live through it too and all you can think about is going home. Then you make it back and I dunno, something's missing. You can never quite put your finger on it. You don't miss the bombs or the blood. It's great being able to walk down the street without being shot at and you swear to God you will never go on another tour. But within months you're packing your kit again because life is just too fucking quiet. Do you know what I mean?'

'I think so,' says Hannah, although she's not sure if she does.

Craig sighs. It's a deep, aching sigh.

'It's like going back to visit some place you knew as a child. You remember it but it's never the same. It doesn't look the same, doesn't smell the same. But it's not the place that's changed. It's you. All I'm saying is to be ready if things feel different. It's normal.'

Hannah is touched by Craig's words. More so because they have come from a real tough guy. She goes over to him and gives him a big hug, leaving her hands flapping in the air like enormous white moths. Craig grunts in surprise and hugs her back.

'You'll be okay, Hannah,' he says. 'You're a fighter if ever I met one.'

Hannah smiles. 'Thanks to Gates,' she says.

'Thanks to yourself,' counters Craig.

The Sunday traffic is light with the school term in progress and cooler weather keeping families indoors. Hannah and Craig stop twice at the services which breaks up the journey but also makes it long and tedious. They're both lost in their thoughts as the countryside rolls past and Hannah finds herself caught in a limbo between a longing to be back in her flat, ensconced in her normality, and the knowledge that Gates won't be there.

She's aware that with Sullivan gone the dynamic between the two of them will be changed. Without their joint project to find Tina's killer, without their common goal, what will be left for them? While Hannah has found her freedom and her confidence, Gates has lost Olly. He has also lost his livelihood as a hacker. What will his future hold?

Hannah's brain is aching with possibilities, not all of them an appealing prospect. By the time they pull up outside her flat she has a thumping headache. Craig parks in the road directly behind Gates' car. *How the hell did that get here from a Welsh forest?* thinks Hannah. When it had four flat tyres to boot. Gates really does have a way about him.

Hannah pauses on the pavement so she can scan the street in either direction. No pedestrians, no parked cars with strange men in baseball caps. No police cars. *Will life always be like this now?* thinks Hannah. *Constantly checking?*

'Would you like to come in, Craig?'

Craig shakes his head. 'If you don't mind, I'd like to get home. The wife will be worried sick.'

'Of course.'

Craig gets out of the car to help Hannah unlock the front door to the flats.

'Can you manage from here?'

'I can. You've been brilliant, Craig. I hope we get to meet again. In better circumstances.'

'So do I. It's been a blast.'

He leans down and kisses her on the cheek, blushes bright pink then leaves with an embarrassed flick of his hand that Hannah interprets as a wave. She stands on the doorstep and watches him pull away. With a final wave Hannah shuts the front door. She pauses next to Gates' door and listens to the silence. She knew he wouldn't be here but even so the emptiness is deafening.

As she climbs the stairs to her flat, Hannah is overcome with a loneliness so powerful it's a physical pain in her chest. She unlocks her door with difficulty and enters the flat. It smells musty and unloved. She surveys her living room with a new eye. She recalls Gates sitting on her sofa with his croissants. Without him there it's just a lump of furniture in an ordinary room.

She throws open the windows and leans out to look at the garden, already overgrown again.

On an impulse Hannah telephones Gates using the end of a pencil to press the buttons on her phone. It goes straight to voicemail and Hannah leaves another inane message. She slumps down onto the sofa. Is this what Craig warned her about? This feeling of total emptiness. A life given back to her but a life that sits in front of her, empty and abandoned. A life that she doesn't want anymore.

What the hell does she do now?

53

Hannah sits in her flat for four days. She understands that she's at a crossroads and whichever turning she takes will shape the rest of her life.

I'm lost, she thinks.

Four days. She orders a delivery of groceries, eats when she thinks about eating, sleeps when she thinks about sleeping. The rest of her days and part of her nights are spent sitting and thinking as she Googles and takes copious notes. Her time with Gates has served her well and she works with efficiency. Hannah is planning.

She doesn't know when Gates will be back. She doesn't know if he will come back at all. But because she has hope, she arranges everything for a couple. She will go anyway. She hopes she doesn't have to leave alone.

For the first time in years, she dials +39 for Italy. Her call is welcome.

'Ciao papà,' she says.

***

On the fifth day the sun shines, and the sky is blue. Hannah goes outside to the communal garden and leans on the fence.

She gazes across the park. She remembers her flight in the semi-darkness with Gates, not knowing where they were going or what was going to happen. Was it only three weeks ago? Despite the beautiful day, the weather is cool, and Hannah senses the turn of the seasons amongst the first fall of leaves across the grass. Winter will soon be nudging its way forward. That's okay. She's almost done. There's just one piece of her plan missing.

Except that isn't true. Not anymore. Because she *feels* him. She feels his presence long before she hears the swish of his boots in the grass or senses the air particles disturbed by his shape. And when he says her name, she is expecting it.

'Hannah.'

She turns to face him.

'Gates.'

He gazes at her, and Hannah is immersed in a tidal wave of feeling that drowns her ability to leave the support of the fence. She is breathless, dizzy, and disoriented. His face is an atlas of fading bruises, but the grey eyes are unchanged. They rest now on Hannah's still-bandaged hands, and he reaches for them.

'Do they hurt?'

'Not anymore.'

'I'm sorry, I wasn't there.'

She shakes her head.

'You were somewhere much more important.'

Hannah knows it's the truth. He had to be with Alison. It was his way of closing that chapter of his life in a good way, a noble way. Because that's what a good, noble man does.

He meets her eyes with his own. His gaze is studied.

'I'm sorry I didn't get to return your calls. There was so much I needed to do after she died. Paperwork, legal stuff, funeral arrangements. It was intense.'

Hannah searches his eyes but there's no sadness.

'I'm so sorry.'

'It's okay. I'm glad I was there. No-one should die alone, and I was all she had. It was peaceful and now it's over.'

'You did the right thing.'

He releases her hands.

'But a lot of other things are over too, aren't they?'

A sliver of ice lodges in Hannah's heart. What does he mean? What else is over? Is their friendship over? Hannah thinks of her computer upstairs and the neat pile of printouts. All her plans.

'What do you mean?'

Gates hesitates before tipping his head towards the house.

'I owe you a latte or two. If you've got some milk?'

Hannah fetches milk from her flat and is soon snuggled into Gates' sofa.

'This is how it started,' she says, as she takes a mug of coffee from him.

Gates gives her a hard stare.

'And this is not how it has to end,' he says.

'What do you mean?'

Gates swallows a mouthful of coffee.

'How does it feel, Hannah? Being back here?'

Hannah thinks while she sips her own coffee. The truth. She must tell the truth.

'It's weird. Everything has changed, Gates. I've changed. I feel as if my life is pointless. As if I'm marking time just for the sake of being alive. It's not enough anymore. I can't go back to the life I had before that call. My head tells me it was just one call, but my heart tells me it's so much more than that. It's a boundary. It marks a before and an after. A then and a now.'

Gates is nodding.

'I feel the same.'

Hannah doesn't know where this conversation is going.

'What are you saying?'

'My ties are broken. I've done a lot of thinking over the last couple of weeks. I can't tell you what I want exactly. But it's not this.'

He waves his arms to take in the flat.

'The last few weeks have been the first time I've feared for my life and for the life of someone I love.'

His eyes meet Hannah's and the fluttering in her chest strengthens.

'What is it you want?'

'Something different. Something meaningful. Something legal.'

Hannah blinks. Her heart is thumping, hope stirring inside her.

'Something with you.'

Her voice cracks.

'With me?'

Gates turns to her. He cradles her bandaged hands in his and smiles.

'Whatever I do, wherever I do it, I want you to be part of it, Hannah. I love you and I want to spend the rest of my life with you. But...'

'But what?'

'Are you up for an adventure?'

Hannah giggles as she thinks of her days of Googling. Her giggles turn to laughter as she thinks of the papers stacked on her desk upstairs and only when Gates has finished kissing her does she catch her breath and manage to speak.

'No. Are *you* up for an adventure?'

Gates squints at her.

'What?'

'It's sorted,' she says. 'Is your passport up to date?'

Gates looks into her eyes and smiles. 'You little beauty,' he says.

Acknowledgements

Behind every published book is a village of people. You know who you are. But some of you deserve an extra special mention.

To my precious daughters Eleanor and Amelia. What beautiful, clever, outstanding young women you have become. Since the day you were born, everything has been for you.

To Doctor Geoffrey Williams, my third time lucky who has nurtured my writing in so many ways, but mostly by allowing me to firmly shut my study door and get on with it – except when the door is firmly shut and a small tap is followed by the question, 'Are you writing?'

To my writing groups, Zoomwriters and Nashers. Thank you for the support and the laughter and especially to Derek, France was a blast! Everything a writing retreat should be.

To Jericho Writers. Your endless down-to-earth, practical advice and support has been instrumental in getting me to this place. If your dream of becoming a writer is still just that, a dream, sign up and start to develop your craft. The Ultimate Novel

Writing Course gave me skills I didn't know I needed and left me with lifelong friends. Becoming a Friday Night Live finalist at the Jericho Writers Summer Festival of Writing in 2022 was the epitome of success for me and having the Nashers in the audience cheering and applauding was the icing on the cake.

A huge thank you to all the lovely bookstagrammers who, if they did but know it, have spent many hours in bed with me sharing recommendations, book news and gossip. And photos of their pets. Nothing is more cheery than a bunch of new pages to scroll through even if it means my tbr will never be finished.

If you buy, borrow, read and review books, you are a star. An interesting and lovely person beloved by other readers and by the writers you support.

And finally a huge hug for my adorable little doggie, Poppy. Whether I am reading, writing, or even sneaking a nap, that cute little bundle of white fur is never far away. Funny how she gets more likes on Bookstagram than my Book Reviews. Well, why not? She deserves every one of them.

And if you enjoy *One Call*, please leave a review. You know I want you to.

Thank you all.

Wendy Williams
Instagram: @wendywilliamswriter